Stigmata

a Knights 1
by Carl Michael

Episode One

Cape and Swordstick Press

Gladstone, MO 64118

www.capeandswordstickpress.com

The characters and events in this book are fictitious. Any similarity to real persons, living or dead, is coincidental and not intended by the authors.

This is a work of fiction intended to be in communion with the Holy Catholic Church. It does not bear an imprimatur or a nihil obstat, but the authors have taken pains to ensure it does not conflict with anything the Church dogmatically teaches. If the authors have missed a detail that does conflict, the mistake belongs to the authors; The Holy Catholic Church does not teach error when it comes to faith and morals.

Cover art by Patrick Sayles

Cover layout and lettering by Chuck Regan

Copy editing by Catherine Lueckenette

Stigmata Invicta
By Carl Michael Curtis

From Joe - to my wife Rachel, thank you for walking next to me on this adventure, being my anchor when I try to fly too high, and supporting all my dreams, schemes, and ploys.

From Ryan – to Donna, for whom I do everything. To Joe, who suggested we do this in the first place.

Rescue the lowly and poor;

deliver them from the hand of the wicked.

Psalms 82:4

Site of operations:
Arithraw, fourth planet in orbit of G-Class star Geti-12, Hurivok solar system
On site resources:
Spec Ops Unit #7-1a, Brigid, F. Commander
St. Joshua, Eidolon-class stealth cruiser, Bernhard, A. Captain

3rd Commandry of the Knights of Those Washed in the Water and Blood from His Side ("Knights 15 13")

Mission details: stealth extraction of asset from planet's surface by any **just** means necessary in accordance with Knights 15 13 Rule of the Order, CLASSIFIED location coordinates

Mission designation:
UNSANCTIONED by the Federal Interstellar Governmental Network/FedNET

UNSANCTIONED by Arithraw planetary authorities ("National Civilians' Authority Council" – officially designated as hostile)

SANCTIONED/UNSANCTIONED by local solar system governmental authorities is not applicable/none exist

SANCTIONED by Knights 15 13 Supreme Commandry in accordance with Christ the King's commandment to LOVE THY NEIGHBOR AS THYSELF and TO RESCUE THE LOWLY AND THE POOR; TO DELIVER THEM FROM THE HAND OF THE WICKED

COMBAT PERMISSIONS:
Granted in full

Patron Saint(s) assigned to ops to request intercession from:
Saint Michael the Archangel (*Angel*, eternal)
Saint Martin De Tours (*Homo Sapien*, Earth, 316 or 336—397)
Saint Xohig SomphambiXo (*Quasi-homo/anthropomorphus Gecarcinus*, Ionus 7, 2704—2769)

Part One:
Surface

Mission Briefing

"Glory be to the Father and to the Son and to the Holy Spirit," the six Knights of The Brotherhood of Those Washed in the Blood and Water from His Side, recite in perfect unison as they kneel. The supplicating position is difficult because they all must shift their heavy-caliber weapons out of the way to honor and praise God.

In the ready room of the *St. Joshua*, an Eidolon-class stealth cruiser, the warrior-monks gather for the last time in peace. The rays of the solar system's sun crest a wave across them as they keep station behind the largest moon to an antagonistic planet. Called Arithraw by its lone species of inhabitants, the small and desolate backwater place unfolds beneath them like a ring of Hell in Dante's *Inferno*.

Arithraw's largest moon glacially rolls along its axis. The moon is nothing more than a dead gray rock bespeckled with red, glass-like shards of frozen liquid that was the result of a comet impact thousands of years prior. A color palette like an adorned skull. The *St. Joshua* banks with jets of positional thrusters as the crew finish their preparations.

In ten minutes, the ship will cloak and enter the upper atmosphere of the planet. All of this surreptitiously; Arithraw despises everything these men stand for.

"As it was in the beginning, is now and ever shall be, world without end. Amen." They all make the Sign of the Cross in reverence and stand. The clink of their gear resettling is like a thousand bolts cocking back. Dressed in high tech, close-fitting armor, each with the emblem of his Order and rank above that adorning his left chest plate. A few have cups of coffee in one hand. One, his Rosary. Each with the quiet confidence of tried and tested operators. Each with the greater confidence knowing his Creator loves him.

"All right, brothers," Commander Brigid says as he taps on his podium console. "Let's go over the particulars one more time before we roll. Pull up the mission details in your Visuals with me real quick."

The Knights put on their helmets and queue up the mission dossier. It unspools along the inside of their visors, and Brigid gives his men a moment to orient themselves. "Pretty basic stealth op on paper." He pauses. "*On paper*. We insert into the infil location. Local time, it's late and we're dropping into a field outside a farming community. Sweep it, make contact with our guy. Move to the cargo point, take possession. Brother Gonzaga, that's on you."

Gonzaga, who, on the last mission, pulled a rotting tree out of the ground and used it to batter open a door they needed to get through, simply nods. "Roger, sir."

"Then we move to the exfil site, take liftoff. Rendezvous with the *St. Joshua*. Then our part is done. Anything changes our plan, we react accordingly. Any questions?"

Each man shakes his head. As the commander said, on paper the operation is basic. Brother Santa Cruz clears his throat, "What potential problems are we looking at?"

"Getting seen by local authorities is the biggest risk," Brigid says. "The bridge has reported there's a military patrol down in our location, but I guess there's a patrol in every settlement no matter how small. Governmental iron fist, I guess.

"So, that's one thing. Intel says patrols are commonplace, but I don't like seeing them pop up where I'm getting ready to go." He shrugs. "The main thing to remember is stealth. The planet is small, consisting of only two continents, and neither are all that big. The Thraw live as hostile to most other species and especially guys like us. So, if we get picked out, we're not getting back to the ship with much ammo left."

The small cadre of Knights—Commander Brigid, Santa Cruz, Gonzaga and Brothers Cleopas, Pio, Nonnatus—stand in silence for a moment, the tension of their mission beginning to sing within them.

Cleopas rolls his Rosary through his hand. The beads are a dull iron color, crudely cast; droplets of slag allowed to fall into a quench and then drilled through to tie the cord. The crucifix stands out in sharp contrast, a meticulously detailed image of Our Savior during His Passion.

Santa Cruz asks, "The Thraw are the ones who martyred something like seventy-seven Catholics on a humanitarian mission there... oh, a few years back? Is that correct?"

"Yeah, it was them," Pio answers from two seats over. "*Eventually* they martyred them. Word on the intel network was it took a while."

Nonnatus says, "The Thraw government will martyr any Catholic. Any and all. Always have since they first heard the Gospel."

"Correct," Brigid nods, shuffles through their mission details and highlights a portion. "I'll summarize here: the government—a single oppressive regime across the entire planet—is virulently atheist. Rule with a rod and sword. Dissenters get the usual treatment—hard labor, starvation, execution. Arithraw has a decent-sized underground church and the government hates it. Wants it dead. Intel network says it's hidden well enough, but anytime the government gets its hands on a Christian it tortures to try and get info. Other members, church and holy locations. Mass times. Anything. I guess they're not doing too well on rooting it out. Never have."

"Why don't we just get word on the intel network to rescue whoever's left and then glass the planet?" Gonzaga asks. Young, bald with dark eyes and a face full of scars already, he towers over his brothers in both stature and anger. "You guys know when I was a kid that Neo-Gnostic Movement, they did that to us when we wouldn't convert. Folks like this, that violence, that's what they understand." He scratches his neck and shrugs. "That's all they understand."

Gonzaga looks down at the filial ring tattooed on his left hand, the ink barely two years old. He remembers getting it the morning after taking his final vows into the Order. The insect pinprick of the needle amidst the constant buzzing of the implement itself. "I should have gotten this the day before my vows, not the day after," he lamented to himself as the artist-brother working the tabooing machine made a swirl along the patch of skin.

"I wouldn't have done it then," the artist said, wiping the work clean and continuing.

"Why not?"

"I'm not tattooing a man with his filial ring just to have him back out last second. You get this emblem after you commit. Not near it."

"I'm not going to change," Gonzaga said with a grunt.

"Then you need to let Christ work in your heart some more."

Gonzaga grunted again and started thinking about something else. The artists finished the ring, and the newly minted member of the Knight 15 13 needed to move on because another newly minted brother was waiting for his turn in the artist's chair.

After being received into the Special Operations division, Gonzaga trained for eighteen months and was assigned to Brigid. This is his fourth mission with the team.

The filial ring was on the same finger he jammed as a child when falling and bracing himself while fleeing. One day at his old colonial settlement's school, the sky was sandy yellow and orange with the noonday sun. Then it was black with falling bombs.

The Neo-Gnostic movement entered the Verities System, his system, and bombarded them from the lower atmosphere. School buildings exploding one by one. Fires, craters. The chaos of his playmates running around frantic. The hopelessness of it all and his lefthand ring finger swollen and throbbing.

But then his father, by divine providence a maintenance man at the school, plunged out towards him from a thick, drifting cloud of debris smoke. Bleeding from his scalp. Grabbing him mid-stride and running to shelter. He did what he could to herd other children as well, but the constant barrage of new explosions killed any higher thought in those moments. It was all basic survival instincts, and the children scattered. How many of them never saw their parents again?

The warm colors of the sky were blotted out by the ashen smoke of the attack, and it only became red with blood as the neo-Gnostics set their boots to the ground. Gonzaga was orphaned in the following weeks and filled with rage at their tyranny.

He was always bigger than his schoolmates, and clever. He could read others. After his father was injured when an explosion knocked him off his feet and never woke up a day later, Gonzaga was alone. By then the new dawn, one glazed over with the smoke and dust plume of ruination, was cold. Dew helped ash cling to every low surface. Gonzaga huddled under the meager cover his father found and died within. Knees drawn to his chin, he wanted nothing more than resolution.

Staring at his father's still face, eyes closed, and lips sealed in what would otherwise be a simple slumber. The Neo-Gnostic Movement tromping around the landscape, killing those who would not covert. Gonzaga wanted a cleansing fire against his enemies. And what child would not? Newly orphaned and hurting. Gazing at the last of his family connections, passed away.

But a single dot in the sky floated through the blood red skies, light shimmering across it as it came nearer. A lone ship, filled with warrior-monks, come to answer their prayers. Directed by God, out of love, to bring what was needed.

The Brotherhood of Those Washed in the Blood and Water from His Side, or the Knights 15 13, had rescued what was left of his colony during their purge years ago, fought the Neo-Gnostic Movement back to the gates of hell from where they'd come, and raised the orphans as their own sons. Brother Gonzaga was still tamping down the embers of his fury as he took his final oaths to God and the Order.

"No," Brigid says now. "You've seen how much good comes from them, if they only accept Christ. How many have come to believe the Gospel? It was wrong of those pagans to slaughter your colony for not accepting their beliefs, it is wrong of the Thraw to slaughter their own for having our beliefs, and it would be wrong of us to slaughter the Thraw."

"I know. I know."

Brigid watches Gonzaga for a moment and then clears his throat. "Okay, if you've never seen a Thraw in person, check the mission brief. They're an ungainly race. Bizarre movements. Even the way they turn their heads is strange. Before we left on this mission, I got to meet a Benedictine priest from down there. He was smuggled out about a decade ago, now. The Roman collar on him was neat. They had to adjust the fit of it because of the triangular shape of the throat."

"Commander, what are these huge things?" Cleopas asks, quietly going over the mission details in his Visuals. He sends a digital marker of the being in question to Brigid.

"The ones labeled Skreeve?"

"Yes."

"The Skreeve," Brigid says as he crosses himself in sadness. "The Skreeve are mutated Thraw. Real quick, the Thraw are oviparous; they lay eggs. The eggs develop and hatch fairly quickly—in about four to five weeks."

"That is fast."

"But, since they recognize no God, they have no fixed source of morality. During what's called oogenesis, as the egg develops, they'll inject it with a serum of some kind to mutate the child into one of those things."

The Brothers shake their heads, sink inwardly. The digital image in the mission dossier is a semi-blurry photo, shows a single Skreeve in mid-attack. The thing is easily three times the size and girth of the unmutated and relatively lithe Thraw. The look on its face betrays its insanity, its abject bloodlust. Mindless.

Brigid says, "Intel says the Skreeve are feral. They don't use a language. Nothing as sophisticated as using utensils; they cannot be educated. Absolutely violent. Their lifespans are severely limited. A few months, usually. Kept in cages, fed from slop tossed onto the floor next to their waste. Otherwise, when sent into battle, they'll just keep charging and beating and destroying whatever they're pointed at until their bodies literally quit. They collapse, DRT."

Gonzaga raises an eyebrow. "DRT?"

"Dead right there."

"I'll say it again. Glass the entire planet," Gonzaga murmurs. His brothers ignore the comment.

"Tech? Armament?" Santa Cruz asks.

"Intel is sketchy on that." Brigid says as he sifts through digital reports. The better ones include pictures. "Seems like down on the planet, they've got the universal basic guerilla package. Hand-me-down firearms, some explosives. Their maintenance kits are mostly tape and bubble gum, so that's their level of sophistication. Whatever has four wheels and can go *vroom* they'll retrofit with a gun and brush guard. Maybe some helicopter-type stuff."

"We'll have superior firepower, for sure." Nonnatus says. "Although I was reading in—hang on... here we go." He flips through some of the intel reports in their dossier and finds the one he wants, sends his brothers a tag for it in their Visuals. "The Thraw have been inquiring about buying tech from other civilizations. It's open-ended. We might be in for a few ugly surprises."

"Buying? With what currency?"

Brigid clears his throat. "Everything I've heard—mostly from that Benedictine priest—is they'll pay in flesh. Sell their undesirables as slaves, whatever. Their entire society is based on a caste system, and one cannot move upwards from where he was born. Although I guess one can always be dishonored and moved *down*. Doesn't matter. Just be ready, as we always should be." The group nods. Then, "Questions that don't pertain to glassing the planet?"

No one responds. Brigid says, "Pio, check with Father Cho and see if he's ready to hear our Confessions. We've got eight minutes to go stealth. I want silence when we throw cloaks."

"Yes, sir," Pio says. He heads out the hatch into the passageway. The others finish their coffees and begin last-minute checks.

"Now, Brother Gonzaga." Brigid says, approaching the new Knight as the others leave the room. Just the two of them, Brigid leans in and places his forehead near the young brother's. With the kindness of a father consoling a child who has scraped a knee but with the firmness of a military officer speaking to someone who should know better, he says, "When God blinks, who vanishes?"

"No one, Commander. God does not blink."

"God, with the universe on His shoulders, when He shrugs, what falls off?"

"Nothing, Commander. God does not shrug."

"So, God has made us?"

"Yes."

"And we respond to His graces by trying to live by love?"

"Yes."

"And we are to love, in accordance with the second greatest commandment, as God loves?"

"Yes, Commander."

"God loves the Thraw, despite their evils. He does not blink and let them vanish. He does not shrug and let them fall. And while He does not love their sin, He loves them. He loves us, but not our sin. I hope to avoid killing any of the Thraw, but if we must, it must be accordance with His justice. Glassing the entire planet is no way to show them the love of God. There are plenty of innocents there."

"I know, Commander. I'm just— I've got a long way to go."

"We all do, in our own ways. And you'll get there. You'll—"

Pio swings back into the room. "Confession. One minute each for whoever needs it. Strict. We're getting ready to throw cloaks and move in."

Pio ducks back out the doorway. Proudly etched into the arch over it is a passage from the Gospel according to John, chapter 15, verse 13: *Greater love hath no man than this, that a man lay down his life for his friends.*

Brigid slaps Gonzaga on the shoulder. "We are warriors," he begins, "We defend those who cannot defend themselves. I will not hesitate to use force. But it must be acceptable to God, through His teachings."

"Yes, Commander. I'm working on it."

"I know," Brigid says as he touches a double pendant around his neck. "All the time, I am too."

He breaks away and withdraws his TechHaft. Ignites it. A large Merovingian battle axe blazes forth, crackling with the contained energy particles used to forge it on command. He examines it with a smile, rotating it about as thin streams of energy crawl up and down it; Gonzaga admires it as well. Brigid swings it once casually, just to feel it move, extinguishes it and the particles dissipate into nothingness, leaving only the haft. Gonzaga instinctively reaches down and grips his own TechHaft.

Brigid nods, says, "Now, if you have mortal sin, confess it, so you may better prepare for war."

Throwing Cloaks

The Knights secure themselves inside the *St. Joshua*'s combat dropship seating, their backs to the port and starboard side walls, facing inward towards each other. Sliding doors are situated on either side for rapid deployment. This dropship is more spacious than others they've been inside, with enough room for ten Knights in their armor. RADAR-absorbent coating along the exterior to complement its fractal shape helps deflect sensory equipment. Wings with rotors built into them, pivoting with their turbojet engines next to the body. Aerodynamic nose cone. Weapons systems. A two-meter-tall print of Jesus and His Sacred Heart on the forward bulkhead. Nothing else.

The dropship itself is drone-piloted and the Knights are the only souls on board. Commander Brigid likes it that way; it's better if he only has to worry about his Knights and not a pilot and crew if things go south.

The *St. Joshua* buzzes with its cloaking measures. The sound is unsettling on a subconscious level as the skin of the craft starts actively trying to defeat both visual and electronic detection measures. The resulting effect is like an aura or some bubble they're ensconced inside. The effect is in the air. The Knights do one last check of their weaponry and tech, then without a need for prompting, they all take out their Rosaries.

"We won't have time for a full one, but maybe a decade," Commander Brigid says as he removes his. "What is today, local calendar?"

He looks up, trying to think. Brother Nonnatus sees him doing some kind of conversion math in his head and sighs. Responding with his flat, sandpapery tone, "Monday. Monday local time. The Joyful Mysteries, Commander."

"Ah, yes. Joyful. Well, then. In the name of the Father, the Son and the Holy Spirit—" They get seven prayers in and the ready light starts flashing. Brigid completes the prayer and tells his Knights to secure.

Brother Gonzaga looks around, says, "I don't see any fire controls or anything. Are these dropships armed?"

Nonnatus says, "I'm pretty sure they have a couple of those telson rockets—they're solid red and two meters long. Really thin. You can carry them around with your bare hands. Air-to-air guys."

Brother Santa Cruz smiles. "If you ask the Commander, he'll tell you about how he got into serious trouble in the Academy when he saddled one of those things, magboot-ed to it and rode it like a horse or something."

"Did not," Brigid says with a smirk. "Urban legend."

"What's a horse?" Gonzaga asks.

"It's like a telson rocket, only with legs. They have manual controls on the outside of them," Nonnatus says, winking at Santa Cruz. "Why would they do that if they didn't want you to ride them?"

"Won't it explode, though?" Gonzaga asks.

"At some point," Santa Cruz says. "Just get off it before then, right Commander?" He winks. Brigid laughs and waves it away.

"So," Brother Pio says. He smiles, excited. "Stigmata, huh? When I read that in the mission briefing— boy. You guys all must know my namesake Padre Pio was a well-known stigmatic. I can't wait to ask—"

"Yeah, but you're gonna wait," Santa Cruz says. "Until we get all the way back up here."

"I know, I know," Pio says and makes a fake growling face. "If you'd let me finish, you'd have heard me say that."

"Sure," Santa Cruz says, putting a piece of gum into his mouth and flicking the wadded wrapper at Pio. Pio catches it and flicks it back, hitting Santa Cruz in the eye. The wrapper falls into his lap. "I let that happen."

They all laugh quietly.

"T-minus twenty minutes to maneuvering into the outer atmosphere," Captain Bernhard, the skipper of the *St. Joshua* comes across the comms system. "We're cloaked up. We should be reaching atmospheric turbulence in those twenty minutes. We'll clear the drop ship for launch directly afterwards. All hands, prepare to drop."

"All right," Brigid says. "You heard the captain."

The Knights ready themselves as they feel the ship outside them begin to move.

"Saint Michael the Archangel—" Brigid says.

His Knights chime in, "—defend us in battle. Be our protection against the wickedness and snares of the devil, we humbly pray. And do thou, O prince of the Heavenly hosts, by the power of God, thrust into hell, Satan, and all evil spirits who prowl about the world, seeking the ruin of souls. Amen."

Pio continues, "Lord protect us from every evil, and bless our mission today, so that we may receive your blessing here in this dark hour and preserve the embers of the fire You have kindled here, yet another planet and another people who need Your love and Your graces. Bless us and even our enemies, dear Lord, that we may all yet come to know Your truth, holiness and love. May the Saints and our guardian angels intercede for us. In Jesus name we pray—"

"Amen." They all finish.

Brigid says, "From here on out, maintain all audible discipline unless mission critical."

The silence in the drop ship impregnates the small space. Every external mechanical click and groan, every last gasp of hissing air from the *St. Joshua's* pneumatic systems filled their ears. The dropship shifts once as the final adjustments settle out and then a true blackout occurs. A single electronic light ticks on and off in the depths of it, the utter silence of it broken only by its beeping.

Almost ethereally, a subtle glow of red and blue emanates from the blood and water flowing from their Savior's sacred heart on the wall. There is no light source, and each Knight might believe he is only imagining the minute radiance. But they all perceive it.

The Knights grip their straps. All peer forward on the dropship as that light turns on, turns off. They are fixated. Here it comes.

"All hands, begin mission." Captain Bernhard orders, and the *St. Joshua* jolts violently under the sudden and extreme propulsion.

†

The thrusters on the ship dilate fully open and the blazing glow of the propellant grows to a blinding white. From behind the dark side of the moon the ship rockets forth. The distance between the moon and the planet is almost four hundred thousand kilometers. To cross that in the twenty minute minutes the captain spoke of, the ultra-high output of the thrusters is pegged in the slim space between near-divinely efficient and suicidal.

The ship, cloaked against satellite and land-based detection, soars towards the brilliant penumbra surrounding Arithraw.

The planet rapidly approaches on a collision course. Cuts its thrusters. Begins reverse propulsion to counter their momentum. As the blanket of exosphere begins to caress the *St. Joshua*, it banks in a long arc. As it matches the curvature of the planet the ship levels out and the portside hatch opens. The dropship ratchets forward on its two receiving bollards until its beak leans out into the world. The *St. Joshua* maintains a steady distance from the surface of the planet, banked slightly to the north.

"Dropship in launch position in T-minus one minute," Captain Bernhard says. "God bless you, gentlemen. And God bless our mission."

Brother Gonzaga rolls his head on his neck, alert. Brother Cleopas is still with his Rosary in his hand, prays silently to himself. Brothers Pio and Nonnatus wait patiently as all the gears of the mission begin turning, involving them and their part to play. Brother Santa Cruz watches the *status ready* light blink steadily on his rail gun.

"Drop ship in position in T-minus thirty seconds." The thirty seconds pass, ticking one after another off into oblivion.

"In position. On my mark."

The men steady themselves and pray to their patron saints. All time for complaints, for adjustments, for refusals, all that time has passed in the blink of an eye.

"Now is the time to do, for God. Be men who use their strength for the benefit of others, my brothers," Commander Brigid whispers.

Captain Bernhard says, "Mark."

The dropship ejects. Within seconds of being shed from the *St. Joshua*, the atmosphere's deafening roar passing by screams all around. The turbulence of freefall sends every man's gut into a jiggling mess of nausea. Shattered equilibrium.

Each Knight's Visuals begin a ticker counting down the distance between them and the surface. From tens of thousands of feet, so quickly dissolving to thousands. The eternal sunlight flowing through the stratosphere begins to wane as they descend into the troposphere, sinking into the murky dark of the planet. Night descends.

"Positions," Brigid says with eager intensity. "It's here."

The Knights hit a single buckle on their chest, a quick release for their straps. All stand, taking one large stride to the ready rail running down the center of the ship. Each grabbing an overhead loop dangling from it. All six hands grip and pull, notifying the automated safety system they're in place and ready, and the sliding doors unlatch with snaps like gunshots and draw backwards.

The rush of the cold atmosphere floods into the belly of the dropship. Winds whipping, the roar of the air screaming. The Knights endure as the thin clouds whoosh along inside with them, the night swirling and sapping all their heat.

"Ten seconds to jump," Brigid says. "Ready the tech."

In response, Nonnatus reaches to a small square controller he has mounted on his left shoulder. His thumb flips a switch and behind them in the cargo area numerous blue lights blink to life and auto adjust their brilliance down to avoid glare in the ambient darkness.

"Engage active camo."

Each man in his stealth suit; a form-fitting outfit designed for mobility and small-caliber engagements. Printed from Ceramatex, a polymer/ceramic/carbon fiber development that provided the protection of old Earth ceramic plating but allows the ease of movement unheard of for the durability it provided. It's almost impervious to conventional small arms and bladed weaponry.

Woven through the skin are nanotech emitter/receiver that observe what is directly opposite them and display a low-res image of it on the opposite. Using the surface of the suit itself as a screen, it displays in front of the Knight what is directly behind them, and vice versa in a 360-degree manner. Not true invisibility, but something approaching it.

Brigid says, "Coordinates are in your Visuals. All degrees are relative based off the dropship's nose. I'll be at zero-zero-zero. Nonnatus, you're at one-eight-zero. Cleopas, zero-four-five. Gonzaga, one-three-five. Santa Cruz, two-two-five and Pio, you're at two-seven-zero. When you touch, mark that lat and long as the exfil, then secure a spot fifty meters out and wait for the all-clear. Then we head east. Five seconds to jump."

The Knights bend at the knees, then rise to the balls of their feet. One hand on his overhead loop, the other drawn in close. The electronic hum of the vertical landing and take-off system cuts and whines in reverse for a split second. Everything goes quiet.

"Jump," And Brigid steps out the door into the nothing just beyond it.

†

Two hundred feet beneath the dropship, the tall field grasses outside of an oppressed farm town wave in the midnight breeze. The delicate droning of the Arithraw insects carry on all around. A chirp here and there of something looking for dinner in the night.

Two feet hit the ground in a muffled slam. The Ceramatex suit clinks as its Kinetic Effect Reception Systems rolls that energy up conductors sewn into the legs and into a battery/capacitor combo on the Knight's back, storing it. Might come in handy later.

Two more feet hit, then four. Then another two. As they land, they drop a digital marker in their Visuals to save that latitude and longitude as the rendezvous point for extraction. The Knights fan out in a 360-degree pattern, each one covering all space between the shoulders of his brother to either side. Brother Nonnatus uses eye flickers in his helmet to send commands to the drones. All four of them exit the cloaked, hovering dropship. Their dim blue lights are like bioluminescent sparks in the night. The drones, small enough to fit into two cupped hands, soar out in the four cardinal directions.

The Knights meet their fifty-meter perimeter and take up positions. Their active camo settles out and to the naked eye at such low light conditions, the Knights smear into the shadows. The bland nighttime color palette only aids them further. So little contrast to blend into.

The quiescence of night lays down heavily against them. In stark contrast to the noise, rush and cavalcade of the *St. Joshua* and the drop, now the silence is so piercing it raises their hackles.

The drones fire up their scanning arrays. Tour the small town and the surrounding area, nitpicking the entire electromagnetic spectrum. Each drone is equipped with specific arrays, so a few minutes pass as every drone makes a full sweep. Nonnatus takes in all the raw data in his Visuals. The onboard software in his system overlays the scans to add layer upon layer of detail. He reduces the informational noise and clutter, sharpens the images and pushes them out to his brothers.

"Nothing useful in the radio waves, microwaves, gamma and ultraviolet. I do have contacts with infrared, visible and X-rays. They're all marked in the Visuals," Nonnatus says.

"What are the contacts?" Commander Brigid asks.

"Just Thraw life over in the town. Inside the buildings, houses, whatever. Usual stuff, looks like. Everybody settling down for the night. Nothing looks like it's alerted to us."

"Okay. Indications of military watchtowers, overflights, potential hostiles? Anything remote?"

"Looks like a patrol on the far side. At least a kilometer away and moseying along. Closer to us, I see two ground vehicles parked with their engines running. On heading two-eight-one. Might be another patrol, but if it is, the soldiers are inside a building. They're not with the vehicles. Nothing tall enough to be a legitimate manned watchtower. I don't detect a radio or comms tower, either. First impression is they're relying on goons to patrol."

"Roger. Anything else worth mentioning?"

"No other signs of electronic detection, no laser trip wire kind of stuff. Not even cameras."

"That's the nice thing about tyrannical regimes," Brother Santa Cruz says. "Oppression doesn't do much for advancement. We're fighting low-tech brutes here."

"We're not fighting at all," Brigid says. "We're slipping in and out. Nonnatus, do you see our contact?"

Nonnatus checks his watch, says, "Supposed to start up in about twenty-six seconds, on the hour." He sweeps the drones' arrays towards the town.

On the outskirts is nothing more than a few trees. Sparse foliage, thin trunks and branches, short. Hefty stones scattered amongst the semi-barren ground. Nature has been pruned back to allow for a flattened, earthy plain on which the Thraw built their settlements. The town's plot is circular, a few kilometers in diameter. Clusters of small buildings have been thrown up and are now wearing the dilapidation of a century.

Brother Gonzaga stands in the combat ready stance they drilled into him in post-academy schools. Knees bent, up on the balls of his feet. Arms at weapons ready; established grip and finger indexed along the trigger guard. Just swing up on point and let fly. Head on a swivel.

A small insect flutters up on two pirs of wings, lands on his transparent forearm. Tucks its wings behind two long elytron like throwing daggers. Four spindly legs. Four segments to its body with ungainly, bulbous eyes. It scampers along on his forearm, a single moniliform antennae rotating like a RADAR dish on its head. He gives his arm a quick jerk and the thing flutters away into the Arithraw night.

He flashes back to a similar insect on his home world. As the bombs fell, swarms of them lifted off in coordinated sheets. Snapping in the blasted winds and swirling in a dark undulating tube formation. Away from there. Strange to be jealous of a bug.

"Time," Nonnatus checks his watch again, sees the counter roll over to the top of the new hour. The drones broaden their sweep. In moments, a flashing burst of UV light illuminates a small spot. Quick successions. "I see the beacon. Heading two-six-nine relative."

The Knights turn that way, see it for themselves. Nonnatus triggers the drone equipped with the responder beacon to communicate back to the contact. The Thraw beacon changes its flashing pattern in response.

"Signal received. They know we're here."

Brigid takes a deep breath. "All right, move. We make contact."

The formation acts, liquid shadows on top of the night lit only by the moon. The grasses in the field give way to the stonier rim of the town, which gives way to the abused earth the Thraw scratch a living off.

Black Robe's Cargo

Ten meters out, the Knights halt and reassume defensive positions while the drones make a final scan.

Weapon barrels high and ready, trigger fingers floating above the mechanisms. Alert; the tension from waiting worse than active engagement. Each man has developed his own tic, something in particular he has tuned into. Brother Gonzaga listens for twitching in the tall grasses, a twig snapping or some earthen crunch. Brother Pio lets his eyes crawl along windows, a quick flash of light or shift in the shadow. Brother Santa Cruz searching for vehicles. Being armed with the rail gun, he looks for heavy or fortified targets his projectile can punch through and keep going.

The drones finish their sweep, report back. Brother Nonnatus says, "Single heat signature where the beacon presented. Matches Thraw biology. Nothing hiding, so far as we can tell. Contact is unarmed. Looks to be the real deal, sir."

Commander Brigid nods. "Blessed Virgin be with us. So be it; fall in on me. I'm making contact."

They draw in their formation in and close the gap to the contact. Nearing the closest building, the taller grasses and sparse trees give way to drudged earth. A strange, intentional ululating whistle rises in the stirring night. Two quick notes, the last one hits higher and slides down in a trill allowed to fall off into quiet. A pause. Repeated.

Brigid's helmet speakers are programmed with the call-and-answer response. His system factors the distance between himself and the contact, plays the answer through directional speakers at a volume loud enough to reach without drawing unwanted attention. The return whistle grows urgent. Brigid does it once more and a single note comes back to him. Pio says, "Eyes on. I like the way he dresses."

He puts a mark on the contact and the Knights receive it in their Visuals. Brigid says, "Make it."

They drop their active camo and move forward. As they near a wall, a lithe bipedal form rises from crouching in a shadow. Its arms—the two primary ones—are so long they almost appear as legs for as low as they hang. The secondary arms are clasped in prayer at its chest, the apex of the fingertips just under the white block of its Roman collar. Its black cassock bound by a rope, strung through with prayer beads. A crucifix dangling on a chain from around its neck.

No matter what race the alien is, it is always a source of great spiritual light to see a priest.

"All praise be to Jesus Christ, King of endless glory, for having delivered you safely to us, my brothers in Christ. We are in need of you," The contact says in his thick Arithraw accent.

The Knights are equipped with a small piece of tech they commonly called a universal translator. Though far from truly being universal, it does do a better-than-decent job at interpreting foreign languages on the fly, in real time, but only if the user knows to preprogram it ahead of the encounter.

"Greetings, Father and thank you for your priesthood," Brigid says, lowering his weapon and drawing within arm's reach. "The Brotherhood of Those Washed in the Blood and Water from His Side have sent us to help. Thank you for meeting us."

The Thraw priest smiles—a bizarre-looking expression to the eyes of a human. But it is serene. So much peace like a flower in search of the sun, growing through the cracks in the forceful oppression of the atheist and domineering planetary regime. "Crusaders. Here, with us, now. God is good."

The priest reaches out, and with its thumb rubs a cross on the forehead of the Commander's helmet. "Blessings, blessings."

"Thank you."

The priest motions with its secondary arms. "Please. Come. We must hurry. There is always a patrol, you see."

†

The Knights fall into a single-file line and follow the nimble, quick priest as they make into the town's rim and through shadows across several squalid buildings.

Commander Brigid sends a text scrawl along the others' Visuals which reads *take note how fast this species moves. Now imagine the combat.*

They stop outside a blocky and featureless building that could be any one of the town's structures. In the darkness, everything seems as gray and lifeless as any heavily oppressed settlement, no matter the planet. No matter the variant of regime. Brigid looks up to the stoop framing the door. It is sunk deep into the building, and on its ceiling a small cross is carved. He smiles. That symbol, from so long ago on a distant world, has traversed time and space to these alien creatures. It has made a home with as much meaning, wonder and hope to them as it did to those first humans who actually watched the God-man crucified. It became their symbol. Millennia atop millennia later. Here. Now. It is the Thraw's symbol as well.

"Glory be to God, indeed," Brigid says.

The priest follows his gaze and returns the smile. "To think... Jesus came here. To us. *To us.* We were little more than slaves to our masters. A commodity to live and die according to their whims. Used and thrown away. Our government, godless and military. My father and his father before him, laborers in the fields and the mines. Those men... when one would die, another would step right over his body and take his place. Such was the way for the plebian Thraw. We were not born into the highest caste; therefore, we were not even worthy of being given names.

"But... *He.* Our Lord and Savior Jesus the Christ from a faraway planet, His good news was brought here to us by the Blackrobes. He came to us. *To us.* He came here to let us know we are loved and worth being loved. We are as valuable as the highest caste. It was near insanity. The Blackrobe priests, clandestine evangelists proclaiming the Good News of Jesus Christ, they snuck in here, on this planet, and preached. They won souls, converted us. They brought the greatest threat to our government: hope. Something more powerful than it. They brought Jesus. God bless them.

"And now, that is my mission: to let others know. The love of our Savior. *Our* Jesus Christ. I am one of them, now. An underground priest. Glory be to God, as you have said."

Brigid looks into the priest's eyes and sees tears of joy. "Indeed," Brigid says. He pauses and then asks, "Is our cargo inside here?"

"Yes, of course, my friend."

In the cluster around them, Brother Nonnatus nods in acknowledgment. Follows standard spec ops protocol and prompts one drone to follow them and set the other three to a collapse and hold formation. They trace a quick path close to the ground and go off into the nearby field. Those three all fold their maneuverable parts inward and set, one atop the other in a stack. They hover a few inches off the ground near a tree. The fourth stays in an alert status, scanning and hovering a meter above the heads of the Knights.

"Let us help you."

"Yes, of course." The priest says. And he leads them inside.

†

A motorized Arithraw patrol is drawing nearer to that side of town. Announced from far off by the buzzing hum of the vehicle's small electric motor and the chains clinking from around the necks of the two Skreeve they have pacing beside them.

The driver maneuvers the vehicle towards the outskirts of the town, dipping the vehicle down off the flattened earth and onto the grassier untamed stretches.

The gunner, standing on a small platform at the rear, its secondary arms manning a crew-served automatic gun, barks harshly at the driver. The driver returns with a similarly harsh comment, waves the gunner away dismissively. He then drives the vehicle towards a copse of trees and parks. Gets out, mumbles something over its shoulder and walks off into the shadows of a tree. With its back to the rest of the patrol, it unzips and begins relieving itself.

The two Skreeve, now not being pulled along by the vehicle, take the opportunity to meander about as far as their leashes will allow. Dragging their fingers through the dirt, leaving deep ruts and picking through the clumps of grass and vegetation that come up in their palms. Finding digestible roots and chewing on them.

A cloud shifts, refracting the light of the moon. An unnatural twinkle catches the eye of one of the Skreeve. It snorts, freezes. Takes notice of something small at the base of a nearby tree.

†

"We have hidden her—Sister Stella Nessa, that is her name—and we have hidden her here for the past two moons. Our physician—Lord, grant unto him eternal rest—had examined her numerous times before he passed." The priest says as they descend a flight of stairs into the small building's basement. The steps are hewn from rock and scaled to accommodate the Thraw's sprawling gate. The Knights navigate them, leaving Brothers Nonnatus and Santa Cruz at the top near the front door.

Commander Brigid sends another note to his Knights reading *Arithraw lunar cycle is approximately forty-five (twenty-four hour) days. They've had her for three of our standard months.*

The priest continues, "Our physician was excellent. A surgeon by trade, he was skilled enough to work on the highest castes if it wasn't so dirty in their eyes to let someone of his caste touch them."

The priest gives what appears to be a shrug. "They would rather die."

Brother Gonzaga grumbles to himself. Mutters, "Animals."

Brother Pio sends a text to him, *Who? The highest caste?*

Gonzaga catches himself before he responds with *most of them.*

The priest says, "The sister's wounds remain fresh, and under our care we have verified she is not doing it to herself. With them comes a scent of flowers, which I love. Our physician could not explain them naturally. She has moments of ecstasy; when I am here for those, I feel extremely close to God. I want to give Him glory just thinking about them!"

"When did they begin?"

"Seven moons ago, now. Even before the bishop could meet with her, church members heard of her and began pilgrimages to her. Asking for prayers. Trying to get a little of the blood on a cloth to keep or touch their sacramentals to her. One of the reasons we moved her here in this safe house is to protect her. Word has gotten out... they captured our doctor."

"Who?"

"Our government." The priest says with a hint of sadness. "Always our government."

"They're Satanic," one of the laymen says. He looks to the priest for some kind of assurance or maybe forgiveness for bursting into the conversation. The priest smiles at him and shrugs.

"The devil has his fingers in all that is fallen."

Brigid nods and asks, "Your doctor? The one tending to the nun? He was captured?"

"Yes. I assume he was tortured until he gave up our secret."

"That's why you so urgently got a hold of us," Brigid says as it falls into place. "I never heard your message—I just received mission orders. But your government knows about her."

"Yes. They want her dead." The priest shakes his head and makes the sign of the cross over himself. "Our government has stepped up its efforts to kill us. I can only assume they learned of her through torturing one of us. They have a copy of our liturgical calendar and have been making raids on Holy Days of Obligation. Major feast days. Our bishop has been here several times, to pray over her and check up. He has officially sanctioned her experience as genuine and miraculous. He would have been here to meet you; except he is very ill at the moment."

Brigid nods, "I understand. Part of our briefing stated he was prone to an illness common to older Thraw males?"

"Yes. We lose our sight and fine motor skills. Rest and water are the best medicines for it. And prayer, of course. Always prayer. But, once the symptoms set in, we know our time to meet our Lord is coming. He is near death. We become joyous about it. Those who remain atheist fear it. The junior males plot against them for power. As it is, the bishop asked that I offer his apologies for missing you."

"No apologies necessary," Brigid says, stands at the base of the steps. His mind shifts and he says, "I've never been blessed to see this in person." The bottom of the stairs turns into a narrow corridor that looks like it spirals around the base of the building.

Even through his helmet, Brigid notices the smell of fresh flowers in the air. Though there are none in the room, and he saw none in the wild coming here. "It smells wonderful in here."

"Yes. Yes, it does. A sign of her holiness. It is beautiful."

They walk to the far side of the room where a Thraw layman stands guard at another door. He is armed with a small pistol. He speaks quickly with the priest. A reverent sound. Then he regards the Knights and a mixed look of relief and renewed concern comes over him.

The priest moves past the guard and enters the room, motioning for the Knights to follow. As each man passes by the guard, he nods his thanks. Brother Cleopas looks down and sees a Rosary dangling from the guard's secondary hand. He smiles in recognition of it. Holds up his own with pride.

He says, "I love her, too." The guard tips his head and clasps Cleopas's shoulder and he goes inside.

Gonzaga is last and he tries to be cordial. A voice in the back of his mind asking about this layman. Trustworthy? Armed? He works to turn his back to him.

In the room, two more laymen stand up to meet them. Each armed; one with a farming tool, the other with a long stick whittled down to a point and slender cantles of metal, like nails, driven through it. They are on either side of a small bed. Near the foot of it there is a table with a lit candle illuminating the room.

The priest extends all his arms out and says, "Brothers in Christ, behold. Her safety has arrived. Praise Jesus."

The Thraw move aside, and the Knights see her, sitting upright on the slender bed with her back along the wall. A Thraw nun, small in stature as the females are roughly half the height and girth of the males. Fully habited, the nun smiles at the Knights and sighs a loving and gorgeous note.

Her bare hands and feet, bearing the Stigmata. The wounds of Christ.

Bloody injuries in her hands and feet, supernaturally appearing on a select few of the Catholic faithful whose devotion to Christ is so thorough that they desire to unite with His suffering as He became the ultimate sacrifice. The wounds are real and tangible, subject to scientific examination. And her continued examination proves to be authentic. They bleed, though she never suffers the effects of prolonged blood loss. They emit a pleasant, floral odor to aid in their recognition as a gift from God rather than some masochistic cry for attention. Divine gifts.

For her to receive such blessings, she must be intensely in love with the Lord. Focused on nothing, not hunger, not passions, not the strife of her world, not herself, but only on Him. So rare, even amongst the religiously devout.

"Praise God," Brother Pio says. The Knights make the sign of the cross over themselves.

"Yes, my friend," The priest says. "Sister Stella Nessa, she is a stigmatic. The first Thraw ever to bear the wounds of Christ."

The guard armed with the sharpened pike turns, clears his throat. With anger in his voice he says, "They have been searching for her. To kill her. They know what she means to us."

"Proof of miracles. Proof of God," Pio says. "A threat to the entire planetary regime, like the father said. Hope." He beams with happiness and steps to the nun. Looks at her and says, "My name-saint, Padre Pio was a stigmatic as well—"

"Save it for the *St. Joshua*," Brigid says. Peers at the Nun and her serenity. "Can you walk? We came prepared to carry you—"

"No," She smiles, and Brigid can see just how few teeth she possesses anymore. "I am not fast, my son. I am old. Nearing two hundred of my years."

"She must be carried," The priest interjects. "She is frail."

Brigid nods, smiles. Looks to his men. "Gonzaga, you're up. Let's get her off-world."

†

As the first Thraw patrolman takes a step near the unnoticed cluster of metal by the tree, the gunner, who has also exited the vehicle, seizes him by the shoulder. They bark and rasp at each other for a moment, and they come to an agreement.

The first patrolman withdraws a set of binoculars and looks about the fields and beyond. Something has bothered their Skreeve, and it is near here. Behind them, the Skreeve become more and more agitated. Their chains rattle, their feet pounding on the earth.

Another vehicle pulls up alongside and a third patrolman gets out. A single Skreeve rides in the back of the vehicle, better trained than the two on chains.

The chained Skreeve respond to him as if he is their wrangler, and mewl as he hisses forcefully. But they are agitated, excited. They do not settle for him. When the Skreeve cannot let go of their building energy, the wrangler jabs the nearest mutant with a prod. A sharp electrical snap and a smell of burnt flesh wafts up. The chastised Skreeve makes a pathetic sound, recoils. The other continues its bestial commotion. The wrangler bares its teeth at that one and takes a large step to cross the distance. Jabs the second Skreeve at the base of its neck. The creature snarls and barks at the face of the wrangler. The wrangler, undeterred, slaps the Skreeve along the head with a loud fleshy thump, daring it to bite at him.

After it satisfies itself with its last snarl, the Skreeve eases and turns away. Picks at the ground again and finds a root to chew on.

The wrangler turns to the patrolman with the binoculars. "Something has them irritated."

The gunner chuffs and asks, "You need to be a wrangler to know this? Look about. What is it?" The patrolman and gunner return to their vehicle, look all around down below and then upward. Somewhere in the stars.

The first Skreeve begins again, can still barely contain itself. The second is digging grooves in the soil, finding grubs and woody roots. The first finally snorts deeply, clearing its nostrils. Extends its lengthy forearms to the ground and assumes a quadrupedal stance, its nose-member extending like a short snout. As it sniffs the earth, it exhales out through gill-like slits just below its eyes. It begins to check the ground all around. The wrangler recognizes its behavior, snaps his fingers.

The patrolman looks over and the wrangler says, "Free it. Let it root it out."

The patrolman unsnaps the quick disconnect on its leash and it begins to move with the possession of an animal in the hunt. The wrangler is near enough it, as intense as the mutant is. The others watch as it searches for a scent. Roars when it finds one. It lumbers towards the tree and the clouds shift again. The drones hover perfectly still, but that makes no difference now.

The gunner yanks his weapon in the drones' direction, and they spring up into the air. Move behind the tree and then vanish. The gunner curses. The patrolman begins to shout about what he's just seen, and the wrangler picks up their comms device, begins speaking.

†

Brother Gonzaga kneels before Sister Stella Nessa and sets a small ring on the floor. He presses a button, and the ring releases a dark, thick gas that is instantaneously electrified, lining up its molecules and forming a malleable mesh-like netting. Gonzaga uses a special tool to grab the netting and draw it upwards, eyeballing how tall the nun was.

"All right, let's get you inside."

"My gratitude," she says as the Knight's large hands gently lift her under her primary arms. She folds her long limbs inward and becomes a small ball wrapped in black with a habit framing her face. Gonzaga sits her inside the ring, grabs the rescue litter with two backpack-like straps, and shrugs her on himself.

"Please, gather to me," the priest says, hands outstretched. The Knights do, and the priest crosses himself. "In the name of the Father, and of the Son, and of the Holy Spirit. Lord, You have blessed us beyond measure with the selfless gift of these brave men. Now, bless us again by giving them safe passage as they transport Your holy daughter to a place where she may experience Your love and grace. Continue to pour forth Your love on we who remain, ever seeking holy union with You and with the Sacred Heart of Jesus. And for the conversion of those who persecute us, may they too see Your love and Your plan for their lives. In Jesus's name we pray, amen."

"Amen." A resolute word spoken by unified voices.

The nun looks around, concerned. "My Rosary..." she says, not seeing the prayer beads on the bed or floor nearby. One of her guards takes the single sheet on the bed and fluffs it, haphazardly folds it up. Sets it aside and begins to search about.

"Would you like to pray on mine?" Brother Cleopas asks, holding out his hand. The nun takes the beads and feels them over once. Cleopas nods towards them, says, "Those, they're very special to me. When I was a novice member of the Knights 15 13, on our first combat mission, a missile punched right into the ground in front of me while we were pinned down by enemy fire. Right in front of me. Like, as far away as me to you. Never exploded, though. They kept us pinned down and we spent two days there, exchanging small arms fire, all that. Our demolitions expert wound up defusing the missile. I took the casing and when we finally escaped, I melted it down. Fed droplets of the slag into water until I had those prayer beads."

"It is gorgeous. Thank you," she says.

"Stories later." Commander Brigid says. "Brother Nonnatus? Brother Santa Cruz? Read me?"

The Knights upstairs acknowledge in clipped whispers.

"Good. Here we come, cargo in hand."

"Coast is clear. Ready to exfil."

The Knights move, the priest and laymen behind them. As they reach the top of the winding stairs Nonnatus and Santa Cruz move out the front door, covering their exit. The Knights spill out behind them, Brigid in the rear with the priest next to him.

"Pray for us, Father. We'll be back with help. I want to bring an entire command and free your people, Catholic or not."

"As the Lord wills it. I am here for Him, by Him and to do His bidding until He calls me home."

"We all are."

"God bless you. Be off."

Brigid nods sharply, says, "Move out."

They step out into the night and a flash in the distance catches their eyes, raises their hackles.

"Incoming!" Brother Pio shouts as the small building behind them explodes with the artillery.

Exfil

Another flash appears before the smoking fragments of the building have finished raining down. Blasted debris trail tails of dust and fire through the air as the concussion blast hits the Knights from behind. Shoves them off their feet. Falling face first onto the gritty alien dirt. The building cracks and begins to collapse.

By divine providence, Brother Gonzaga spins a hundred and eighty degrees as the whistle of the first artillery sings overhead. The explosion hits him square in the front. He prays he got enough of his body between it and the nun as he bursts backward. He collides into the ground on his shoulder, dragging a trench through the soil as the blast shoves him away from the ruined building.

He coughs and groans. Under his breath he says, "Hope these savages are worth it." Out loud, he shouts, "Sister, you all right?" He tries to shout over his shoulder as he shoves up, grabbing his weapon. "Are you all right?"

"Oh, yes, yes," she says, calmly. "God bless you for saving me."

Gonzaga can still smell her pleasant odor. Feels a joy radiating off her like light from a bulb. But as a rapid line of small arms fire pops to life, walks towards them, it's enough. Gonzaga pitches away and makes sure to take the rounds along his chest where his armor will protect her. Gets up, aiming in the dark where he sees the muzzle flash and returns fire.

Commander Brigid pushes up off the ground. "All right, do it the hard way. Engage fall back. Get to the dropship," he turns to make out the way they came as another artillery shell hits directly on their path. Then another behind it.

All the Knights turn on their active camo. As their silhouettes vanish from the battlefield, the enemy fire begins to open up. Throwing darts at the entire wall to hit an invisible bull's-eye.

"Secondary location?" Brother Cleopas asks over the immense clatter of noise.

"Gonna have to. Get the dropship piloted over there." Brigid says. "Nonnatus, the drones?"

Brother Nonnatus is pressing himself against a block of demolished wall, one hand on his shoulder-mounted controls for the tech. "Already on it."

"Get eyes on that—" Yet another shell hits, and Brigid watches as the final standing walls of the building detonate outwards. He spins, seeing two of the laymen guards face down, sprawled out and deathly still in the rubble. A third layman is crawling away from the damaged building as the next shell strikes, and he disappears in the whoosh of fire and smoke and dust.

Gonzaga looks at them, focuses on the one layman still struggling. The one at the outer door armed with a pistol on whom Gonzaga didn't want to turn his back. Rosary still wound up between his fingers.

"Lord, ease his suffering," the nun says over Gonzaga's shoulder. The scenery around them getting chewed up by the attack, bullets ricocheting. Small explosions foretelling larger ones. Fire. In a moment the layman stops struggling, goes still. The nun says, "Lord, eternal rest grant—"

"In a minute, sister," Gonzaga says as a sliver of memory flashes through his mind's eye like a blade cutting. The Knight shakes it off and stands up. Bolts over to better cover as rounds chase them.

Nearby, the priest lays on his side. Brigid runs to him; sees how badly he is hurt. Brigid's Visuals begins to run a diagnostic on the priest, but these stealth suits don't have the sensor suite and capabilities to give a good report on someone not wearing the suit, and beyond that, on Thraw biology. All the basic diagnostic states is SEVERE. Then it recalculates and states IMPENDING FATALITY.

Brigid snarls. Says, "Brother Santa Cruz, rail gun us a way out of here."

"Getting ready to rock and roll, sir," Santa Cruz is on his feet, running to a perch he'd seen to where he can even the odds some. Around them, spats of small arms fire begin springing to life, snapping into the dirt and walls. Santa Cruz sprints past Brother Cleopas huddled up behind a massive stone half buried in the ground, radioing the *St. Joshua*. He runs past Brother Pio who is on one knee, returning fire.

As Santa Cruz races to an exterior staircase leading to the roof of a two-story building, another artillery flash appears on the horizon and the approaching whistle foretells the outcome. The building he's running to explodes. Santa Cruz pitches off to the side to avoid shrapnel and flame, landing in a tangle near a tree.

"They just shelled where I was headed," Santa Cruz says. "I'm looking for a new spot."

"Stop looking and find one," Brigid says. He kneels beside the priest, who, even as injured as he is, is still so serene. "Anybody else got eyes on?"

"I see muzzle flashes here and there," Brother Pio says. "Watch out—" a new explosion in the soil several meters away from him kicks up a plume of debris.

"Be very careful with return fire," Cleopas says. "I've got civilians running out of their homes into the woods."

"Roger. Mark them on Visuals as best you can," Brigid says. "And zero in on the muzzle flashes," Brigid brushes away a flat piece of wooden debris that landed across the priest. His Roman collar is still clean, bright white. Below that, Brigid sees blood. "How are we on the drones?"

Brother Nonnatus can hear the small devices hum over his head. Their locators flash on his Visuals. "On scene." The three on sentry join the fourth and they swoop off at a hard angle, rise to thirty meters off the surface and unfold their formation to cover the entire battleground.

"I'm marking muzzle flash and artillery spottings," Nonnatus says. The Knights' Visuals light up with designators as they begin to digitally map the battlefield.

"Found a perch." Santa Cruz said as he spots a fifteen-meter-tall tree towards the center of town. With the active camouflage distorting his silhouette, he races, muzzle forward. Jumping around divots in the earth, small pockets of flame and shards of debris stabbed into the ground. Remnants of explosions.

Another artillery flash on the horizon, then another again. Santa Cruz doubles his efforts, engaging his suit's KERS to turn his strides into leaps. The Kinetic Effect Reception System absorbs the shock of his footfalls and projects it downward, effectively allowing each step to act as a trampoline. The forward pitch of it hurls him towards the tree with every step.

Two explosions land around the Knights as small arms fire strafes. Pio gets hit along the chest and shoulder in a multi-round burst. They ping off but sting his body. Damage a few of the active camo emitter/receiver cameras. He returns fire, moves to find better cover. He gathers himself behind a spit of bushes that had been partly blown out of the ground and now rest with their jagged roots exposed, the whole plant canted at an angle. He joins Gonzaga there, huddles close.

"You hit?" Gonzaga asks.

Pio brushes a hand along where the rounds struck. The active camo in that spot is slightly frayed and his invisibility image is distorted. "Yeah, but the Ceramatex took it. Charged my batteries a little bit, too."

"We're surrounded," Gonzaga says as he turns in a circle. He peers over his shoulder at the nun, wadded into a ball but still with Cleopas's Rosary beads hanging out of her petite fist. Praying. Totally at peace. She tilts her head back, ecstasy abounding in her gaze.

Pio looks at her, the serenity coming off her like a balm to his firefight anxiety. "She's amazing. You can tell just by being around her... I'm better for it."

Gonzaga can feel it too, and a small bloom of regret opens inside him for wanting to erase this planet. Bullets strafe in two separate lines along them, drawing trails. He snarls.

"We'll get you out of here, sister. Don't worry," Gonzaga says. The Thraw answer with another shelling.

Nearby, Brigid gets an arm under the priest. "We've got to get you back to our ship. Our medical unit."

The priest weakly takes his hand over Brigid's, stills the Knight's hand, says, "What prophecy it was, that just a moment ago I told you I was to be here until the Lord called me home."

"I know. I know, but—"

"But nothing. I am here. And the Lord has called." Maybe it's a demonstration for the Commander's benefit, maybe coincidence, but the priest raises another hand to supplicate the Knight before him, and it's covered in blood. The priest pats the Knight on the shoulder, then he coughs harshly. Fresh blood wets his lips. "The others?"

Commander Brigid looks around, sees the laymen's bodies. Another explosion violently fells a nearby tree and rains a hefty spatter of dirt and pebbles down everywhere.

"They're dead, Father. I'm sorry."

The priest smiles. "God loves you. And God has given them the glory of martyrdom. What joy. Then our secret is with the Sister. Only her. Save her. All is with you and her. If she is captured alive, it will be—"

"I know."

"No, you don't," The priest coughs again and makes a small choking sound. Brigid rolls him on his side, and he relaxes, eases into comfort, and after another breath he goes completely still.

Another explosion wakes Brigid out of his pause. Gunfire erupting from his Knights.

"Pio, what's the word?" He asks.

"We've got coordinates for the exfil. *St. Joshua* says they're maneuvering around, but they've got contacts on their RADAR, closing in from the upper atmosphere. Far side of the planet, though. Gonna be a minute. Looks like they're going to be engaged too. This went real bad, real fast."

"Yeah," Brigid says. "This looks like they were waiting for us."

Gonzaga says, "Well, if she got sold out by the doc, it was only a matter of time."

Another artillery round drives into a two-story building off to their side. The building's guts punch out and the thing cuts in half, the top caves into the bottom without effort. Crashing and snapping fills their ears.

"Santa Cruz?"

"Eyes on," Santa Cruz says, lying prone on a branch in the tree, his barrel square on the Thraw artilleryman who even now is loading another shell. The cannon itself is a small, trailer-able installation they can tow behind one of their small vehicles. Three crates of shells beside him, only the first one opened. "Contact." Santa Cruz says, and he pulls the trigger.

The thin electrical line from the barrel to the target sizzles a brilliant blue and vaporizes into nothing as it magnetically propels a small tungsten nugget between points A and B. The barrel hisses and flushes out a jolt of electrified smoke. The weapon kicks hard, booming into the battle. The projectile is conducted nearly instantaneously from Santa Cruz's weapon into and through the artillery at Mach 6.

The Thraw and its artillery setup disappear in a vast explosion. Flames roar up and curl, belching out oranges and yellows. A domino effect of one shell going off and within a split second, the others as well. All three cases. The explosion tears apart the safe ground the Thraw hold. Opening a way out through their defensive perimeter. The rest of their soldiers scatter everywhere as flames like hands of an emerging titan explode from the ground up. Soldiers toss about. The gout of flame on the horizon is like a volcano erupting. Devastating.

"Nothing like a boom to teach some guys a lesson," Santa Cruz said as he finds his next target.

"We've got a window. Make for the exfil site," Brigid says and stands. "Fall in on me."

The Knights started running straight up the middle through the devastation. Searing hot smoke and debris still settling, gouges in the earth big enough to swallow a vehicle. They dodge and weave through it, snapping off little bits of defensive fire to keep the enemy at bay as they push through the ruined center of the assault.

They make it through and cut to the east towards their new rendezvous. All five of them falling in on Brigid, and Sister Stella Nessa bobbing around in the basket with them. Ahead are several tightly packed buildings, cluster after cluster with narrow alleyways and lines strung between them. Clothes dangle from some of the lines; others look like rudimentarily hung utilities.

"Up top. It's our best bet."

The Knights begin stomping every step. Building up a reserve in their KERS. As Brigid makes the first leap from ground level clearing the rooftop, they hear a terrible roar, joined immediately by others just like it.

Four Skreeve crash out of the tall grasses like nightmares barreling down from a dreamscape into real life. Clamber after the Knights, gnashing teeth and screaming for blood.

†

"These creatures, poor souls." The nun says as Brother Gonzaga takes his next leap. They careen from rooftop to rooftop, jumping across the alleyways. The shrieks of the mutated Thraw following them. The cluster of Skreeve stay in a tight pack, limbs thrashing, galloping and bounding. Closing the distance at a rapid rate.

From the north side of town, new volleys of artillery and small arms fire erupt. As the first explosion impacts against a building, Commander Brigid spins midjump. "Maybe this wasn't our best bet. Looks like we've got to get off this stretch of buildings. They don't care; they'll kill civilians."

"There's woodland and fields to the south," Brother Cleopas says.

"Lead the way."

Brother Nonnatus sends the drones zooming ahead. Gathering a fly-over 360-degree view of the terrain, charting out a path of least resistance as they rush towards the pickup. "In your Visuals." Each Knight's heads-up overlays with the newly calculated path. They shifted towards it, one after the next clearing the last building top as they divert.

Brother Santa Cruz brings up the rear, hearing the grotesque howls behind them. "Those things, they're those mutated eggs, right? The berserker-things?"

"Roger," Brother Pio said.

"Yeah, well, they seem like they're following us dead-to-rights even though we're cloaked."

Sister Stella Nessa says, "Thraw nose is exceptional. They track." She holds up her hands, uncurls her legs enough to see her feet. The wounds of Christ. Their wonderful scent. "Leave me. It may very well be my wounds they smell. I am not worth your lives."

"Nonsense, Sister. We'll be okay," Gonzaga says. He races up the edge of the last building mid-stride and says, "The nun says the Skreeve can follow our scent."

"Gaining?" Brigid asks, even as his Visuals show a bird's-eye view of their contacts.

"Constant bearing, decreasing range." Cleopas says.

A shell hits the street below them, flaring up a plume of fire. In its flickering brilliance, Santa Cruz sees the watery, ephemeral shadow his active camo casts along an exterior wall before him, translucent like a crystalline reflection off a pond's surface. At the same time, he sees the very solid shadow of a Skreeve right behind his, flash frozen in that flicker as it heaves up to strike him.

He leaps, his KERS launching him. Spins about. Rail gun spiraling around and him, startled to see there are barely three meters between him and the lead Skreeve.

The rail gun blasts, lighting up the rooftop in electric blue. The lead Skreeve evaporates at point blank range, the nearest one behind it devastated as well. It flings off to the side, half-destroyed under the force of impact.

Gonzaga cheers at the sight of it. He hears the nun's voice, quiet as the wind through grass but deafening as a sun collapsing, "Why do you celebrate? Life is lost."

The Knight feels deeply chastised at such a simple question. Another explosion brings him to the present. He keeps running.

"Two down," Santa Cruz says. He fires again, and the two remaining Skreeve dodge. They spread out, clinging low to the surfaces and skittering. The sizzling blue fire line of the rail gun lights a path through the evening air, draftsman-line straight. Santa Cruz reaches the last rooftop and plummets to the field below. Hits the ground hard enough to break a rock he lands on. He rolls, digging his shoulder in hard. Jumps up, keeps running.

"Still got two more on our tails, but they're not as bold about it now."

"Good work," Brigid says. "Two hundred meters and we're piling in."

"Such loss," The nun says. "Such terrible loss."

Gonzaga turns. Sees the burning town. Even in the firelit shadows he can see Thraw silhouettes running about in the destruction.

Rescuing those in the rubble, fighting fires. The cost of it all. Another flash of his terrible childhood. His only half-joking request to kill everyone. "You know anybody around here?"

"Some, yes."

"Reminds me of home, actually," Gonzaga said. "Reminds me—" a renewed whistling sings into the air. Then a second, and a third. Then four more.

"Incoming!"

Explosions hit like crashing meteorites on both sides. Trees on fire, blasting over. Dirt and debris catapulted up in titanic bursts. The Knights brace as they charge along, tide after tide of raining detritus crashing around them.

"Worst aim ever," Cleopas said. "And thank God for that."

"Thank God and our active camo," Pio says.

The whizzing sound of engines come sprawling in behind them as new patrol vehicles tumble out of the streets and into the fields. Zinging up on two wheels as they correct their course, the gunners on the backs of the vehicles cocking their guns. Muzzle flashes like fireworks as rounds scream through the night.

"Gonzaga! Get in front!" Brigid says. Gonzaga sends a forceful pulse through his KERS to propel him to the head of the group, putting all the Knights and their armor between Sister Stella Nessa and the gunfire.

"Santa Cruz! Mortars!"

Still in the rear, the heavy weapons specialist dials in a lock on the front three vehicles. Along his upper back, a mount containing the artillery pops several shells into the air. Eight meters over their heads, the shells ignite their primary charges, cut spiraling paths towards the rumbling vehicles.

As the Knights came to a wooded portion of their trek, the vehicles behind them light up with jets of fiery explosions. Tires fly off, one pitches forward and its nose shovels a rut into the soil. It flips, hurling occupants headlong and unprotected at furious speeds. Another vehicle abruptly banks and the tires dig into the ground, flipping it on the long side. Striking the ground so hard everything breaks. But through their wreckage, four more vehicles appear out of nowhere. Gunners loosing volley after volley of chasing gunfire. A new pack of Skreeve comes galloping as well.

"I got more," Santa Cruz says.

"More what?"

"Bad guys. But, I got more mortars as well. We're good."

"Doubt it," Nonnatus says. The drones show him far-ranging views. Larger vehicles including aerial ones as well as troop transports are busting through town in their direction. "We got a lot of company in route. A lot. We need to lift off."

"Thirty meters."

Santa Cruz sets off a second motor volley. A new line of fresh explosions behind them. As the Knights cross through a thicket of trees, there the dropship waits, hovering a meter off the ground.

"None too soon," Brigid says. The Knights pile in on both sides, Santa Cruz taking position to start firing. The dropship's vertical take-off and landing wings rotate. Already warm for emergency maneuvers, the dropship revs with a high-pitched whine and blasts upwards. The whole thing thrusts into the sky. Sizzling blue lines appear as Santa Cruz lays down suppressing fire from above. Small rounds plink and ricochet off the dropship's armor. Vehicle gunners bring their weapons to bear, but they fair no better.

"Airborne contact," Pio says. Points out the open starboard side door to heavily armed helicopter closing in.

"That looks much newer and better than those jalopy vehicles they're driving down below," Gonzaga says.

"Intel said they were trying to buy better stuff," Brigid says. "I guess they did." He turns to the controls. "This thing is armed, correct?"

Nonnatus grunts and leans over him. Pulls up an automated defense screen. "Telson rockets, sir." He activates the system, watches it target the incoming gunship.

The gunship opens fire, spraying white hot rounds in their direction. The dropship banks, fires off two rockets. The gunship releases a volley of fire at them. One rocket explodes. The second twirls out of the way and down. Swoops up at a hard angle and catches the gunship under its chin. The gunship explodes, the tail-end tilting violently down and then falling, trailing flames.

"We gotta get out of here before a few more of those show up," Cleopas says. "Though, judging by how cold it's getting in here, the air is getting too thin to support the rotors."

"Shut the doors before we freeze out the nun." Brigid says. They do.

Gonzaga turns his back to the Knights and Santa Cruz catches Sister Stella Nessa's eye. "If you ask the Commander, he'll tell you about he got in serious trouble in the academy when he saddled one of those rockets, magboot-ed to it and rode it."

The Knights laugh and half of it is the immediate release of the tension from the fight. Brigid leans over to her. "I did not." He turns to Santa Cruz, says, "You've got to stop telling people that."

The dropship continues to ascend into the heavens above the stifled planet. On the ground below, the forces of the Arithraw regime roar in frustration, beam communications off world.

Threat Realized

Breaching the outer atmosphere, Brother Cleopas squints as he looks at the awe-inspiring outline of the planet Arithraw. As they change angle while rising, it is as if daybreak is befalling them. The sun's light strikes along the planet's outer delineation, peeling back the darkness from both ends of the horizon in tandem with that brilliant source of light in the middle, revealing the vast majesty of God's creation in such dramatic fashion it can only be attributed to a deity.

"Oh, how glorious," Sister Stella Nessa says. Their universal translators do a good job of capturing her love. Her joy bubbles over. "Such splendor only our Creator can give us. No being on these planets could ever make something so vast, so flawlessly in harmony, so tuned to perfection. Imagine, this ongoing ocean of stars and planets and life, all the product of His love. All of it within His glorious hands. How can we not love Him in return?"

She weeps at the beauty of the star-bound space before them. Her primary hands clasped together at her chin. The Rosary woven between her fingers. Her secondary hands clasped as well, just below the others. So captured by the breathtaking visage her old eyes must be struggling to see.

Brother Gonzaga can feel her vibrate in the ring basket. Trembling in awe. Her own world, spreading out underneath them like a majestic tapestry. Her sun, which she has seen for nearing two hundred of her years only under the firmament of Arithraw, now naked and beaming before her.

"In my young days when I reached maturity, I laid many eggs. Me, and the females of my lowly caste, we were kept in stables on government grounds. They took the eggs as I laid them. I assume they were fertilized by the soldiers, though I do not know. Many probably became Skreeve. I am from the northern regions, and they like our physiological build from there to make the Skreeve. But I don't know."

She looks pitiful, but lovely, as though she has decided to remember her misfortunes as opportunities to offer up in sacrifice. To love in any way she can. "I imagine any males that came from me are long since passed. Maybe some are with our Lord now. I pray so much for that to be true. And to think, those that chose His love, they get to see this with their perfected eyes. Indeed, the entire universe from the atoms to the biggest galaxies. Oh, how beautiful it is right now to us in our fallen nature, and we see so dimly."

Sister Stella Nessa smiles again and closes her eyes. Settles her forehead on her wounded hands and prays.

"Why do you pray for them after they treat you like that? Two hundred years of that kind of abuse and you still feel something for them?" Gonzaga asks quietly. His fellow Knights can see he's not asking to feed his rage, but rather his heart needs the answer. "I would think after a single incident, I'd... I don't know. Never forgive them."

"You wear His mark," the nun says. Gonzaga looks down to the crucifix molded into his armor. "Forget that He is God and He commands forgiveness. We all want to be forgiven, yes?"

"Yes, sure. We need it."

"Did you offer your blood and your very life for those that have hurt you?"

"No."

She smiles. "But we try to be like Him. If we do not, we should never forgive, nor expect to be forgiven. And if we need to be forgiven..."

Brother Santa Cruz turns from the nun and his brother. Eyeballs the expanse of space. Sees a cluster of foreign objects. "No way," he mutters. "Those can't all be missiles."

"What do you mean?" Commander Brigid asks. He puts one eye on Sister Stella Nessa. Concern draws a scowl over his face. "What do you see?"

"There's a fleet coming from the far side of the planet. All firing at once."

"Show me," Brigid says to Santa Cruz and he steps over to the window. In the starlit expanse of black space, a thousand unnaturally colored dots stand between them and the obvious silhouettes of a star fleet. Growing from twinkling pinpoints and stretching out in the lanky streams of propulsion exhaust as the projectiles draw nearer, Brigid groans. "They *are* all missiles."

Far off, clusters of munitions with glowing aft ends rocket towards them. The thin, needle-like missiles spin around each other as if they are alive and swarming; patterns developed on the fly by their coordinated onboard offensive systems to aid against being tracked and shot down.

At the dropship's console, the three-dimensional RADAR system flashes red. Brother Pio motions along the touch screen and expands an information box. He double taps it, eyes flicking up and down the text. "Confirmed. Scans indicate the ships are Darvian in origin. Next system over. That intel Brother Nonnatus talked about was right. The Thraw must have used their resources to buy a better fleet than they could engineer for themselves."

"Resources," Brigid says with disgust. "They sold enough of their people as slaves and test subjects to buy a better fleet," Brigid says.

"And they're coming right for us," Santa Cruz says, looking between the incoming fire on one side and the approaching *St. Joshua* on the other. "I see one mothership. Maybe three fast attacks. I also see a bomber or two."

"We could try and maneuver out of way of the fire," Nonnatus shrugs. "We've got time to dodge it all."

"Yeah, but not the attack ships. That'll be worse. We'll be overwhelmed. We've got to dock, throw up shields and counter-defenses and punch it towards the wormhole gate."

Brigid looks to the approaching *St. Joshua* and back to the incoming fire. All the Knights know they can't dock to the *St. Joshua* or any Eidolon-class stealth cruiser with its shields raised. Taps his comm link with the ship. "*St. Joshua*, you guys see the incoming?"

Their shared receivers chirp. "Affirmative. AI defenses are set to respond. TPAs are warming up. Give 'em two more seconds. We're maneuvering now to receive you port side. T minus ten seconds. Stay on board until the outer hatch seals. It'll be close. Really close."

"Close?" Cleopas asks with a raised eyebrow. "Lord willing, I can handle close."

"I hope the Lord only wills *close*," Gonzaga says. "I don't want anything more."

The *St. Joshua's* Terminal Point Autocannons come on target and unleash a barrage of 20mm rounds. The cloud of incoming missiles begins to scatter—auto defensive maneuvers—but here and there explosions light up in tight spirals of flame before vaporizing in the coolness of space.

Brigid turns and regards the approaching fire. "We're going dock and at least one of those missiles is going to hit. I hope they get the hatch sealed in time."

"If they don't?"

"I don't want to imagine."

In a single continuous motion, the *St. Joshua* swells alongside the Knights, portside bay hatch open. Swallows the dropship without having to reposition. At the same time the *St. Joshua* fires a hail of proximity mines towards the coming forces. The TPAs continue their million-kilometer-per-hour gatling gun chatter. In turn, now in range, the fast attack ships open fire as they begin twirling in wild evasive maneuvers.

The first of the two receiving bollards clicks into place on the dropship's anchoring points and the hull of ship comes alive with Thraw blaster fire.

"Hang on!" Brigid shouts as all at once everything shudders violently. Pounding sounds of blaster fire pummel from every direction, like hammers on thin steel. The first missile strikes. Then the second. Explosions outside the *St. Joshua* indicate that at least some of the other missiles were shredded by the hull-mounted turrets. The second bollard moves to connect as a third missile hits. The bollard misses, crashing into the dropship exterior.

The dropship leans heavily out of position and stresses the first bollard too hard. It snaps. Despite the lack of gravity inside the bay—fully exposed to space—the ship twists and rolls. Clatters with a wallop onto the deck of the bay, canted off to its starboard side as blaster fire rains down through the open bay hatch. Riddling the interior bulkheads.

The exterior hatch lowers, gets two meters from sealing when the first Thraw ship rams its nose into the space. Wedging between the hatch lip and decking, it squeals to a near-instant halt. The impact is tremendous. Shudders through the *St. Joshua*, and even though the thraw ship wasn't traveling at full speed, it is enough.

The second and then a third fast attack do the same wedging plunge and the hatch exerts against them to no avail. Their wreckage successfully keeps the bay of the *St. Joshua* open, and Thraw begin to crawl out against the outgoing rush of the bay's atmosphere.

"They're inside!" Cleopas shouts as he swings open the dropship door, gun raised. The retained atmosphere inside the dropship condenses and whisks out into the bay, now a vacuum. Cleopas starts firing. One hand on the dropship's frame to hold himself steady in the gravityless chamber, the other working his gun. Invading Thraw start dropping from the fight. Return fire is sporadic but with every passing second, another enemy gun is added to the fight.

"How are they surviving the void?" Pio shouts.

"Who cares? They're in here! Help push them out into space!" Gonzaga shoves down low to the deck, returning fire. Behind him,

Sister Stella Nessa says something like, "Thraw biology is capable of—" but the firefight drowns her out. She collapses back into a small ball, serene with her glorious wounds and the Rosary.

Brigid readies his own gun, and he kicks off the opposing wall, floats to the door. "Mind the vacuum! Fall out in formation and get to the main passageway. We'll choke them there!"

The docking bay in full alarm mode. Lights cut. Red emergency beacons snap to life, shading everything with the LED quality of blood and spilling shadows everywhere their poor light cannot reach. Emergency klaxons ring a thousand strikes a moment, drowning out the exterior sounds. The snap of gunfire is consumed by the alarms, reduced to pockmarks of muzzle flash. The bay's HVAC system cuts off now that the exterior hatch is jammed open. No sense in wasting the ship's recycled atmosphere with a leak into space.

The squad disembarks by using their KERS to kick off the dropship. The bay's remaining atmosphere howls by in constant gusts, dying out to nothing. Pulling them and they have to find something to land a foot on and shove off of before being sucked outside. Thraw soldiers dipping and ducking, flailing and grabbing onto features and detritus. Finding cover to return fire. Suddenly a fourth ship rams so forcefully in between two of the wedged attack ships that it crushes them, killing a handful of Thraw in the process. One of the battered fast attacks is hit so hard it unwedges and tumbles out into space. The nose of the new ship opens and Skreeve pour out.

They launch themselves off a surface inside the nose and cleave through the winds of atmosphere like fish swimming upstream.

"Getting worse!" Santa Cruz says, seeing that. He stabs a code into a keypad on an explosive.

"That thing is the size of a decent Christmas present," Gonzaga says as he makes sure his body is between the enemy and the nun. Gun jabbed into his shoulder; he fires constantly.

"Yes," Santa Cruz says. He tosses it right at the Skreeve transport. "Now watch what gift it contains."

They shove back to where Nonnatus is working at the hatch leading inside. "Might want to take cover."

"Why?" Brigid asks. Without receiving an answer, he turns to Nonnatus. "You got it?"

"Explosive." Gonzaga says.

"Trying another override," Nonnatus dials in a few numbers, switches to a different screen, keeps going. "With the damage... breach... the safeties on this thing—"

A detonation so strong it dangerously unwedges the Skreeve ship. A boil of rapidly decaying flame expands out. Consumes nearly all the Thraw and the vacuum of space sucks the mess out into the void. One fast attack remains, and a new wave of Skreeve races out from behind from the swirling and vanishing flame.

An RPG flings out of the wreckage, corkscrewing a small smoking trail behind it. It strikes the hatch Nonnatus is trying to open. Talon-like grippers from the nose of the explosive scrape a hold into the metal, and Nonnatus sees a flashing red dot on its body.

"Get away!"

They dive and the RPG detonates, knocking all the Knights further back to the deck. Nonnatus shoves off and rolls his feet up towards the RPG. Lets his suit's KERS roll the blast wave up to his battery/capacitor combo mounted on his back, just below his comms system with the drones. The capacity meter on his Visuals red lines. The explosion puts him into a whirling spin.

"Too much!" Cleopas shouts as he sees Nonnatus's battery/capacitor combo swell pregnant and burn red in a near-instantaneous move. The glowing color of it there and gone, there and gone as Nonnatus pinwheels in the absence of gravity. Nonnatus feels the intense heat as the capacitors melt down and hits his disconnect switch. The combo flings off right at Cleopas and the others. Cleopas grabs a dented handrail next to him and kicks at the combo. It flies off all of six meters before exploding. Shards of molten metal shrapnel everywhere. The Knights brace themselves for it, get peppered.

Nonnatus groans as Pio catches him, steadies his twirling. He looks over to the Skreeve, sees so many of them floating limp in the chamber. Shards of molten metal embedded in them. Others still clawing at the deck or ceiling, coming this way.

Nonnatus gets to his feet, sees the RPG tore a hole through the hatch he couldn't open. More atmosphere flowing through it and out. The Knights move, make it through the ruined hatch into the main passageway, but even so another small device comes rolling from the melee to between Nonnatus's feet. It bounces off his ankle and settles out nearby.

"EMP!" He shouts and lurches forward, swinging his arms to try and contain it as it explodes. The electromagnetic pulse blast wave sweeps over and past him, echoing down the passageways and licking every Knight as it passes until it finally weakens and dissipates. Everything electrical touched by its disruptive field shuts off. Dead right there.

Corridor lights blink out. Emergency lights snap to life, small red beacons up and down. A blast door slides down in place of the exploded main hatch, separating the bay from the passageway. Drawn down by the ship's Delta V dampener-induced gravity, it thumps in place at the bottom and rests. The hatch's control pad blinks out, and so does the electromagnetic lock that would otherwise seal it shut.

Brigid sees his Visuals fail and go black. Comms go silent. A small indicator in the bottom corner of his viewer flashes that emergency environmental systems are running at sixty percent. All other systems are rebooting. A minutes-long countdown begins. He yanks off his helmet just in time to see the door get hit by the first on the other side like a battering ram. Then a second. Then two at once. The thing begins to bow inward. "We're low tech! Low tech! Fall back! Gonzaga, get the nun back!"

Gonzaga rolls and sees the nano-pack that held Sister Stella Nessa has also failed. She lays there, Rosary still in one hand. She speaks in a tiny voice, her native tongue. Gonzaga's universal translator fritzes and struggles against the effects of the EMP.

"What?" He says as he scoops her up. Their size different enough to where he can cradle her body—long and lithe but so little weight—in his left arm. A gun in his right. "Say that again."

She understands his plea and extends her neck towards his ear. He leans his head in. The translator is garbled and half-effectual. "I— honored— die forrrrr— Savior," she says in a sweet, thin voice.

"I'm going to keep you alive. *We're* going to keep you alive," he says as they back down the main passageway, darkened against the eerie red glow of the emergency lamps. The Skreeve's pounding drowning out half his words.

"— kill me—" she whispers into his ear.

He looks stunned. Stares at her placid and beautiful face, that odd Thraw smile along her lips.

"What?" He looks from her to a distracted Brigid and back. The Knights are withdrawing down the passageway. Setting up for battle as the *St. Joshua* rushes away from the fleet. Their suits slowly rebooting from the attack. The warped blast door scrapes upwards as Skreeve hands reach under it, lifting. The going is hard after they've distorted its shape, sliding up in its track.

"You must kill me," she says again and his translator suddenly gives a smooth dictation, adding to the shock value of her plea.

"But— I can't—" so confused. "Why?"

The digital distortion smears her words in Gonzaga's ears. "Many pilgrims came— my wounds. Seeeeeee the miracle. I know— much. Too much. So mmmmmmany. They w— brain harvest me. Learn— locations. Many. Mmmmmmmost. Gen—"

"What?" Gonzaga asks and the door down the passageway caves in. A Skreeve stumbles through. Gunfire erupts, but Gonzaga leans in, asks, "What did you say?"

"Geeeeeeeenocide." She says. Sister Stella Nessa speaks more, and he can't understand over the noise. Gonzaga looks up and Pio is there also, down on a knee. "My translator caught some of that." He says.

"And?"

"If she's captured alive, they can do something to her brain." Pio says, grabbing Gonzaga and lifting him up. Gun aimed down the passageway. Gunfire lights it up. But a second one comes through also. Then a third.

Gonzaga grabs the nun and they begin to retreat. "Her brain?"

"They've got tech to read it. Brain harvest, she said. All the underground church that came to her wounds on pilgrimage. They'll identify them. Get them."

"Every pilgrim," Gonzaga sneers under his breath. "Get them alive, do the same thing."

"Like dominoes, brother." Pio says. "They'll murder every last Christian on that planet. That's what's at stake here."

Sister Stella Nessa nods. "—better I die thannnnnn— captured." The blast door caves in, spills out of the track with a crash louder than anything they'd ever heard before. Skreeve pour in like a flood.

Swallowed in the Vacuum

"Saint Arthelais, pray for us." Sister Stella Nessa says as another EMP grenade flies over the herd of charging Skreeve twenty meters down the passageway.

"EMP!" Brother Santa Cruz shouts as he drops to his knee. Aims. The vacuum penetrating the destroyed blast door whistling the atmosphere around them. The grenade wobbles in the flow. Santa Cruz fires his small-caliber weapon, every third round a tracer. The little spits of red starbursts catch in the rising rush of air down the passageway. Out to space. Their straight trajectory arced as they're overpowered by the breach.

The EMP grenade fairs no better and explodes as it skitters backward along the deck.

The Knights hit a second time. Systems shut down. They fall under the weight of even their light armor. Ten meters down the passageway, the Skreeve make such abominable sounds it's as if a rift into hell has opened and the soundtrack of the damned spills out.

"Up on point!" Brother Gonzaga shouts as he struggles to get the nun behind him. His gun up. Five meters down the passageway the throng of flailing claws and teeth roll towards them. Stomping, pounding against the continued flow of vacuum.

"I'm trying." Captain Brigid says as the first beast reaches them. He is able to twist and slump, rotating his gun around. Pulls the trigger. Something yelps. He fires again and one of the Skreeve kicks his gun from his hand. One of them picks up Brother Cleopas and hurls him against the bulkhead. He falls back into the pile.

The Skreeve barrel through, swinging their clenched fists like hammers into the struggling Knights. Kicking, roaring. One of them grabs Brother Pio by the back and Santa Cruz by the head, smashes them into each other. Lets them both drop to the deck, limp. Gonzaga is able to overcome the weight of his armor enough to aim his weapon at the one directly before him. Squeezes off a shot into its open mouth. It jerks and falls limp, landing across him. Pinned.

Small bursts of gunfire erupt behind them, further down the passageway. Petty Officers Johns, Franz and Bonilla begin strafing the beasts. Crewman on the ship, they're not frontline combatants but they are trained in weapons and shipboard fighting tactics. They frog-leap their way forward, trying to fight long enough for the Knights to regain their systems.

It makes no difference.

Even as the Knights all groan and struggle to overcome the EMP effects, the beatings, Sister Stella Nessa rises in the air. Rosary in hand, that serene smile on her face. Her wounds flowing forth with precious crimson. She begins to sing, and her melody rises above the tumult and the voracious winds pulling ever backward.

She seems to float, and for a moment Gonzaga believes some miracle has overcome their situation. Horror dawns as he sees she is aloft in the consuming grip of the Skreeve.

"Sister!" He bellows and fights twice as hard to shuffle off the dead thing. The pulsing mound of feralized aliens pulls back with their religious prize, retreating five meters down the passageway.

"They got her! Get up!" Pio calls. His system's emergency protocols finally boot up and he gets enough juice to sit up. Takes aim.

"Don't hit her!" Brigid says, his own system booting up.

Pio fires and one of the Skreeve immediately jolts downward, rounds hitting its knee or close to it. It continues to move, limping. A gruesome look of satisfaction along its face. Ten meters down the passageway, the other Knights get emergency systems back online.

"They want her brain! She's the key to the underground!" Gonzaga calls, taking aim.

"That's an order! Don't hit her!" Brigid says as his Knights open fire, shooting low. The Skreeve react, being pummeled and pierced twenty meters down the passageway.

"Get her!" The Knights rise to their feet, helmetless and struggling against the weight of their systems. "The vacuum!"

The Skreeve begin to disappear into the blast door's hole. As quickly as they poured through, slobbering mayhem and all, they file back as if their writhing mass, such large beasts squeezed together in the narrow passageway, have carefully orchestrated their exit.

Gonzaga scoops up his helmet and thrusts it on. He and Santa Cruz race down the passageway, the other Knights close behind. Their guns first through the hatch and the full pull of the vacuum bites into them. Still pitch black, accentuated only by the red emergency beacons, the percussive klaxons sounding, pockmarks of gunfire bursting throughout as they chase their enemy and their prize.

The full force of the vacuum hits them as they enter the docking bay. They react instinctively and lean back against it. It sweeps their feet out, they fall to their backs and slide, free hand grasping at the deck, digging in their heels. Gonzaga catches and grabs Santa Cruz's backpack. Holds him in the gusts. Gun still on target, Gonzaga fires into the engine cowls.

The other Knights crowd the hatchway, brace up. Leading with the barrels, they spray the fleeing crowd. Brother Nonnatus chucks two grenades, careful of their kill radius versus where the nun is.

"Shoot out the engines!" Gonzaga shouts direction. Santa Cruz drops his small caliber rifle and it floats in the vacuum before him, tethered to his chest by the strap. Pulls his rail gun from where it is slung around his back. Pumps a shot off. The kick of the weapon goes all the way through the weightless Santa Cruz and up Gonzaga's arm. Without their suits on full strength, the recoil of such a weapon is almost too tremendous. It doesn't stop him. "Again!"

Santa Cruz fires, the electric blue trail of energy appearing instantaneously between the muzzle and the impact sizzles and evaporates into a puff of fizz in the roaring vacuum. He fires again. The long barrel of the gun turning red.

The projectiles pierce an engine cowling. Gonzaga hopes for a much larger explosion than he gets. A snap, crackle and pop, an electronic whimper. Something fiery flickers aggressively inside the cowl and sizzles, Dies out in the exhalation of the bare space's vacuum. Smoke bleeds out. "Do it again!" Gonzaga says.

Santa Cruz takes his eye off the rear sight, examines a digital read out on the receiver body. Taps a palm on the barrel and jerks away, even in his suit. "Already overheating."

"How? It's freezing in here! The wind is whipping around! C'mon!"

"Blow on the barrel, then! What do you want me to do?"

Gonzaga huffs and yanks Santa Cruz back to him. Pulling against the vacuum, he slams his brother Knight into the space between his own legs, shouts, "Hold on," and lets go of him. Santa Cruz does hold on. Gonzaga pulls out his own rifle and starts peppering the Skreeve with a volley of well-aimed headshots.

One after another drops, scoots along limp in the atmospheric surge and fly off into the nothingness of space. Specks falling off a greater cluster. All the while, the nun's fragile form bopping up and down inside the mass. Gonzaga empties his magazine and changes out. Begins again.

The Skreeve pile back into the open maw of their ship's nose. Wedged into the hull hatch, its engines still at the ready. Thraw gunners provide cover fire and Sister Stella Nessa disappears inside. As her habit vanishes from the view of the Knights, the maw shuts. The Skreeve left outside know what they must do and begin pushing against the ship's nose.

Dislodge it from the *St. Joshua*.

With a final surge, the ship unwedges and falls out, turns on its wounded propulsion and rockets away the best it can. The Skreeve pounding at it fall out the closing hatch. The void of space devouring them. The hatch shuts and all at once the raging tempest ceases.

The klaxons die off one by one as if they were wind-up drummers, and their arms got tired one after the next.

The red beacon lights continue to accent the blackened shadows of the small bay. The toppled dropship. The severe damage in all the surfaces.

"Where is she?" Pio asks.

"They got her," Gonzaga says.

"Not for long." Brigid says as his comms relay comes fully online. He beeps at the *St. Joshua's* skipper. "Captain Bernhard, you copy? Captain? Adam, you have comms?"

"They're heading back to that mothership," The captain says, the electronic connection snapping to life.

"Get us alongside," Brigid says. With a snap gravity restores to the bay and the Knights drop to the deck. Brigid stands and shrugs the dust and debris off his shoulders. Checks the load on his gun. "We're getting her back."

Part Two:
Void

Full Frontal Assault Kits

From the bridge, Captain Bernard comes across the ship's 1MC as the Knights rush through the main passageway. "There's no way we can catch that light ship. I'm pretty sure we can come alongside the mothership it's docking to, though."

"Can you shoot out its engines?" Commander Brigid asks as they come to the end of the passageway to their weapons locker.

"Their starboard engine is toast right now. We could shoot the port, but their velocity is set regardless. Their maneuvering thrusters will get them inside their docking bay—we can't snipe all those. Too delicate. We'll get you alongside the mothership."

"Our port side. We'll be ready in two minutes." Brigid says as he slaps his palm print onto the hatch's ID reader.

"That's all you'll have."

The hatch slides open and the Knights shove inside. There are ten slots, deck to overhead, each a storage for gear and munitions. Each labeled with a Brother Knight's name. Each with a small devotional on one shelf with pictures of the glorious Jesus Christ and whatever private items the men keep close to their hearts. Brigid has a photograph of two women, a mother and daughter. Standing behind them with arms curled around both women is a younger version of him. No gray in his tightly cropped hair. No scars along his face. No beard at all. A proud smile. He puts a fingertip to it, then to a double pendant around his neck.

Brigid clears his throat and comms up to the bridge. "Captain, we need three dropped off by the docking bay and three on coordinates I'll give you as soon as I have them, but it'll be close to the engine compartment."

"I think we can do that," the captain says. "We're already taking fire."

"Roger," Brigid looks to his Knights, says, "Get the frontal assault suits. Entire kit. Pack to the gills with ammo for whatever you're carrying. Two MDEs a piece. Check the batteries on the shields; this is gonna be a full contact sport in just a minute. Brother Santa Cruz, you load up with the really mean stuff, and get a second doggone barrel for a change-out on your rail gun. Brother Pio, bring the biggest ordinance you can carry while running."

"Does this ship have a breaching craft?" Brother Gonzaga asks. "Are we going blow a hole in the side of that mothership? I don't get—"

"Hey," Santa Cruz smiles. Holds up a round device in his palm with a thick blue and black ring around it. "MDE."

"I hate those things. My guts always hurt after going through one," Pio says as he locks down the final retaining bolts on his suit. Turns to Brother Cleopas, "Buddy check?"

"Sure," Cleopas says as he runs down the Knight's armor, slapping the ammo cans and making sure all the connection points between segments are secure. Presses a recessed button that blinks a minute indicator light twice. "Verified good. All locks secure and internal electrical comms are up. Ping and ping back. Do the same, eh?" Both men turn around and Pio checks Cleopas.

"MDE?" Gonzaga asks.

Brother Nonnatus holds up one. "Yeah. This guy right here," He clips it next to another one on his suit.

"Verified good," Pio says and gets done with Cleopas. Nonnatus taps him on the shoulder and motions to himself. Pio begins checking him.

Gonzaga grits his teeth. "I haven't used these things in real life yet. MDEs. Why would my guts hurt after using it?"

"We'll fill you in," Pio says. "We've got to hurry."

"Quiet. More gearing up, less throwing away our time," Brigid says. "I already said every man take two. One in, one out."

"Might make it three," Cleopas says. "Might drop one during the extraction."

"Where you going to carry it?"

"I'll find a spot."

"Yeah. Find a spot for four. I need an extra as well," Santa Cruz says.

"Fine," Brigid says. "Gonzaga, come here." He begins to check the warrior-monk. "Now. Our ROE is as follows: that ship we're chasing is going to dock with the larger one before we can intercept. Captain Bernhard isn't firing on it—obviously. We must consider the crew of the larger ship to fully know what it's doing: stealing the nun. Doing the brain thing to locate other Christians and kill them. They're culpable for their actions. Assault only those who aggress us. The ship's crew most likely aren't going to try and kill a Knight 15 13 in his full-frontal assault outload. Incapacitate if you must but work very hard to keep it non-lethal. Nonnatus, let's do what we can to their automation and bridge, though. We don't have to make it easy for them or harder for ourselves. Got me?"

"Yes, commander."

"Good. The rest of you, Hail Mary, full of grace—"

The others chime in with the prayer. Pio crosses himself and admires the pictures of the Blessed Virgin on his devotional shelf. Brigid looks at all the men, checks his watch. Thirty seconds.

"Finish up on the way to the port side exterior platform. Double time."

The men continue with their prayer as they rush out of the weapons locker. Racking rounds. Donning helmets. The metallic clack of the frontal assault kits booming down the passageway.

Each man encased in a full suit of bulky armor. The first layer, a skintight suit lined out with a medical sensory array as well as ballistic impact gel and a cut-proof outer coating. Then the armor in huge chunks they step into and screw-gun together. Torque down. They snap a few comms cables together throughout the armor and connect their helmets with a pneumatic hiss, locking in.

Armored suits too big for KERS or active camo. These are the wearable tanks.

Painted with ancient images of angels before they were neutered into fat babies with harps and feathery wings. Instead, the men are adorned with the Old Testament icons of six-winged Seraphim or Thrones, composed of numerous rings sphered around each other, all lined with eyeballs. Flaming swords. Armor plating. "The cool stuff, the stuff that made me want to believe in Christ," Pio once said.

Loaded down with guns, ammo, explosives, magnet-equipped boots in case their combat goes into zero G environments, the men shuffle out of the locker and down the passageway.

Captain Bernhard comes over the comms, "The fast attack has just docked with the mothership. We're keeping pace, closing the gap. You'll have to move quickly now."

"Roger that," Brigid says. As they move, he slides up alongside Gonzaga. "MDEs. You at least drilled on them in the monastery, correct?"

"Drilled once, I think. But—"

"Okay. It's just like the drills go. We're going to use them to breach. You throw it, stay right behind it. You'll have about three seconds to get through before the breach closes."

"Only three seconds?"

"In the moment, three seconds is a lifetime," Brigid says. "Believe it or not, I once saw Santa Cruz jump through and jump back out in that three seconds."

"Jeez," Gonzaga says. "The disassembly? Right, this is a molecular disassembly something?"

"Yes. And don't worry about your stomach hurting or whatever Pio said."

"Why?" Gonzaga asks as they arrive at the hatch for the exterior platform. The other Knights are geared up and Santa Cruz has his hand poised on the latch. Brigid gives him a nod and he opens the sealed hatch. They step into the foyer that serves as an atmosphere barrier between open space and the ship's corridor.

"I mean, it'll hurt, but you won't have time to feel it," Brigid says.

Father Cho rushes up to the Knights and flicks holy water on them in quick showers. He makes the sign of the cross over the group and says, "O crux bona, protégé hos et opus manuum benedicat Dominus. Amen."

"Amen."

"God bless you, brothers. Pray without ceasing. We will do the same," The priest steps away and shuts the hatch behind them.

Brigid double checks that the interior hatch is sealed and locked against depressurization. Starts the cycle. The atmosphere inside the lock vacuums out in a soft humming noise that decreases in tandem with the air level. Warning strobes go off; an indicator light for the exterior door turns solid green. Brigid strides over to the exterior hatch and takes hold of the handle. Above the hatch, as is in every hatch inside the ship, a small crucifix.

Brigid points to it. "For His glory."

The Knights say in union, "Amen."

He throws the handle and the hatch hisses, slides open. The vacuum of space regains its foothold inside the ship and the Knights, prepared this time, step out onto the small exterior platform. The ship is hurling through space, maneuvering alongside the Skreeve mothership that is actively yawing and rolling to maneuver away. "Stay low, be ready. Watch out for the cannon fire," Brigid says.

The Thraw mothership spins a topside double-barreled turret and takes aim at the *St. Joshua*. Gonzaga swings his anti-artillery launcher up on his shoulder and flashes a projectile off. The turret takes the projectile hard on its righthand side. The explosion, while dead silent in the void, snaps something loose in its gearing and the turret lazily drifts off target, limp. The metallic surface of it marred and torn.

Gonzaga smiles, takes aim at the next turret.

Nonnatus rushes out, a different set of drones in tow behind him. These are half the size of the ones he used on the planet's surface, and with different functions. Each one loaded down with an explosive pack. He uses his Visual to lock onto four of the exterior cannons strafing the *St. Joshua*. The drones zip out into a quickly narrowing chasm between the two ships, spread out. As each exterior turret rotates, firing at the *St. Joshua*, the drone slides alongside and deftly stabs the explosive pack between its two barrels. The drones get halfway back to Nonnatus and the turrets flash like brilliant sparks of electricity.

Both barrels of one turret shatter and float free, becoming just two more pieces of detritus in the vastness around them. Another turret has one barrel so deformed it scrapes along the hull of the ship and jams up, locking the gun in place. The other two turrets fail as well.

The mothership has more exterior guns, but they don't have fields of fire where the *St. Joshua* is and remain dormant.

"Praise God," Nonnatus says, collecting his drones and moving to his brother Knights.

"Captain Bernhard, we're in position," Brigid says through his comms piece.

"Copy. We're matching speed and spatial coordinates. They're not going to make this easy." Captain Bernhard said. "God bless you, gentlemen. And God bless our mission."

"Santa Cruz. You knock first. Gonzaga and Cleopas with him. We're near enough to the docking bay where she just landed. Recover her. First exfil point is to MDE out back onto the *St. Joshua* here. Second is back in the docking bay, if needed. Two meter-spacing on your landing. Lord, be with us and no one can be against us."

The beautiful and endless void of space rotates around them in a never-ending planetarium, speckled in shotgun blasts of stars and faraway worlds. The brilliant glow off Arithraw casts a blaze across the *St. Joshua*. As the ships move and twist, chasing one another, the planet's corona peeks and disappears.

"Coming alongside now," Captain Bernhard says. The Knights line up on the platform as the spaceships maneuver and counter-maneuver.

Nonnatus turns to the others, asks, "Does anybody know what it'll look like inside? Will we, you know, fit or whatever?"

"Well... the Thraw are taller than us. Lankier. I think we'll be fine." Pio says. "Darvians make custom spacecraft for a lot of different races. They're typically pretty good. Consistent, anyway."

"Okay, I just don't want another Bilm spacecraft, is all." Nonnatus turns and sees the question on Gonzaga's face. "The Bilm... we did this same thing to them a few years back. Their passageways were narrow—"

"They were filled with jelly." Santa Cruz says. "We MDE'ed into a spaceship literally filled with goo and we had to fight in that."

"But not here, right?" Gonzaga asks.

"We'll find out right now." Brigid says. "Drop it."

Captain Bernhard says, "In position in T minus five seconds."

Gonzaga rolls his head on his neck, alert. Cleopas painted a Rosary on his chest armor, touching a dot and praying to himself. Pio and Nonnatus wait patiently as all the gears of the mission began turning, involving them and their part to play. Santa Cruz watching the *status ready* light blink steadily on his rail gun.

"In position. On my mark."

The men clench themselves and pray to their patron saints. All time for complaints, for adjustments, for refusals, all that time has passed in the blink of an eye.

"Now is the time to do, for God. Be warriors, my brothers," Brigid whispers.

Captain Bernhard comes over PA. "Mark."

Santa Cruz smiles. Molecular Disassembly Explosive in hand, hurls it at the surface of the Skreeve mothership. As soon as he swings his arm, he leaps after it. The MDE strikes the surface and explodes, sweeping a glimmering, almost liquid-like blastwave outwards. The surface shimmers and crackles, becomes vague and rippling, breaking the atomic bond of the bulkhead.

Santa Cruz, gun first, strikes the disassembled exterior and phases straight through. He bursts inside the mothership in a massive spat of distorted light and lands on his feet in a corridor surrounded by his Thraw enemy. They startle; too shocked at the absurd sudden appearance to react. Like being dunked into a nightmare.

"Hello," The heavily armored Knight 15 13 says, not unkindly. And he opens fire.

Rescue

The first volley of gunfire sweeps the corridor and the Thraw buckle at the knees, collapsing. Two more Knights come phasing into the space in brilliant bursts of light and crackling energy. Brother Cleopas drops to a knee, sees where Brother Santa Cruz is firing and he spins to cover the opposite side. Opens fire that way at oncoming enemies. Brother Gonzaga tumbles through the MDE portal and rolls across the corridor on his shoulder.

"Oh my gosh!" He shouts and gets to his hands and knees. Shakes his head to clear it. The corridor glows a sickly orange with yellow highlights. It hurts his eyes but his full-face shield adjusts to filter out the harsher qualities of the Thraw light.

"C'mon, brother," Santa Cruz says as he grabs him by a shoulder plate. "She needs you."

Gonzaga takes the nausea from his first MDE experience and forces it down. Coughs and stands, pulls out his gun. Shouts into the ship, "We're here, sister."

"This way!" Cleopas shouts as they move. The three men race aft on the ship, knowing they MDE'd approximately thirty meters forward of the docking bay. "Hopefully on the same level," he says.

"Should be right through there," Santa Cruz says as they make it to a sealed hatch.

The passageways in the Thraw ship are wide but low. Gonzaga assumes the Skreeve would have to clamber along on all fours in these spaces. He looks around and doesn't see any scratches, excrement, or signs of one of them going wild. Nothing. "If they're allowed in here at all," He mumbles to himself.

"What?" Cleopas asks.

"Nothing. Just wondering if they let those huge mutants in here."

Santa Cruz shrugs. "Might have separate tunnels for them, something like that. But if they are, we put one down and it'll be a good roadblock for the rest." At the hatch, the low overhead flares upwards in a bizarre design aesthetic. He looks up and sees the hatch's control panel embedded in the curve of it, high up where a Thraw arm can get to it. "Goodness, even in these full armor suits that panel is out of reach."

Gonzaga turns to a sound of footfalls down the passageway, spins. "Hurry up and get taller. More bad guys are coming."

"I hear them," Cleopas says. He steps forward of Gonzaga, braces himself and extends his left arm. In the middle of his forearm a circular device pops out of the armor and rotates, drawing an energy shield wide and tall enough to effectively provide all three of them cover.

"Save some of that battery life for the rest of your suit," Gonzaga says. "We might be here for a minute."

"No, we won't." Santa Cruz says. He jumps, slaps a rocker button on the panel. The hatch slides upwards and beyond it, the docking bay is laid out. "Head's up."

Gonzaga rushes through, gun forward. Santa Cruz follows. Cleopas walks backward towards the hatch, shield still extended. As the first of the Thraw blaster fire cuts down the passageway and hits him, he shouts, "They're here!" and returns fire.

✝

"...I agree. Just get us alongside," Commander Brigid and Brothers Pio and Nonnatus are held magnetized by their boots on the exterior deck, watch the MDE dissolution on the Thraw mothership's outer skin from the other Knights' entry fizzle out into nothing. He's been in contact with Captain Bernhard, finalizing their insane plans.

"We've got to blow those engines," Brigid says. "If that ship gets back to the fleet before our guys succeed..." he stares out across the surface of the planet, across the void at the approaching cluster of Arithraw ships. "... it won't matter if they get her or not."

Pio nods. "We'll be overrun."

"Yes, which is not good for business." Nonnatus says. He has three drones with him, each carrying a charge. His Visuals display the status of the small, circular machines; little more than deep gray toadstool cap-shapes hovering about him, a brick of explosive clasped on their undersides.

Captain Bernhard comes across the comms. "MDE infiltration site is being sent your way. Scans show it's a large open room in the belly of the ship. Not the engine room; that's dead center of the thing. But it's not very far, either."

"Seems good enough," Pio says, shrugging belts of explosives around his arms, making sure they're attached to the built-in clasps of his sapper-model armor. His, the only set with larger blowout compartments filled with CQ4 explosives. No one liked standing next to him when he wore the suit; he was a miniature atom bomb on two legs. Every enemy's favorite target. Santa Cruz had painted *don't shoot me!* across the back of Pio's armor once. Even Brigid laughed.

The *St. Joshua* rolls sharply and accelerates inward, invading the personal space of the mothership one more time. As it does, three more exterior turrets come alive. Unfold and spin their way.

"Just got into their line of sight," Nonnatus says. "Oh, good."

"Better make this quick, gentlemen," Captain Bernhard says. "Jump as soon as you can."

The *St. Joshua* screams in tight enough to where the shadow of the mothership falls over it. The first of the turrets charges up, barrels glowing with the building energy burst.

"Now!" Brigid shouts and they throw their MDEs. Jump directly afterwards. Their feet leave the ship and the *St. Joshua* peels off, rolling even sharper to avoid cannon fire.

The MDEs hit, blaze to life in that near-phantasmal ripple that cascades with various colors as the fabric of atomic reality wavers. The Knights hit in and plunge right through. Landing on their feet and squatting, nearly falling forward with the sudden effect of gravity on them.

Their vision turns to complete darkness as the room they're in has no lighting. Their suits compensate immediately, flipping through the light spectrum and turning on an infrared laser, then reading it.

The first thing they see are a horde of Skreeve staring their way, most still covering their eyes from the spectacular MDE light show. The Knights look around, see very quickly where they are.

"A corral for the mutants," Pio whispers. The room is large and square. Containing nothing but some alien type of dead grass for bedding. Along the rear bulkhead a feeding trough splattered with animal parts, clearly picked through by hungry mouths. The foreword-most bulkhead has a set of doors in it.

"Are we locked in here with them?" Nonnatus asks. No doubt those doors are secured from the outside against these things from breaking free. The side facing inward has no handle to pull, no knob to turn.

The first Skreeve roars. Blood on its fists, smeared around its jaws. The others join in, and while their eyes are blinded by the MDE brilliance, their noses are right as rain.

"Lord have mercy... to the doors, now," Brigid says, dropping a marker in their Visuals. "MDE our way out."

The entire herd of Skreeve drop to all fours and race, closing the gap with the Knights in just a few gallops.

†

Brother Gonzaga goes to the right, Brother Santa Cruz to the left. Before them is the ship that stole away with the nun, pockmarked with their fire. Even now the engine they shot out is blackened and stinking, tendrils of oily smoke lifting off its ruined edges. It sits on its landing gear, nose cone left open, and gangplank still extended from when they landed and exited.

"Mercifully small space," Santa Cruz says as they clear the room. It's big enough for four of these sized ships, but only the one is inside the bay. Gonzaga goes up the gangplank as Santa Cruz makes a round through the entire bay.

Inside the dropship it's tight. Not meant for the full frontal assault kits. Blood everywhere. Gonzaga rushes through, stops only when he sees a Thraw soldier slumped in a corner. One hand pressed with fingers splayed open against his chest, wet from bleeding out.

"Was that my bullet?" Gonzaga stares at it, trying to see if maybe this dead warrior looks like the sister. One of her eggs. They have that species familiarity—as any species does—but Gonzaga can't see anything beyond that.

"Still, you're somebody's son." He says and doesn't know how he feels about it. He snaps out of it and moves off.

In the bay, a wide rectangle of an opening serves as the entry and exit into space. It's set into the mothership's side, as if whoever built the ship forgot to put that final block of paneling into place. Leaving the belly open to space. A crackling line of an energy field is set inside it, serving as a barrier. Somehow it contains the atmosphere inside the ship.

"Ghost town," Gonzaga says as he rushes down the gangplank. "Nothing inside but two Thraw that died of their wounds between the *St. Joshua* and here."

They both look at Brother Cleopas, steadfastly holding the hatch with his shield engaged. Blaster fire smacking into it like rain falling. His own gun shouldered into his suit, barking back.

Gonzaga looks at the docking bay entry as they rush over to Cleopas. Whistles. "I like that. No airlock, no nothing but an energy barrier. It's like an open door out into it all."

"New tech, but don't trust it."

"Why?"

"That barrier loses power... you better hope they installed an emergency dropdown," Santa Cruz says. "We've got to start scanning for her. Something. There's got to be a trail starting at that ship." He looks around. The newest spate of gunfire has already chewed up the area surrounding Cleopas. Little bits of ruined plastic and metal lying about; a spark from a damaged electronic in the entry frame spits out nearby.

"We don't have any spare seconds to spend digging," Cleopas says. "Just find it." As if to accentuate his point, a burst of heavy fire hits his shield, the impact knocking it aside for a moment. It's enough for a second blast to come through, hitting Cleopas several times. He stumbles, takes another volley along his back, then turns and gets his shield back in place. Takes two RPGs in rapid succession to it. Returns fire.

"Good point," Gonzaga says. He yanks a grenade off his armor and tosses it towards the Thraw's cover down the passageway. "That'll buy the second we don't have. C'mon."

Santa Cruz steps inside the hatch and throws a chunk of debris at the control panel. It hits the rocker switch he operated earlier, and the door drops as best it can in the blasted framework. It closes much of the way, and they have a moment of uncomfortable silence without all the gunfire.

Cleopas looks at him, says, "You have the luckiest aim."

"*Blessed. Blessed* aim," Santa Cruz says. "That's why I'm the sniper."

The three fall back, Cleopas drops the shield and rushes into the bay. Gonzaga runs back to the drop ship's ramp and sees a bloody handprint. Thin, delicate fingers splayed open and a concentration of blood at the center, in the palm.

"Her..." Gonzaga says. He uses his suit's onboard sensor-based detecting/tracking array to scan the chemical signature of the blood. Sets his suit to it and puts it on active detection. He looks around frantically while his brothers keep their eye on the hatch. He stops stiff, shouts joyfully. "There! Let's go!" He points to another red spot on the far bulkhead, which in his Visuals becomes encased in a flashing green box. Identified as a match. The Knights run to it as the damaged hatch behind them opens. Thraw scuttle inside, spreading out. Gunfire erupts.

Gonzaga runs to a corner in the bay where the nun left another print on the bulkhead. Near it, obscured by the curve of the bulkhead itself, is a single, slim hatch.

"Saint Anthony is praying for us, all right," Santa Cruz says, looks up, sees another control panel. Cleopas shoulders past him and jumps, slaps at the rocker switch but falls short.

Santa Crus leaps and hits it. The hatch opens. "Your battery, was it charged before we came out here?"

Cleopas shrugs. "It read fully charged when I put it on, but those RPGs hit me right dead center. But still—"

Santa Cruz grabs him and rotates him as they go through the hatch. "Yeah. You got damage here, right along the conductor plating. Battery's going to drain prematurely."

"Great," Cleopas says as Santa Cruz shuts the new hatch. "That's what I get for covering you two."

"No more shield for you."

"Yeah, sure."

"C'mon. The sister is marking the path to her," Gonzaga says. Something in his heart is leaning towards the nun. He can feel his filial ring tattoo itch, almost as if the Holy Spirit is running a ghostly finger along it. *Then you need to let Christ work in your heart some more.*

The new passageway is, so far, unoccupied and only leads one way. The Knights run down it.

What Do Guardian Angels Pray For

Brother Nonnatus jumps forward towards the locked doors of the corral, throwing his second MDE. He and his drones—stacked innocently along his back like feeder fish on a whale—hit the pool of shimmering light and burst into a passageway. Commander Brigid follows next.

Brother Pio grabs a single brick of explosive off his belts and flips the charging switch, drops it. A parting present. Throws his MDE and crashes through. Rolls off to the side with his partners, watches the fluttering colors of the MDE peter out.

"Get ready for the first boom," Pio says.

"Alright, now we—" Brigid begins.

A Skreeve plunges through the MDE portal, lands on its knuckles and snarls. Two more tumble through. Rolling, crashing into the opposing bulkhead and kicking to right themselves. A fourth begins to phase through and only gets halfway when the MDE effects die out. The beast phases solidly with the bulkhead and thrashes violently for a moment before it settles and mewls one last time. Goes limp.

The three who made it out turn and face the Knights. Suddenly a blast from inside the corral shakes the entire level of the ship. The doors punch out and nearly come flying off, straining their hinges and locks. Severely distorted. They won't be holding back much very soon. Screeches from inside rise and fade away and smoke escapes through the wrecked angles of it all.

"Time to go," Brigid says as he lifts his left forearm up. A barrel rolls out of the side from a folded compartment and fires a pressurized bolt deep into the eye of the first Skreeve. It collapses as the other two lunge. He spins to take another shot, but claws rake down his chest. The armor is impressive, but the force of the swiping arm nearly buckles his knees. Brigid dips backwards and rolls, comes up as his men lay down cover fire.

The Knights run. Nonnatus types into his shoulder keypad and multiple displays appear on his Visuals. The three drones unfold and drop off his back, hover. They race off forward into the ship, wind around, trying to find their way upwards.

With the two Skreeve in chase, the Knights run down to where they see a new paint scheme of safety-colored stripes. Their Visuals throw a heads up about it, report that a universal standard for Darvian-designed ships is to make these designs around primary engineering sectors.

There are two extra-large doors, sealed shut. Machinery tracks embedded in the decking like inverted rails. A space at the top for a hoist to move in and out. The rumble of thrust and power becomes omnipresent.

Still running towards it, Pio looks up and sees a tremendous label in two languages. "I'm guessing that reads something like *Engine Room* in Thraw and Darvian," he says, pointing.

Nonnatus nods. "My Visuals translated it. Yup."

"We've got to get those doors open," Brigid says. He shoots his gun at the door, punching rounds into where there ought to be a mechanical lock. The door shudders but remains closed.

Even as he does the fastest Skreeve lunges like a tiger descending on its kill. Arms and jaws open wide, claws and fangs like some nightmare coming to shroud them over. Pio tackles Brigid and they fall. The Skreeve overshoots them, swiping as it tumbles forward. It swings upward to try and stop its motion but only swings through thin air. Hits the doors dead center. Like a wrecking ball. They fly apart and the Skreeve rolls inside in a heap of limbs and slobber.

"I planned that," Pio says with a smirk as they get to their feet. The final Skreeve comes rushing, and Brigid again swings his left forearm at it. Fires another pressurized bolt. The Skreeve head snaps back. Topples like its strings are cut, slides along the deck. Crashes at their feet, motionless.

"Damn them for doing this to their own babies," Brigid says as he considers the placid face of the thing. It settles out at his feet, and he kneels, lovingly runs an open palm along its still head as if he was brushing hair out of a little boy's eyes.

Pio, gun raised as he looks from the engine room door to the commander, says, "It's crazy. That thing came from the same species as the nun. Rational souls, open to Christ. They all have guardian angels just like us, right? I wonder what its angel prays for?"

Brigid clears his throat. "Same as ours. To intercede for us, so we can obtain Heaven."

"These poor creatures are utterly ruined before hatching," Nonnatus says, warily looking inside the engine room. "I'm sure God takes that into account in judgement. Culpability must be almost nil for them."

Brigid points inside. "Thoughts for later. Right now, where is the other one?"

The two Knights go silent, staring at the smashed door. Pio shrugs. Nonnatus ominously says, "It went in there..."

The mothership shifts. Somewhere off in the distance, they hear gunfire. Santa Cruz's team. "C'mon. Let's blow this thing."

The Knights get inside, an absolute cavern compared to what they've seen so far. Stuffed with machinery. Low output from the spare overhead lights. About equal in strength is the glow from various LEDs and monitors spaced about.

"Plant the explosives, we'll post up to guard you. We're not alone," Brigid says. Pio takes a full three seconds to look around for the best place. His scanning array mapping, overlaying. Making educated guesses while his instincts have him follow the loudest rumbling noise. Material composition and thickness. Anybody can plant an explosive charge. Only the talented folks like Pio have been trained on how to sonically tune the CQ4 to really squeeze the most out of it.

He strides over to a massive cylinder laying on its side. Easily twenty meters long and four high. A stack of rotors on one flat end all spinning in synchronous patterns together. Columns of metal piping swirl and bend with long runs down into it. A coolant piping system strewn all along it, branching off in some kind of spider's web made of 45- and 90-degree angles. The reactor hums in harmonic notes; a melody as alien as anything else in space. Eerie, impressive and beautiful and ugly. All in equal measures.

"That's a good girl," Pio says as he pops open one suit compartment for explosives. "Engine's reactor core. Give me thirty seconds."

They turn and the last remaining Skreeve roars again from in the room's deeper belly. Inside with them, stalking. It echoes through the space; everywhere and nowhere in particular all at once. "You've got five," Brigid says. "Hurry."

Significant to Severe

Fifty meters down the passageway and Brother Gonzaga is the first to a sealed, double-wide hatch. He turns in a circle under where the typically low overhead flares upward. He looks for a control, a rocker switch.

"Nothing," he says, looking again.

"Maybe it's only on the other side," Brother Cleopas says as he jogs up. "One-way door? These right here are different than the others."

"Yeah... could be. Why not?" Gonzaga says, puzzled. He moves over to the bulkhead near the deck where a smeared handprint like a breadcrumb on her kidnapping trail. "We've got to get through it, and now."

"Want to blow it?" Cleopas says as he stands back, one hand on a grenade.

Brother Santa Cruz comes up. "Let me try something." He pulls out his TechHaft and ignites it. A swirl of energy blazes forth from the sword hilt-type device. The energy shaft spirals up, forming an upside-down stair-step cone that is nearly a meter tall and half a meter wide at its base.

"That thing looks like a stepped drill bit," Gonzaga says. He gets down on one knee and gets his weapon ready to cover their rear. The Thraw can't be far away.

"It works like one, too," Santa Cruz says as he flicks a switch on the haft. The bit begins spinning and he smiles as he thrusts it into the door. The energy tool begins to melt the metal, and as the molten ruins of it drip down to the deck, slivers and chips of shaved metal fling about. Santa Cruz keeps constant pressure against it as he forces the TechHaft a little further through, and then a little further still.

From behind him, Cleopas says, "Contact."

Gunfire crackles off the double-hatch high and to the left. Gonzaga and Cleopas let loose with a volley of their own. Santa Cruz presses into the TechHaft and feels the last of the energized drill shove through. He yanks it back and looks through the hole.

"No Thraw on the other side, but I do see a handprint."

"Praise be to our Lord Jesus Christ," Gonzaga shouts over his shoulder as he takes aim at the enemy's muzzle flashes.

"Indeed."

"Press forward, then, for glory."

Santa Cruz rams the TechHaft back into the hatch near the first glowing hot hole.

†

The Thraw racing down the passageway stop as they communicate back and forth from the command on the ship's bridge. The one carrying the nun takes a deep breath and shifts her in his arm.

"What did she just do?" One asks the other. The crew of them, eight in all, turn and every one of them focuses on the sister. On the soldier carrying her.

The soldier stands soberly, withers back a tad under the weight of scrutiny. He looks to her, minuscule and rolled up as tight as she can collapse, then back to his squad. He supplicates, says, "Nothing? I do not know. I think she prays."

"No. She just bled there," one says and points to the bulkhead behind them.

The soldier turns around. "Yes. She bleeds. Have you not seen her hands and feet, fool?"

"You are the fool. She just reached out and touched the wall while you were moaning about carrying her."

"I do not moan. I am the one returning our prize! You—"

"Wait," another says as he walks forward. Kneels and examines her handprint. "Done perfectly." He says, lost in his ruminations. "So... perfect indeed..."

He stands, looks down the passageway. Walks far enough to see another handprint. Also perfect. Peers down the passageway. Comes back, rage building with every step, takes the nun by the head and turns her to face him. Leans in and snarls. "Are you leaving them a path which to follow?"

She blinks serenely and says, "… all my bones will say, "Lord, who is like You, who rescues the afflicted from one who is too strong for him, and the afflicted and the poor from one who robs him?"

"What?"

"Malicious witnesses rise up; they ask me things that I do not know.They repay me evil for good—"

The one holding her says, "An incantation to her god. She blurts these out ceaselessly."

The third one looks back to the bloody handprint, then down where they'd come from. Ponders for a moment, trying to remember if he'd seen her doing it in the past few minutes. Finally, a thought occurs to him. He walks over and stares at the nun. "Give me the comms handle. I have a plan."

†

The drones swirl about each other as they zoom through passageways. The drones are a lightweight model designed for recon and sabotage. Under their bellies, bricks of explosive swell like pregnancies. The lead drone scans the layout and runs anything that looks like a plaque, lamacoid or other labeling through its small onboard processor, programmed to Arithraw and Darvian written languages.

There is stenciling on a bulkhead directly next to an open hatch with a stairwell leading both up and down. That catches the drone's onboard system's attention. The three stop as the lead processes it. The words NAV AUTOMATION and BRIDGE get greenlit flashing approval. The drones enter the hatch and buzz upwards in the tight stairwell, the light noise of their hover motors and blades almost covered by the other ambient shipboard sounds.

The drones reach the next level of the stairwell as three Thraw soldiers come running to enter it through the open hatch before them. The drones surge upward and angle off to the side, huddling in a tightly collapsed formation, hover motors killed. The stomp of the Thraw running downwards reaches a sufficiently low volume that the lead's onboard system interprets as safe to resume running. The lead fires back up and hovers, scanning. The coast is clear, and the others join it.

They sling out of the hatch the soldiers just ran into and travel down the passageway. They pass by another hatch painted solid blue that stands out among the rest of the ship. Overhead, several unique pipes turn ninety degrees and run into the space over the hatch before the overhead, leading inside. It is labeled LABS 01-05.

The lead stops and scans inside. Sees a single Thraw in an exterior space suit loading canisters of liquids onto a cart. On his face is a scar along his jaw deep as a cavern. He leans over the canisters, jots down some notes onto a digital tablet and taps one of the gauges. Behind him, also dressed in an exterior suit, another gruff-looking Thraw male rolling his head on his shoulders, stretching out. This one appears quite cruel, and his skin is marked all along by scars and poorly healed wounds. His face is tattooed in a jumble of geometric lines, some thick and others whisp-thin. They're getting ready for something. But the labs are not the nav or bridge, so they continue, their group reaches the closed hatch labeled NAV AUTOMATION and the two following the lead break off. The lead continues.

The first of the other two flies over to the keypad beside the hatch. Analyzes it for a moment. Extends an articulating arm, several rail thin supports with micro-servo motors for joints. A fingerlike protrusion taps on the button and the hatch opens. Both units slip inside.

The navigation automation control center is small and unoccupied by anything besides the four massive banks of computing processors.

The two drones shimmy about to the rear of the processors. Jungles of cables run in and out of their backs. Massive power conductors, thin, light-voltage input and output cabling, comms cables and more.

The drones float through them, adjusting their hovering force to not get snagged and bound up. The plant their burdens under the cabling next to the processor bodies. If the explosions don't wreck the processors themselves—and they should, being ten kilograms of pre-tuned CQ4 each, they're enough to level an armored personnel carrier—it'll ruin the cabling. Same effect.

Bricks planted; the drones buzz out. The one taps the controls again and the hatch shuts. No immediate evidence the space has been invaded. The two drones travel back down the passageway and find a corner and tuck in a shutdown formation, awaiting their exfil signal.

†

Brother Santa Cruz yanks the TechHaft out of a fourth hole, making an impromptu circle in the locked double hatch. Inside the circle is the remaining chunk of metal precariously held in place by the thin strips of unmelted steel between the holes, and all are still red hot and rimmed with molten metal.

Brother Gonzaga stands up from his cover, still firing. "Watch out," he says, and mule kicks the portion of the hatch in the center. His massive, armored foot bursts through. The remaining hatch section clatters onto the deck on the other side.

"Good enough for the women I go out with," Gonzaga says and shoves through the breach.

"What girls? You're a monk," Brother Cleopas says, following, keeping his gun up and popping off rounds.

Santa Cruz makes it through, and they run, covering their forward advancement the entire way. No Thraw have come to meet them head-on.

"There are surprisingly few enemies here, given the circumstances," Cleopas says.

"We took them off-guard, even back on the planet. Might be that they're scrambling still."

"Lord, please make it so," Cleopas says. His Visuals battery indicator is creeping further into the yellow, leeching off power through the damage.

†

In a passageway further down, a Thraw hand grips the nun's frail arm and extends it out, forcing her palm against the bulkhead. Withdrawing it, her crimson breadcrumb remains.

The other Thraw smirk and smile conspiratorially. Their work done, they carry her further down the passageway and around a corner past the tripod mounts of their trap.

"Solutions come to those who work for them, eh?" One says. The others squat down, breathing easier now. Sister Stella Nessa closes her eyes and continues to pray on Cleopas's Rosary.

†

They reach the handprint and Brother Gonzaga touches it as he has done all the others. Finding some connection with her, getting her blood on his armor, and using it to draw a cross. A nun blessed with the graces of sharing the wounds of Christ.

"As underserving as I am, to think she united with His sufferings, how holy she must be," Gonzaga says through clenched teeth. "I can't believe I lost her."

Brother Santa Crus slaps him on the back as they continue moving. Smiling, he says, "We just laser-drilled a hole through a sealed hatch on board an enemy spaceship while wearing a quarter-metric ton suit of robotic armor, all the while taking gunfire so we could recover her. Fear not."

"I'm not afraid," Gonzaga says. "Not of... well, I *am* afraid of where they're taking her."

"I have to assume they're running towards that brain-thing machine?" Brother Cleopas says. "I guess it's a machine, right?"

"If it's even on this ship," Santa Cruz says. "They might just be running from us, hoping we die in a gunfight. Or leading us on a wild goose chase. Buying time until they get back to the fleet."

"Or the surface of the planet," Gonzaga says. As they round a corner he startles, shoves his gun forward. And there they are.

A crowd of soldiers behind an encampment of tripod mounted machine guns blaze to life. A row jampacked from bulkhead to bulkhead of barrels. Multi-bore, large caliber. Machine gearing rotating them, spitting a barrage and coating the passageway.

Behind it all, the nun in the fierce and unrelenting and cold grip of the enemy.

The hail of gunfire sprays across the Knights. Cleopas kicks his shield back up but it immediately fractures and crackles with static. Thin sections of energy appear and flicker, here and there in a constant dazzle of inconsistency. Gonzaga shoots low, trying to clip feet and legs while keeping an eye on the nun in the arms of a Thraw.

"Fall back!" Santa Cruz shouts. He fires as well, trying to cover his maneuvers.

"No! She's right there!" Gonzaga says, his vision clouded, pinpoint focused on the nun. Even as he begins ducking, leaning his massive suit into the onslaught, trying to press forward against it, he shouts, "We've got to get her!"

"Fall back before we're shredded!"

"No!"

The passageway is mauled by the firestorm. The bulkheads and overhead chewed apart in an instant. The recessed lighting begins popping and dying. Darkness captures sections of the distance between them. Other sections flicker and spark. Ricochets and red-hot projectiles bouncing all around. Clearly this is the Thraw's last and grandest stand. Gonzaga's suit lights up with alarms at the incredible rate of fire it's deflecting. "They can't keep this up. This is their own ship—"

"They don't care!"

Gonzaga sees a small crowd of the Thraw soldiers part and from it emerges a mortar cannon. "They wouldn't fire that inside here—"

The barrel violently jitters and the fire and smoke-filled *whoosh* from its muzzle answers his thought. Another RPG careens the twenty meters at the Knights. Gonzaga bullheadedly fights his way through thousands of rounds as he charges down the middle of the passageway. No cover. Absorbing it all, if only he can make it to his goal. In a split second Gonzaga feels so foolish, throwing away his life this when he could have been so much smarter about his mission.

The explosive like a comet hurling through the passageway with time stopped everywhere, gun bursts frozen mid-flight down the space, damaged lights flickering and paused in their death throes, Gonzaga sees the nun and feels guilt. Guilt for not performing as he now knows he should have.

Guilt for wanting to glass her planet, deemed unworthy all because the little boy in him watched his own colony razed to the ground. *Then you need to let Christ work in your heart some more.* And her blood, shed by uniting to Him, now the medium he used to inscribe Christ's image on himself.

And as the explosive closes the last few meters, suddenly a fritzing energy shield folds over him and Cleopas body checks him off to the side. The detonation on the other side of the shield still knocks Gonzaga back off his feet. Cleopas collapses beside him and all time and space rush in to fill the void. The smoke and fire of it all mushrooming out, rolling to lick every surface in the mutilated passageway.

Gonzaga sits up as the gunfire barrage resumes. He sees the Thraw holding the nun turn and start to run away, whatever it wanted to see apparently done now. The mortar cannon goes silent as the operator goes to load another shell. Cleopas groans and rolls over. Santa Cruz grabs him and heaves him back behind cover around the corner. Santa Cruz looks behind them, from where they came. He sees Thraw reinforcements coming.

Cleopas groans and rolls over. Santa Cruz eyes widen. He grabs Cleopas, says, "Did that explosion tear through your suit? You're bleeding."

Cleopas says nothing as his Visuals flash a schematic of his body next to his drained battery life. An injury report points a red line at his torso where he's hit, the word SIGNIFICANT next to it.

"I'll make it. We're almost done here."

Around the corner, Gonzaga does the math. A round strikes his helmet and pings off. Another one against his chest plate. Then a third. The barrage resumes full force.

"Saint Michael, guide this effort," Gonzaga speaks softly. "I beg of you, for her."

He takes his remaining MDE and activates it, chucks it towards the gunner's nest. It careens through the firefight, and even though there is a veritable wall of projectiles coming against it, not one strikes it. Gonzaga smiles as the MDE hits the deck, bounces and rolls. Settles right in between all the tripods and pinballs between their feet before spinning itself in place and going still.

"Thank you, my dear archangel friend."

The disassembly grenade explodes.

Its brilliant whir of distorted colors ripple out. The sound of it jangling the atomic structure on such a monumental scale bursts into the world. The deck becomes a pool of deconstruction. A flowing mess, unorganized, energized apart on a level one would need a microscope to witness. The entire gun nest drops through the phasing ring underneath like a trap door was pulled under them. They bottleneck into a pile, jamming inside the wavering circle-like shape.

But so temporary.

Whatever falls all the way through misses the worst of it. Whatever jams and remains is severed as the MDE dies out. All that is left is a jarring sight. Thraw cut off at all levels of their bodies. The tripod guns missing whole sections, disintegrated. The mortar destroyed.

"Let's go!" Gonzaga shouts as he clambers to his feet.

Santa Cruz heps Cleopas to his feet. He steadies himself, makes a show of patting himself up and down.

"Thanks," he says. "Just been getting the wind knocked out of me. Our Lord took more abuse than I have."

"He has authority over death, though," Santa Cruz says as they go around the corner, see the devastation. "If you can't resurrect yourself in three days, I'm going to ask you to play it more carefully."

"Yeah, yeah."

They run past the mess. Cleopas crosses himself as he picks his way around the remains; arms and barrels sticking out like thorns in a bramble. They move on at a fast pace to close the gap between them and Sister Stella Nessa.

Cleopas hopes the others don't log into the shared stats and view his battery life. The final two bars are flashing red. His bodily injury report updates, changes from SIGNIFICANT to SEVERE.

All in Bursts of Sunflare

Renewed vigor washes over the Knights like the inundation of a tsunami wave. A long stretch of passageway lays before them, uninterrupted by either more Thraw or zigzagging turns. No handprints, but stipples of blood here and there. Whether the sister's or one of the soldiers, they don't know. Yet. Brother Gonzaga charges in front, rushing forward now that he has her so close in memory. Furious pursuing.

"Inventory, total package," Brother Santa Cruz says, staying close behind his brother. "We're pretty tapped out for only being here for a few minutes."

"Has it only been a few minutes?" The battle-weary Gonzaga asks, realizing it has. "It's been a gunfight since we stepped foot in here. I'm down to thirty percent already in about everything."

"I'm at... almost fifty. Almost." Santa Cruz says. "Cleopas?"

Brother Cleopas can't hide his deepening limp from the wound he sustained all the way through his mechanical armor. "Battery is low. Ammo is okay."

"Got numbers?" Santa Cruz asks as they run past a small pile of discarded equipment from the Thraw. Weighing them down with little benefit, apparently. "Words like *low* and *okay* are pretty fuzzy to a guy like me."

"Not good. Don't worry. I'll make it."

"Same fuzzy category, brother. I need numbers. *How* are you?"

Gonzaga snarls. "Dead ahead! I see 'em!" He raises his gun and slows his run. The Thraw soldiers are grouped together, the nun in front. All guns to her head. "Last stand."

Santa Cruz notices how Cleopas matches his stride, limping. Intentionally stays behind him. Must be a reason for that, and Santa Cruz thinks he knows it. But not now. Guns up, they close the distance to the Thraw.

There the group is, small, weary. Four of them left, all worn out. Probably trading off carrying the frail nun, and now their last major defenses worked through by the Knights 15 13. As Gonzaga approaches, his suit opens four small flip-up pockets on his shoulders. His Visuals comes online and paints a target on each soldier's head.

†

"See that thing yet?" Brother Pio asks down on one knee, slaps a rectangle of explosive onto the bottom of the engine's massive cylindrical reactor.

"No," Brother Nonnatus says. He and the commander with guns raised high, back-to-back as they sweep the engine room. "Can't get penetrating rays in here. Reactor shielding, I assume. Everything we have is visual along the light spectrum. It's hiding."

Pio scoots along the bottom of the reactor, the heat leeching off it is baking him even inside his suit. Gets to the next thin spot in the outer skin of the cylinder, pops open another compartment on his armor. Takes out a brick of consonance quattour or CQ4. A "tunable" demolitions device that uses sonics to create an explosion disproportionate to the size of the weapon. The brick of it, in his unsuited hands, would be too heavy to hold. The armor's strength-assist makes it lightweight, and he sets it in place.

A small block of electronics pressed into the explosive itself interfaces with Pio's handheld controller. He uses the controller to examine to thickness and basic composition of the surface he's attached the brick to. Calculates the force necessary to punch through it, how large the explosion needs to be, what time it needs to detonate to coincide with the other bricks, and several other factors. The controller inputs to the electronics block and that affects the composition of the CQ4. Then the electronic block mates with the others he's already planted, ensuring they explode together. Tuning it for the synchronized explosion. Pio pushes away from it, rises to his feet.

"This is more than five seconds," Commander Brigid says.

Pio huffs. "That's two. Another two—" The stalking Skreeve launches up above him from the other side of the reactor. Pio drops as the thing crashes down, swinging its arm as it does. It rolls, lashes out one more time even as bullets pop to life around it. Along it. It hits Pio across the chest and helmet. Finishes its roll and bounds off again into the higher scaffolding of the cavern. Pio slams hard into the reactor and falls forward. Pushes up with a groan.

"Fine..." He groans as Nonnatus and Brigid scramble around him. The sound of the Skreeve leaping from rafter to machinery back to another rafter as it runs wild is too threatening. "Fine. We do this dirty."

The other two chase the mutant with their gun barrels, popping off tight groupings of fire as the shadows shift where it is, was and might soon be. The muzzle flashes illuminate the room in bursts of sunflare.

Pio pulls out the other bricks of CQ4 and haphazardly toss them along the reactor. "If that doesn't outright blow it to hell, it'll do enough damage. Your gunfire's got to be adding to it all. I can already hear steam leaks. Let's clear."

"You could have led with that, you know," Nonnatus says.

"It's an art, and art needs—"

"You sure?" Brigid asks over his chasing fire. "You sure it'll do enough damage?"

"Yeah, yeah," Pio stands. His suit's read-out is one yellow status bar above the red. And after only two hits. "We could use your pressured dart marksmanship right about now."

Brigid lowers his weapon and pushes the other two towards the obliterated doors. "The other two were within a few meters. Everybody can hit their target within a few meters." He moves, pushes forward. "Nonnatus, cover the rear. We're clearing out."

†

Brother Gonzaga activates his universal translator and projects it through his suit's exterior speakers. "Give her over. Now."

Brother Santa Cruz steps up. Says, "We don't want any more bloodshed. Not you, not us, not her. Let us have her and you can shoot at our backs as we run away."

One of the Thraw spits, works his alien mouth parts around. Irritated, he leans from one foot to the other. His secondary arms clenching unconsciously. Making a fist. Brother Cleopas activates his Visuals and types, "Pre-fight indicators on the far right one."

Gonzaga messages back, "We got all the pre-fight indicators we needed with their guns to her head."

"I know. He's just— he's the worst off."

Santa Cruz messages, "Be cool. We're in a standoff. Excitable bad guys with their backs to a wall are a little rasher than I'd like, so. . . Be. Cool."

The two groups close in on each other in the passageway. Quiet from all around, but even if a war was exploding outside them, the tension here would silence it.

Santa Cruz takes one hand off his gun, holds it up, palm-out. Supplicating. Trying to diffuse. "May we have her? A God-fearing elderly female isn't worth much to Arithraw, is she? But we value her. Let us have her."

The irritated Thraw barks, "Not worth much? You lie so stupidly to me; do you believe me to be of feeble mind? All of us? She is central to— she is key to smashing the cult that poisons our society. She *knows* them. A death cult that worships an alien man, killed for his stupid proclamations! *Killed* for them! Who worships an executed prisoner? Who poisons their world with such filth? You kill many of our people for something like this— this woman. This *harlanlocute*."

Cleopas runs that untranslatable word—*harlanlocute*—through his onboard system. A report populates his query.

Harlanlocute - Harlan Location or Harlan Locus. Refer to the village of Harlen in the Arthrawian region of Biobawa in the southeastern hemisphere. 102 years prior, a severe plague originated. It disrupted the Arithraw gastrointestinal system's cellular walls, resulting in fluid leak-through. Condition is terminal. No medical cure nor treatment. Estimated casualties of 2.7 million that year—or approximately one-eighth of the entire population—before it was contained by burning the corpses and executing the living in affected areas. That number includes medical personnel and caregivers. The term holds a negative connotation; it has become derogatory in modern usage, implying that a harlanlocute is a Typhoid Mary or center for disease.

"She a central location for the disease of Christianity," Cleopas says.

"Central location for the disease of hope eternal," Gonzaga says.

"Hope?" The irritated Thraw says. "*Lies.* She lies to the lower castes. They are all trash. Animals. They have the gall to tell the upper castes they are equal with the lowest ones. Who looks at dirt and calls it gold? Who tells gold it is no more valuable than dirt? A liar. This used-up low-caste waste of breeding, still clinging to her beads and her alien god. Her brain is worth more than every honorable Thraw out here in the black beyond, circling you even now."

"You cannot see she has value beyond what you can steal from her mind?" Gonzaga asks.

"Her value started the day she began laying eggs and was spent the day she stopped."

"This is pointless," Gonzaga sighs.

The irritated Thraw reaches a fever pitch. "Value your females however foolishly you want, but we know the truth of such things! She is here to serve, and her brain—"

The flip-up pockets on Gonzaga's suit cough startlingly loud jets of smoke. Four pencil-thin rocket-propelled darts embed in the foreheads of the soldiers, each skull kicking back as the heavy gauge metal hits with such force that their brains are destroyed before they can twitch and pull their triggers.

Gonzaga leaps forward and grabs the nun as she falls from dead arms. He cradles her for just a moment as the threat crumbles around them. "You have value, sister. I swear it before our God."

She turns to the dead soldiers, heaped on the deck. "Still, they need our prayers even now."

"Yeah, I know," Gonzaga groans. He turns and they place her in back in a ring basket, slung over Gonzaga's back.

Santa Cruz, still eyeing Cleopas who has very intentionally kept his front towards the other knights, clicks on his comms channel. "Commander Brigid, we've got the nun. We're short on MDEs. Heading to secondary exfil location."

†

They pass through the engine room doors and see a tripod-mounted gun swivel their way. "Incoming!" Brother Pio shouts and extends his left arm. A circular device pops up in the middle of his forearm, rotates, springs to life with an energy shield wide and tall enough to cover them.

As it crackles into the passageway, the machine gun chatters a string of projectiles at them. Manning the gun is a small crew of Thraw. One to pull the trigger, one to reload, two to stalk off to the sides and flank. A fifth in the back, loading a small handheld RPG.

"You don't have the battery for that!" Brother Nonnatus shouts. A compartment in the back of his triceps flips open. Inside five matchbox-sized drones tumble out like playing cards in the breeze. Kicking to life and winging about in a loose but coordinated line.

Pio takes the first barrage, watching his shield deteriorate under the load. "You got a better idea?"

"Working on it," The miniature drones zip along the deck. The two flanking Thraw take potshots at them but get only sparks and light shards from the flooring. The little boxes pop off the deck at the last second and cling to the legs and lower rail of the gun.

"Dip off to the side," Nonnatus says as he yanks the other two. The drones, armed with little more than a camera and audio array and a small bit of explosive, blow up.

The trigger man and reloader get enough shrapnel to count them out. Rolling on the deck with shards of burning metal everywhere. The RPG gunner spun last second, got blasted along the back and sent rolling, gun and all. Commander Brigid and Nonnatus use the distraction to unload into the flankers. Both drop, harmless now.

Brigid points down the passageway, past the brand-new mess. "We've got to clear out enough to blow this—" The Skreeve hurls itself out the engine room door, fanged mouth gaping.

Pio swings his shield around as it smashes its entire bulk into them. Gun bursts fling wildly up into the overhead. The armored knights clatter and roll uncontrolled. Pio's shield shatters and dies out. Nonnatus collapses into a heap a few meters away. His gun clattering off to the side.

The Skreeve maneuvers to get to its feet. Sees Brigid's back within striking distance as the commander scrambles to pick himself up. The Skreeve swipes down hard. Drives Brigid to his knees with the force. Metal tearing. He shouts, tries to turn but the Skreeve hits him bare-knuckled. The fist lands between his shoulder blades and sends him across the passageway into the bulkhead. He takes the hit full force and drops.

He groans, turns as best he can. Suit reading only red bars. SIGNIFICANT scrolling along his Visuals. The Skreeve rises to its full height in the low overhead. Bloodlust in its eyes. Brigid thinks he sees revenge in its eyes for its other two members. Maybe for all of them. Fingers wide, flexing. Those talons so powerful they rend steel.

"What are you waiting for? I've confessed any mortal sin. I'm ready," he shouts. The creature roars and rears back.

†

The lead drone runs quiet, peeking and scanning around each passageway, each corner the nearer it gets to the bridge. Ships' bridges have a high foot traffic pattern, and the drone's programming isn't fond of being caught prematurely. Gets in the way of the mission. It has a small onboard gun, but it fires little more than grains of sand. Worst case is to suicide run towards the bridge and detonate when it can no longer hold it off.

But, as it is, by tucking into high corners and keeping its hovering motors to a minimum to retain flight, several running enemies have passed beneath it as it creeps forward in fits and spurts. Finally it meets its objective.

It waits directly over the double doors that lead into the bridge. It scans and finds a controls console. Extends its articulating arm, taps a button. As the doors separate with a hiss of changing air pressure, it bolts inside. Goes high.

The bridge is wide and two levels deep; stair-stepped forward leading towards the massive screens that display the cosmos around them like a windshield. Various scrolls of information populate corners of the screens, moving as they constantly refresh with data. Not the least of which are updates to the gunfights currently going on at the other end of the ship.

With the doors opening, several heads turn to see who's entering. One, a Thraw adorned in deep royal blue and gold sitting in a lone chair in the middle of the space, makes a show of turning in his chair.

At that moment, a deep rumble travels through the metal of the ship. A red square begins flashing on the info screen. Something about the navigation automation center. Everything offline. The ship controls stop responding. Fire alarms. Air purifiers and recyclers pushed into their danger ranges.

One member of the bridge points to the drone and shouts something. The others see it. A few brace for something. Others stand up. One tries to draw a weapon.

The small black circular drone with a single large photo eye in the middle of its form unnerves them. They start to shout. A few get up and begin rushing towards it. The drone spits its EMP landmine as deeply inside the bridge as its pneumatic launching mechanism will fling it. The drone reverses out the door. A single shot *plinks* off the bulkhead near it, spitting a few weak sparks from the metal. The standing Thraw chases it out and the doors close automatically behind them. They watch as the drone buzzes too quickly for them to catch down the passageway. One of the Thraw stops, turns around and looks at the sealed doors.

The EMP, originally designed to be buried and lie in wait for powered vehicles to roll over it, now rigged on a timer release, pulses. Even through the closed doors the impact of it moves like a deep bass sound wave. Inside the electromagnetic pulse disables everything it can, and the bridge is no longer in control of the ship. The noise of confusion rises substantially outside, and the Thraw's shoulders sag as the sound of the buzzing drone disappears down the passageway.

†

"Do it!" Commander Brigid shouts with all the wind he has. The Skreeve looming above him roars and begins to swing its fists like driving hammers down onto him. A belt of explosives lassos around its neck and yanks taut. The thing lunges forward, startled. Along its back, clinging to the belt is Brother Pio, tightening the reins. The Skreeve goes beyond feral, forgetting about Brigid. It screams and bucks, swings madly at the waist.

A wild horse refusing to be broken; Pio wrenching down tightly with his belt of explosives like gripping its mane. He pendulums heedlessly along its back. Clambering up to its neck, Pio risks letting go with one hand to draw his gun. Headshot.

The mutant squats and leaps, ramming him into the overhead. Pieces of it fall away. Pio opens fire point blank. The thing twists its head and leaps again. He takes the hit full along his back and violently slides off to the side. Hangs on. Still firing. It jumps away, then forward. Off to the side. It swings again and his gun goes flying. Pio grabs his last belt and throws it around its neck. Its arms tearing at him, swatting. Clawing. He kicks off its side and uses the belts to swing around as it rakes its own flesh with the talons it meant for Brigid.

Brother Nonnatus and Brigid get to their feet. Nonnatus fires at the Skreeve's heels, sending up errant ricochets from the decking. The Skreeve panics beyond its feeble mind. Does what it knows it can do. Knows what worked before. It gallops towards the engine room.

Pio bounces along it, sees where it's going. Two meters away from the open doors, the darkness and CQ4 beyond, he lets up on the belts and they sag. He drops and the two belts clatter along the deck next to him. The mutant disappears into the cavern and away from them.

Brigid shouts, "Fall back!"

The three battered Knights hastily make their move, shoving past the drone-blasted machine gun. Nonnatus reaches the RPG gunner and grabs the weapon. He shoulders it and fires into the engine room.

The explosion turns the darkness into light and comes barreling out of the damaged doorway. A belch of smoke and fire that roils down the passageway. With nowhere good to run, Nonnatus throws the RPG cannon down and extends his own shield.

"Oh... Saint Jude pray for us," he whispers. The shield extends a millisecond before the racing furnace hits them. Flames curl and charge around the shield. The three Knights packed in tightly behind it, watching the reds and oranges peel around in all directions over the surface of his translucent energy shield, licking and torching.

The surging colors develop a black center, then black edges, and transmogrify into deeply saturated smoke. And that rolls hungrily around the shield and nearly engulfs the men. Nonnatus eases up, and they all wait motionless in the settling cacophony.

"Well, I'm in the red," he finally says.

"Me too," Pio says.

"All of us are," Brigid says. "But the engine is toast."

"Gosh, I hope so," Pio says and laughs in relief. The exasperated huff of the mothership slowing down proves it. "We've lost acceleration. Just maintaining now."

"Lost acceleration, lost maneuvering. Their fleet is going to have to come to us now," Nonnatus says. "That buys us a few extra seconds."

"Maybe," Pio says, putting the explosives belts back in place on his armor.

Brigid pats him on the back. "Good wrangling back there, by the way. I was impressed."

"I'm gonna feel it tomorrow."

Nonnatus smiles. "You're assuming we survive today. A Knight 15 13 knows better."

Pio smiles. "John 15:13. Greater love hath no man than this, that a man lay down his life for his friends. It's in the name, I guess."

And as if by some divine providence, Santa Cruz comes over the comms. "Commander Brigid, we've got the nun. We're short on MDEs. Heading to secondary exfil location."

"Us too, good friend," Brigid says to himself as he touches the empty MDE racking on his suit. "Meet you there in two. Good job, men. Praise God."

Into Inescapable Glory

The secondary exfil location is the docking bay, and two minutes is an eternity. The drones get there first. All six Knights come clamoring down separate passageways, their thick, metal footfalls announcing their arrivals up and down.

Shoving past fallen Thraw soldiers from previous gunfights so close in memory the spent casings are still warm on the ground. They arrive within moments of each other, the entire team and their holy prize. Brothers Cleopas and Pio take defensive postures and hold the two hatches against any unwanted visitors.

Inside, the space is as it was when Brothers Gonzaga, Santa Cruz and Cleopas were inside it forever ago. A large bay with a gaping rectangular hole in the exterior bulkhead. Stars and galaxies past it. A thick band of light running along the inside of the hole's frame, generating a barrier between the atmosphere inside the bay and the space beyond. And beyond it, a field of eternal black stippled with stars and planets light-years away. So peaceful, where God the creator spoke "Let there be light," and scattered His love outward into inescapable glory. Now, waiting for the *St. Joshua* to come right outside. Commander Brigid opens a comms channel to the ship.

"All right, Captain. We're at secondary with our objective. Ready to exfil on your mark."

"Roger. We've matched course and speed. The angle is going to be weird and we're going to catch defensive fire. This is our only shot at it. Coming in hot."

"Hear that?" Brigid asks the Knights. They all acknowledge. "Is Sister Stella Nessa protected?"

Gonzaga has her in the ring basket on his back. Santa Cruz and Brother Nonnatus inspect it. Nonnatus pulls up the read-out into his Visual, says, "Atmosphere is tight and temp will be stable for maybe three minutes before heat leeches out. Gonzaga, brother. Don't stay outside the ship too long."

"Not planning on it."

Nonnatus continues. "She's not tethered to anything inside but the basket is too small for her to really float anywhere."

"Copy," Brigid says. "Any sign of opposing forces?"

"No," Cleopas and Pio say in union.

"There has to be more," Brigid says to himself. "We've got maybe thirty seconds 'til we're out of here. Pray it doesn't turn into—"

"Reeves Station?" Santa Cruz says. "Remember that?"

"I was going to say that op on Milestone, but whichever. I'm tired of shooting my way out of bad situations."

"If God wills it," Pio says.

"I wish He'd will a beach vacation."

Brigid says, "Watch the space; we've got two hatches covered but they might know any number of other ways in here. They've got some way that they herd those Skreeve out of here if it isn't a passageway. Captain Bernhard?"

Scratchy, the skipper's voice crackles in their ears. "Yeah, send it."

"The rest of the fleet? How are they looking?"

"Seems it took them a moment to realize something is wrong with the guidance systems on this ship. They're headed towards us now, but we've got the jump."

"More missiles yet?"

"Not yet, but I wouldn't count it out."

"Roger."

"Coming alongside in thirty seconds," Captain Bernhard says. Two seconds after he speaks, the Thraw ship's defense systems open up. Bolts of red heat flying at the incoming *St. Joshua*. The Knights can see them light up the dark through the bay. By watching the bolts they can see their ride out of here, track its wizened progress.

Brigid turns. "Anybody who's got pocket drones, launch them outside. Get visual on those cannons. If we can, set a charge. Hurry."

Compartments on the Knights' triceps open. Matchbox-sized drones come zipping out and dart through the barrier. Once in space, the men can see tiny flashes of positioning bursts to move the drones. They flutter up and down, following the cannon fire.

"Contact," Pio says. He opens fire down the passageway. The recoil of his gun shakes the remaining belts of explosives attached to his suit. Brigid turns and sees him. Looks to Cleopas holding the other hatch. Crouched in the opening, ready but not firing. Brigid magnifies his view, sees Cleopas's damaged suit in the back. Glances outside as he hears the cannon fire pick up in intensity. The *St. Joshua* now in their field of vision, soaring towards them.

Brigid says, "Cleopas? Anything yet?"

Cleopas adjusts himself and says, "Nothing yet, sir."

Brigid takes a large step to Gonzaga, eyeballing the curled-up nun in his pack. Her hands moving over Cleopas's Rosary, still praying. Praying without ceasing. She rolls one eye to the commander, and it is light and peaceful. He breathes easy looking into it, nods. She smiles and it is ancient and beautiful. Brigid pats Gonzaga on the shoulder. Quietly, he says, "Be ready. You have to make it."

"Yes, sir."

"If the five of us die, *you* have to make it. Keep her alive, hear me?"

"Yes, sir."

He points to Santa Cruz and Nonnatus. "You two. Cover his back."

Brigid pulls up Cleopas's suit on his Visuals. The word SEVERE in a red flashing box. A diagram of his body pops up, labeling lines pointing along him up and down with various maladies filled in. Damage to his armor everywhere. Their suits have onboard emergency foam sealant to fill small damages, but there is a wound too wide for his suit to compensate for.

"Contact," Cleopas says. Begins firing as well.

Brigid rushes over behind him. "I'll take position," he says. "You get that massive hole in your suit foamed up before you step into space."

"Thanks, sir," Cleopas says as he ducks from a shot very close to his helmet. "I've got it ready. Since I'm already here and you're already there, want to do the honors?"

He passes an emergency foam sealant cannister to the commander between returning fire. "More Thraw sneaking around. Maybe they're bringing those heavy guns with them."

"They've got maybe twenty seconds to do it," Brigid says and smirks, takes the can. He uses it to fil the gaps in Cleopas's battle-rent armor with a ballistic foam that will offer some impact resistance and, just as important if not more, insulate him and his internal atmosphere against the void of space. "Almost done, brother. I want you to be vacuum-tight and ready to jump out a perfectly good docking bay barrier into the featureless cosmos and onto the skin of another ship that's under fire, after all."

"Commander," Santa Cruz says. "The pocket drones have accumulated on a few of the external cannons. They're set to detonate when we jump."

"Copy."

Captain Bernhard comes over the comms, "Coming in hot. Five seconds."

"Places, people," Brigid says. "And detonate those pocket drones."

A shudder buzzes through the ship as the counterfire outside eases up. The pocket drones are stock equipped with miniature cameras and small explosive packs. Not enough power to sink the entire ship, but enough that their explosions will leave sizzling holes in metal. That's enough damage to the guns to take them out of the fight. The drones are programmed to land and huddle on weapons barrels. Without the intact precision tooling of a gun barrel, its projectile is hosed.

The *St. Joshua* charges forward on its final press. Pio and Cleopas stand, ready to fall back. They each toss grenades into the passageways and shut the hatches. Begin to fall back towards their brothers. The *St. Joshua* fills the view outside the barrier. Game time.

Brigid sees Gonzaga jump. He flies out the docking bay, the invisible airlock energy barrier rippling as he passes through. Lands magboots first, stomping along the ship's hull towards the airlock. Santa Cruz and Nonnatus leap, being chased by gunfire as Thraw soldiers pour into the bay. Brigid turns around, lays down fire.

He sees something that also catches Cleopas's attention. Off to his side. Behind the damaged ship. "Oh, that's where—" Cleopas says across their intercom and shoves his weapon up. A Skreeve swings into view, taking gunfire and never stops. Appearing from somewhere hidden, something unfound. There were still so many in that corral. The Skreeve claps Cleopas with a blow that would tear through a wall. The Knight goes flying off into the bay, his gun snapped in two.

Pio keeps shooting as Thraw enter both hatches like ants swarming a dollop of sugar on the ground. Several of them lugging in tripod-mounted cannons. These are so much larger than the ones they used in the passageway against the Knights. His Visuals weapons ID system flashes something about them being anti-vehicle munitions before he turns away. Gets on the move.

"Pio!" Brigid shouts and drops a marker into his Visuals of where Cleopas fell. Cleopas's suit has begun signaling the others as it transitions from SEVERE to IMPENDING FATALITY, such is how ruined it is. His medical readouts are nearly as bad. Both Knights continue covering fire as they rush over to him. Pio sees more Skreeve charge into the bay from a wide hatch open in the deck on the other side of the damaged ship. He sees the Thraw setting up gunner's nests. They grab Cleopas and drag him towards the *St. Joshua*, all sides closing in.

†

On the surface of the *St. Joshua* in the vacuum of space, Brothers Santa Cruz and Nonnatus watch as the docking bay soundlessly lights up in gunfire. Their own intercoms give them the others' exhausted breathing and clipped conversation.

Brother Gonzaga checks the nun's specs. "Sister, I love you and you're going to be fine. Bear with me for ten seconds while I help my brothers, okay?"

Her tiny and wonderful voice comes to him like a drink of water to a parched throat. "In the name of our Lord and Savior Jesus Christ the Almighty, do as you need. I am safe in your arms as I am safe in our Savior's arms."

"Oh, that's a lot of pressure, sister. But thanks," Gonzaga takes a knee and maglocks himself to the exterior. Draws out his TechHaft, which glows to life and extends a bow arm from both ends. He draws back the sizzling string as a laser arrow feeds out. He aims and releases. It strikes the neck of a Skreeve charging towards his brothers. The energy arrow transfers all it has on contact, concussing a burning wound into the creature. It falls off to the side, dead right there. Gonzaga draws another.

Brother Pio and Nonnatus look at one another. Nonnatus activates the drones that have collapsed along his back. They set off back into the docking bay, small onboard guns flipping down at the ready. They'll be useless in a fire fight but might draw some attention away from the struggling Knights.

Santa Cruz takes a shooter's stance and locks his magboots. Opens a compartment on his right forearm. A spring-mounted contraption ratchets up. "Recoilless," he says with a smile.

"You're going to snipe from this distance with a recoilless minigun?" Nonnatus asks.

"Absolutely."

Nonnatus gives a confused look, then shrugs as best he can in the armor. "Why not? I've seen you do—"

The spring-loaded device snaps a pellet-shaped projectile up into space maybe two meters. Once free-floating, it activates a small rocket charge, and it zips off towards the Thraw swarm. Somewhere in the boiling mass of the enemy a threat drops to the deck. Another pellet loads up, it springs off. And a third. The fourth, fifth and sixth pellets come faster and faster until the minigun's barrels are a blur, launching hundreds of rounds in moments.

†

"I'm down to half a mag," Commander Brigid says as they drag Brother Cleopas the last twenty meters. Another Skreeve charges over and he fires what he has left at it. The thing screeches as bullets strike along its face and dodges off to the side. Goes behind the ship docked there. The hollow *tick* of Brigid's gun while he's holding the trigger back says it for him. He snaps it back to his chest holster, grabs his TechHaft.

"I'm about out also," Brother Pio says. "But if we can just get him to the lip and toss him, we'll be okay."

"Leave me, brothers," Cleopas says, half-unconscious.

"No." Brigid says. A recoilless round zings overhead and strikes a Thraw. He sees it fall, and then sees that they've got the tripod-mounted guns set up. The first crew is feeding ammo into theirs. "Out of time."

Pio looks, knowing those guns will open up and rain down too much damage on their weary suits and then the *St. Joshua*. Sister Stella Nessa.

The Skreeve Brigid shot at leaps forward from out of nowhere. Brigid ignites his TechHaft in a brilliant blaze of energy, the Merovingian axe, a lethal jewel in the middle of the fray. He swings as the Skreeve descends, cleaving its arm from its body.

The thing hits them like a bull in full charge. The three Knights fall. But divine providence steps in, and as they collapse the first anti-vehicle gun opens up. The crossfire razes the damaged Skreeve and it falls, a miserable but swift death.

"Oh, we're in trouble," Pio says as he activates his forearm shield. "Last few meters, c'mon."

Brigid looks at the distance. "That's more than a few, but we've got it. Santa Cruz, target those guns." He sees the minigun line of fire sweep along the docking bay where the hardest fire is coming from. "Gonzaga, you got her inside?"

"Almost. I'm giving some cover fire for you guys."

Brigid sees another energy arrow fly overhead. Concussively pierce a Thraw gunner. "Get, now. This'll be over in a few seconds one way or the other."

Captain Bernhard comes over the comms. "We've got incoming missiles from the fleet. Estimated contact is forty seconds. Last call for a ride out of here."

"Loud and clear," Brigid says.

Suddenly the first of Nonnatus's drones pops apart in a whisp of smoke as a violent burst of gunfire cuts through it. The second and third swirl away, but the third does not outrun the fierce attack. It takes several rounds as well and plummets down into a heap. The lone survivor dips and swings around, races and tilts out of the docking bay. A single round *plinks* off its surface and it is knocked on a ugly trajectory but it corrects itself and leaves a dissipating smoking trail in its path.

The Thraw line of guns is mobile, creeping ever forward as the Knights make their way to the atmosphere barrier between the bay and space. A small team of the Thraw are assembling a new contraption of multiple barrels stacked in three rows on top of each other. He rolls the last of his grenades towards it, but two Skreeve scramble in its path and as it explodes he sees them gravely injured but the newest weapon untouched.

They cross the last few meters, Pio's shield taking such a beating it begins to fizzle and rupture in sections. "Eight percent left, Commander."

"None too soon," Brigid says as he grabs Cleopas under the arms. Throws him out the docking bay access at his ship. "Go."

Pio turns and jumps. So does Brigid.

†

Brother Gonzaga eases up, shuts down his TechHaft. As Brother Cleopas comes smoothly sailing at him under the power of the commander's hurl, he grabs the damaged Knight and turns with him to stop the motion.

"Gotcha, brother."

Cleopas pats him on the shoulder. "Thanks. I'm uh... well, I've seen some better days."

Receiving Cleopas's suit's SOS, Gonzaga nods. "Yeah. Well. Wouldn't be a Knight 15 13 without the risk of giving your life for your friends, eh?"

Brother Pio and Commander Brigid land on the *St. Joshua*, their magboots grabbing with a powerful click. Brigid says, "Pio, get Cleopas. Gonzaga, get her inside like I told you to."

"Roger, commander," Gonzaga turns to the airlock.

"Bernhard, we're on board," Brigid reports.

"Copy that, prepare for maneuvers."

For a split second the strange peace outside in God's inescapable glory is like a weird skin that drapes over them. A cleansing rain. A breach in the tide of deafening violence they've been mired in.

And then the newest contraption the Thraw have assembled fires from the docking bay, an actual grappling hook and trail line jetting towards them. Then a second one springs off. And a third. The fourth, fifth and sixth come sailing towards them. Then more. The hooks begin catching onto the hull, clamping down with grippers. Thraw soldiers hook onto the trail lines and jump out of the bay, come careening towards the *St. Joshua*.

The Knights start firing at the newest invasion force. The *St. Joshua* rolls hard to its starboard away from ther Thraw mothership. The trail lines tense and actually pull the mothership along.

"They must have those hook launchers secured to the deck." Brigid comes over the comms, "Hit the hooks themselves! We've got to go!"

They open fire as Thraw soldiers touch down on the *St. Joshua* and start moving under fire. The *St. Joshua*'s Terminal Point Autocannons spin around and begin mowing through the new invaders. But more come. Brigid looks back to the docking bay and sees it teeming with every soldier they did not encounter while they were inside.

"We've got to get an explosive inside that bay," he says.

"You've got to get inside," Captain Bernhard comes over the comms.

"They're thinning out," Nonnatus says as he lays down another line of fire.

A final grappling hook comes flying through the mess like a needle propelling out of a haystack. Untouched in the melee, it sails, impressively spot-on to its target. It fixes onto the ring basket and the nun inside it, runs taunt in the blink of an eye, and heaves backwards.

Gonzaga's magboots lock down, and the tug of war is just a hair's breadth in time; it passes and the ring basket's clasps break and the entire package comes free. Those lines are towing a ship. His suit doesn't stand a chance. Sister Stella Nessa inside her basket goes sailing backwards. All the Knights dive for it, save Cleopas, whose damaged suit keeps him from moving swiftly.

Gonzaga cannot turn around fast enough.

Santa Cruz dives and misses by a hair.

Nonnatus lunges and nearly grabs the basket. But only nearly.

Brigid tries as well, but incoming fire tears along his path and he cannot make it.

Pio manages to hook a single finger through the rim of the basket but is hit by incoming fire and loses it.

Cleopas, for all his ruin, darts a single arm forward and cups the basket like he's holding a baby. Engages his magboots, and for a moment his boots hold before the power cuts to them. It's enough for Pio to lunge at him, grabbing him.

"Hang on, buddy," Pio says and more fire dances along the ship around them and walks up Pio's body from his foot to his waist. A shower of sparks spits out from his boot. The power meter for that leg's magboot flickers and drops, and now Pio has lost fifty percent of what was holding them, even for a second.

"Don't let that basket come apart!" Pio shouts.

The TPAs shred through the onslaught, but the trail line holding Sister Stella Nessa is taut. Cleopas manages his other arm around the basket, his helmeted face smashed against it. One eye focuses on the nun. She regards him with a smile, reaches out with the hand holding his Rosary and caresses the basket wall where his head is. She mouths something to him. He can't hear her, can't read her lips. But she is serene and beautiful. Ancient. Embodies a gift from God that some vile force wants to squeeze out and destroy. He smiles at her.

The line yanks hard, and he skids backwards. With whatever he has, he holds. The grappling hook's gripper has three tongs on it, and he tries to take one and pull it back. Loosen it.

The incoming fire increases tenfold, and it rains down. One of the TPAs is hit with an RPG. Explodes. Goes off-line. Another RPG fires in, hits nearby. Cleopas sees several new Thraw preparing to jump to their ship.

"Missiles fifteen seconds out," Captain Bernhard says. "We clear to maneuver?"

"No!" Brigid says. "Things have gone pear-shaped out here."

"Things are gonna go much worse in fifteen seconds."

"Give us fourteen of them, then."

The other Knights clamber towards Cleopas. The hail of return fire pins them, tapping their armor and shields. It's gone from lukewarm to a raging boil. Pio pulls to haul them in, but his suit begins to fail altogether. "We're in trouble, all right," he says to himself. In the near-inaudible static hiss of their microphones, with only their own breathing and huffing to cover it, it sounds scared. Almost defeated.

Cleopas sees the grappling hook articulate its tongs, trying to walk to a better grip. He digs a fist under it, wedging himself between it and the basket. He looks to Pio, nods his head towards the nun.

"Get her. Get the basket. I got an idea."

Pio floods with hope and puts one arm around the basket, then the other. "Got her. Now what's your move?"

With the emergency warning of IMPENDING FATALITY overlaid on his Visuals, he simply says, "To show my love for my brothers."

Cleopas uses his free hand to grab a belt of explosives Pio has on his suit. He lets go of the nun and wrenches the basket out of the hook's grip enough to where it clamps back down on his own hand.

"Run."

Cleopas stops fighting. The grappling hook's trail line yanks him back. Off the ship entirely. Out into the dead of space between the vessels. The horde of Thraw at the docking bay firing round after round like a blinding wall coming at them. The exterior of the *St. Joshua* being chewed alive by the incoming fire, the clear glow of the missile thrusters coming over the horizon to detonate the ship into a cloud of radioactive vapor.

The five Knights and Sister Stella Nessa falling back towards the airlock, all screaming for Cleopas. A handful of Thraw jumping from their own ship to the *St. Joshua*, being shot at and struck even before they land on its exterior. A few do land, take heavy fire. They float off into the nothingness, limp and expired.

"Remember, O most gracious Virgin Mary, that never was it known that anyone who fled to thy protection, implored thy help or sought thy intercession, was left unaided—" Cleopas's calm voice over their comms, praying to the woman to whom he has such a devotion.

"Inspired by this confidence, we fly unto thee, O Virgin of virgins, my mother—"

Inside the bay, the Thraw, the Skreeve, they race into a dogpile. The trail line in the center of them, getting shiorter by the moment. One on top of the next on top of the next, all clambering to grab Cleopas as the trail line rachets him to just outside the barrier.

"—to thee do we come, before thee do we stand, sinful and sorrowful—"

He makes a ripple in the energy barrier, sinks through it. A boiling fury inside there to accept him, lusting after the nun but they'll take what they can get.

"—O Mother of the Word Incarnate, despise not our petitions, but in thy mercy hear and answer us—"

So serene. His brothers hear his voice from the belly of the enemy, "—Praise be to the Lord, my rock, who trains my hands for war, my fingers for battle. Thank you for my brothers, for my life. For this gift right here, right now. May it be enough." The enemy reach out and grab Brother Cleopas, drag him inside their pile. Cheering. Joyous and cheering now that they have him.

"Amen," Cleopas at peace, hands on the belt.

Brigid watches as his Knight, the teeming mass of the enemy, the docking bay, and so much of that quarter of the ship explode with all the reds, oranges and yellows in the entire universe. A mushroom of brilliant color followed by gray and then the black of roiling smoke. The trail lines holding the Thraw ship to the *St. Joshua* go suddenly limp. Flail loose. All ties severed.

Cleopas's final and grandest gift of self, his love for his brothers, his devotion to his mission, his vow to the Church Militant, to save this blessed nun from some other species on some other planet that he's never met before a few hours ago. What charity. The belt of explosives destroys the side of the Arithraw ship in one silent thunderclap, spins it off on a violent corkscrew pattern. The entire ship heaved uncontrollably by the explosion in her side. It flings away from the *St. Joshua*. Casting debris out into the void. Such a Goliath struck down by a single pebble from the sling of Brother Cleopas.

Outwardly cast detritus from the explosion pepper all along the *St. Joshua*, and the Knights must avoid bits and pieces raining down. Their own ship battered and pockmarked by return fire. Tiny breaches in the outer hull like craters on a rock moon. A few where the emergency sealant foam from a deeper breach has filled the wounds, instantly hardening into a little bubble protruding from the surface.

There the Knights stand on the exterior of the *St. Joshua*. Brutalized. Now the kind of quiet that can only be found either in the bottom of a casket or at the very feet of God. Watching as that incredible adversary of a ship twirls away, a wasted hulk gasping and asking itself what it did wrong to lose in such an awe-inspiring way.

Silence across their comms. A unified held breath, allowing for the vacuum to communicate its great nothing as the Thraw danger dissolves in a vapor cloud and a husk of ruined ship. In a voice so peaceful and small, the nun says, "Glory to Jesus Christ, in His love and mercy He gives us this man. Into the Lord's inescapable glory he goes, indeed."

The *St. Joshua* peels off and Brigid shuts the airlock. The ship banks wildly, sending up defensive fire at the incoming missiles. The first time the *St. Joshua* shudders Brigid knows they shot one missile down just in time. The strobes begin flashing inside the lock.

Three more shudders and he breathes easier. All four incoming destroyed. The captain warns of acceleration and evasive maneuvers.

The Knights stand in the airlock as it cycles, and the inner door opens. They remove their helmets silently. Gonzaga takes the nun out of the ring basket. In her hand is Cleopas's Rosary, beads made from melting down a mortar that struck beside him but never detonated.

All eyes on him, Commander Brigid touches his forehead with a single finger. Then his chest. Then his left shoulder. Finally, his right shoulder. "For our Brother Cleopas, dear Lord, eternal rest grant unto him, and may perpetual light shine upon him. May the souls of the faithful departed, through the mercy of God, rest in peace. Thank You, Lord, for letting us have him in our lives."

They all say "Amen," in unison, and in procession they move down the passageway.

Seven Hours

"At full throttle, we'll be at the gate in about seven hours," Captain Bernhard says over the comms. "We've got two fast attacks on our tail, but they haven't fired yet."

"Any idea why?" Commander Brigid asks as he reaches the weapons locker with the others. Brother Gonzaga continues to the sick bay where he's to drop off Sister Stella Nessa.

"No. Could be we're moving faster than their missiles can travel. Darvian ships are pretty decent, but I have no idea what package the Thraw could actually pay for. Could be they want to try and catch up and reacquire her."

"Will they be able to overtake us?"

"Not in seven hours. If they get close enough, we can get one right off our six and drop a mag-mine. We're carrying six of them."

"Okay. Give me five minutes and I'll be up there."

Brigid stands in front of his locker and puts his sweaty forehead against its door. Eyes closed; he pushes down the hurt from Brother Cleopas. The other Knights see him and don't react; they're all waiting for their turn to do it also.

Finally, Brother Pio says, "We'll offer Mass for him. But he went to Reconciliation before this mission. He gave his life for his brothers and sisters. Out of love. Christ's love. I'm sure he's at God's feet right now, praying for us."

"It's a kind of martyrdom, I believe." Brother Santa Cruz says. "I think so, anyway."

"It is."

"Do you think they killed him? Before the explosives went off?" Brother Nonnatus says.

"No. But he was... he was so injured by the end... his suit's onboard med systems weren't online, all that. If we rushed him down here and

131

got him in a surgical pod, maybe. Maybe it could have pulled him back from the brink. But he was really hurt."

Pio smiles. "Ours is a wonderful knowledge that death is only the next step in life. Cleopas will be celebrated. He made it. Our Lord gave His life for all of us as well. What a wonderful imitation of Him. Praise God."

"I know," Brigid says. He touches his double pendant. "Ever since Mitchie and Jadie, I take it hard— harder than I probably would otherwise. And that was a long time ago. Give me five minutes and I'll be at peace with the fact that he is at peace."

"We know, commander." Santa Cruz says, looking away. "I take it hard, too."

Nonnatus shrugs and comes back on topic. "Let's be frank. We were overwhelmed. We were going to lose in a few more moments. That was a tide we weren't turning. Cleopas... praise God. He did it all for us."

"Yeah," Pio says. "Praise God, we had him as long as we did." He begins to dismantle his armor. A slow ritual for all of them, made more cumbersome by all the damage they'd sustained. Parts didn't want to come off now. Pieces bent at the wrong angle, systems offline and not helping to unlock, unbolt or unlatch. Sore bodies trying to move, the adrenaline of battle burned out and hot weariness replacing it.

Brigid keeps his head on the locker. "Alright. Yeah. Pio, let Father Cho know we'll need Mass for him. Put it on the calendar for every month, on this date. Nonnatus, you pack up Cleopas's belongings. I'll go to the bridge and send a sitrep back to the Commandry to put in for Cleopas's cause. Santa Cruz, you and Gonzaga go through our armor and munitions, find what's salvageable, top everything off, prep for the next fight, all that."

"Roger, Commander."

"We're not out of this yet."

Brigid hits the emergency evac button on his blasted armor and it all disengages, falls in pieces arounds him in a pile. He steps out of it, kicks aside a few things so he can open his locker. His men laugh at him. He changes out from his inner layer to a clean jumpsuit and leaves, walks towards the bridge to check in.

†

"Comfortable?" Brother Gonzaga asks as he gets Sister Stella Nessa inside the medical pod. He leans back onto the corner of an exam table and for the first time since he can remember, eases. Truly eases.

She smiles and nods. Through his universal translator she simply says, "I am blessed."

The pod closes and boots up the files it has on Arithraw physiology. Begins a scan of her. Immediately reports the wounds to her hands. Her malnutrition. The other standard things that come with her age; bone deterioration, joint strain, numerous bruises from lying down so much. On an Eidolon-class stealth cruiser, the medbays are equipped with a small automatic lab that custom mixes and administers medications based on physiology factors. A single automatic IV finds a vein through Sister Stella Nessa's paper-thin skin and begins a drip.

"I imagine you've been knocked around quite a lot these last few hours. We really did mean for this to be a quiet, peaceful thing." Gonzaga says with a sad smile. "We weren't planning on getting caught with our hands in the cookie jar."

"I am unworthy of your sacrifices."

"We'd die for any of you, Sister. Brother Cleopas was honored to. I know he was honored."

"I will pray for him even now."

"Thank you."

Gonzaga looks off at nothing in the small space. It's a cream white with gentle lighting and stainless-steel surfaces, same as any medical space anywhere he'd seen. He sees a dot on the wall or maybe he imagines it, but he focuses on it all the same. He reaches inside the pod, takes her small hand in his and is delighted at the touch. As the fatigue sets in, all his muscles finally decide it's okay to begin hurting and burning now, his eyes dreary. Everything overtaxed. His body settling out like a tired engine turned off, quietly ticking and cooling down.

"So, my homeworld was little more than a colony on a small planet. Tiny. There were three colonies that all were founded at the same time by the same group of settlers. They weren't very far apart, and within twenty years they each had a road connecting them to the other two. It formed a triangle.

"A zealous group of aliens came to evangelize us with their corrupted take on God. They learned our religion—we were Christian without putting a denomination on it, though numerous churches popped up—and the zealots started mixing Christ in with their beliefs. A few colonists would nod and listen and maybe one or two started to buy it. But the vast majority of us—I say *us*; I was just a kid—told them no thank you. They left.

"They came back and started to kill everyone and everything. My family included. I hated non-human-based life. The Knights showed up as soon as they could, and I made an exception for the non-humans in the Order. They were okay. But everything else, in my heart I didn't mind it if they all died and died right now.

"There really isn't much to my story besides that. We got obliterated and the Knights beat them back. Saved us. Saved me. Raised me in one of their orphanages. I answered a vocation call from God to serve, and I kind of wonder if He called me because He knew my heart was so hard this might be the only way to help me choose Him."

The nun says, "What immense glory He has, to know you and love you so much as to call you here for your own good. Praise be to our God, creator of everything."

"When they rescued me, I was dirty. Starved. Bloody. Covered in filth. And they put me in a medbay like this one. Right here. I usually avoid these places because when I enter one, I can smell my homeworld. The air stank like gunpowder and fire."

Gonzaga looks at the nun and winks. "But not this time. And I wonder if it will the next time I'm in one of these."

"Christ is working in your heart, my sweet friend."

Gonzaga hears that and nods. Stares off in the distance. Feels his filial ring itch. He rubs it, clears his throat. "So, what's the Church like down there on your planet?"

"Vibrant," she says, her other hand clutching the Rosary across her chest. "So much hope."

"Yeah? Growing despite how oppressive the world government is?"

"They came to evangelize when I was a little girl. It spread so quickly. So quickly. Hope was in short supply when I was young. Not much for our world except labor. The mines, off-world doing whatever they sell you for. Many of my older brothers were sold to be soldiers to other species. My mother, she was executed when she could no longer lay eggs. A mouth to feed with nothing in return. There was so little hope. Until Jesus."

"Oh, my."

"It is why they hate us so. The government. We used to fear it, because they meant death, until we came to learn the truth. Death brings us to God, and neither God nor death is anything to fear."

"Cleopas."

"Yes. I pray for his soul, but he died in love of Christ."

Gonzaga lets the air take their words and pass them out of existence. He breathes in and out, clears his throat again. Asks, "Your government... tyranny, huh?"

"Yes."

"It hates the Church."

"Yes. Our people used to have an ancient faith, many generations ago. It was not Christian, but it was suppressed, stomped out. The government rose to power and killed it. That's why we are atheist now, but the spirit of wanting a god lives on in us. Other religions came to us, even before I was born. But they were murdered and stayed away. Only the Christian missionaries would return. Pain and death would not keep them away. They seemed almost fulfilled by it. We needed love."

"Praise God." Gonzaga says. "Why don't the soldiers convert?"

"Some do. It is very risky to evangelize them. We stay quiet when the soldiers are around. Some try to tell them of Jesus's love, but... but the soldiers, the scientists, the bureaucrats, all those in higher castes, what it takes to get and then keep a good government job. For them to turn away and reach for Christ means a real threat to them, their lineage, their everything.

"When I was first in the underground convent, a politician named FhorHo Quing professed his faith. He was from a very high caste. He was good at his job. His father and his father's father were well respected. His spouse's father was the same. But when he professed his faith, his father and his father's father were executed by dehi-dehi."

Gonzaga looks at her, curious. She recognizes the look on his face and says, "Dehi-dehi is a slow crushing between two slabs of stone. FhorHo Quing's hands were tied to the lever that lowered the upper stone, making him a part of their deaths. He was given the chance to renounce our Lord and they would stop it, but he stood strong in his faith. He would not renounce Christ."

"Sadistic."

"And then his father-in-law as well," She exhales slowly. "And his spouse's latest clutch of eggs was burned. His wife was forced to denounce him, and she herself was humiliated when the government had her next clutch of eggs fertilized by convicts. Finally, FhorHo was martyred. And so was his wife."

"All for Christ." Gonzaga thinks back to when he decided to take his vows. The Knights 15 13 put no pressure on him to do it, and in fact, made him discern if he was asking for this life because he felt called to it by God or if it simply what he'd known up to that point. To think of having this Thraw's bravery, knowing what he was risking, and then to suffer so greatly just because he said he believed in God.

"The government hates us," the nun says. "And they make it clear."

"What incredible bravery."

"What incredible faith. Have you read in the Holy Word, the second book of the Maccabees, Chapter 7?"

"Where the Israelite mother was forced to watch her sons executed by the Greeks for not betraying their faith?"

"That very one. FhorHo Quing, he was an example just like that mother. He started a flood of conversions. He never rescinded his love of Christ. His wife never did either. The government wanted their sufferings to be an example of what happens when you pick basking in the fatherly embrace of God instead of languishing under that boot of theirs. It backfired. So many Thraw picked God that day. The government failed."

Her tears shimmer and fall, and she smiles. Gonzaga concentrates on her hand in his. "I didn't mean to make you cry. I'm sorry."

"I weep with joy. Souls won for our Savior are glorious."

Gonzaga returns her smile and laughs quietly. "Okay. So, when did you discern a life as a sister?"

She beams happily at some far-off memory, warming her like a hearth in the cold. "Oh. I was young. I knew in an easy way. I put on a garment like this in a mirror when I was young—" she touches her habit's veil with the hand still holding the Rosary. It spills along the side of her head like raindrops as she clasps it, "—and I never felt so... complete. I felt beautiful for the first time. I knew then."

"What was it like, getting the stigmata?" Gonzaga's Visuals sends up a message about the seven-hour transit. Orders listed to change out and inventory equipment. He sighs and stretches his back.

"Ecstasy." Sister Stella Nessa says. "I would always imagine myself at the foot of our Lord as He gave His life on the cross. How I would clean His wounds. Wipe away His tears. I was there, you see. Always am I there, to tend to his hurts. Hearing the sobbing of the Blessed Mother, being held by Saint John and the Magdalene.

"I, being pushed aside as the nearly blind Saint Longinus, a warrior of that race called a Roman, comes forward to spear our Lord in His side. The blood and water flowing from that wound, spilling along Longinus. How it cured his near blindness. How he came to believe in Whom he had just crucified. I could see it. I could feel the stormy wind that carried that blood and water. I thanked Jesus for accepting His burden for us. I always do. And after so many years... so many years..." she gently lifts her hands, the wounds on display.

Gonzaga smiles. Puts a hand on the med pod. "Have a hard time with people not believing you?"

"At first, there was doubt. Always. And I was the first one to doubt it. To doubt myself, my mind. I prayed for weeks before showing anyone. I was so scared I was going insane. We have never seen this, you understand. We had heard... Saint Francis, Saint Catherine, Saint Gemma, even Saint Florence of the Ice Belt and Saint Xavier of Ceres. So many saints bearing Christ's wounds."

"Eventually you showed someone?"

"My mother superior, she saw my hands. She was worried it was me doing it, but she could smell the lovely odor from the wounds. She ordered me to keep quiet about them, and I obeyed. She checked them every day, and eventually she contacted the bishop. He examined me, had a doctor and a psychologist examine me. When they became convinced I was not doing it, they prayed a novena to Saint Francis."

"Saint Padre Pio, our guy took that namesake when he took his final vows. Brother Pio. Great guy. He really wants to talk to you about the whole thing."

"I would love it," She adjusts some in the pod and exhales deeply. "Truly. Miracles abound."

The door slides open and Brother Santa Cruz sticks his head in. It's the first time Sister Stella Nessa has seen the sharpshooter without a helmet of some kind. She smiles at him, and the man feels a wash of love come over him.

"Not trying to break this up, but Gonzaga, we've got to go inventory weapons and—"

"Yeah, I know. I'm coming," Gonzaga stands up and leans over to the nun. "Rest up, sister. We've got several hours before we make the jump to Centauri Astoria and get you secured, okay?"

"I am blessed."

Gonzaga smiles. "I'll take that as a yes."

The Knights leave, and the nun closes her eyes, her fingers ticking off Rosary bead after Rosary bead, Brother Cleopas's name on her lips.

†

The bridge hatch slides off to the side with a whisper and Commander Brigid steps inside. Like the galley on board these ships, it's smaller than one might think.

Captain Bernhard is at the central console. Lieutenant Commander Keo, the executive officer and engineering officer, sits before him at her station, central in the bridge. To her left, Petty Officer Bonilla, the weapons tech, a middle-aged man with tightly cropped red hair and a permanently installed patch covering his left eye. To her right, Petty Officer Cavins, the pilot and navigator. Young but confident looking in a way that communicates he's not arrogant but loves a challenge because he can defeat them. Along the starboard rear, Petty Officer Johns, the engineering tech.

Bernhard is intently staring at a screen while Cavins rapidly types away. He stops, chews on the tip of his thumb. Brigid can see his eyes reflected in the screen as they rapidly flick across the information.

"Yeah, older model. Late Delta series, maybe. *Maybe.* Not the Gemini 3s we have outside our place, that's for sure. These Delta rings were cutting edge when my dad was still working the controls. And he quit that job— oh, Dave wasn't in seminary yet."

Bernhard nods. "Older brother?"

"*Oldest* brother, yeah. I'm seven out of twelve. Dave was the first boy, child number two. There are two more boys between us and one after."

Brigid steps nearby. Sees the screen, the operations and diagnostics manual displayed there. "Wormhole gate?"

Bernhard and the crewman turn to look. Says, "Yes. We've already booked passage from this node to the one fifteen hundred kilometers outside Centauri Astoria. Petty Officer Cavins here is pretty sure we can work some magic on this node."

"Magic?"

Bernhard smiles. "Well, I'm not really wanting to bring our enemy back home, you know. He'll hack the master controls, get us through to Centauri Astoria and then put a bug in to make the Thraw ships U-turn right back out into their own system."

"Then it'll scrub the coordinates saved in the log going back a few weeks, just in case," Cavins says.

Brigid says, "Oh. I figured we'd just dump a land mine there and let them run into it."

Bernhard laughs. "They're not *that* close on our tail. I think even the Thraw would be able to dodge it."

"So, we set the land mine a few meters off the ring and blow it after we pass through."

"The node's operator would be rather annoyed with us."

"This thing is owned by Gosnell PTE, correct?"

"Virtually every node is, at least in this part of the galaxy."

"You know as well as I do what they're doing besides the wormhole gate business," Brigid touches his double pendant again. Looks off at one of the ultra-high-res screens they use in place of a windshield glass. He sees the stars outside, the darkness of it all surrounding them. Far off, the Arithraw sun gleams in the furthest reaches of the starboard side screen as they try to out-distance its beams.

Bernhard leans on the console and points his head towards Brigid's neck. "You were civilian spec ops when you lost them?"

"Yeah. I'd just started my third tour of duty," Brigid smiles thinking of Mitchie and Jadie. "I made O4 and was already being looked at for O5. Funny thing," Brigid looks to his feet and then squints as if something off in the distance is twinkling right into his eyes. "We weren't even religious. I never cared much for it. Mitchie and I only had the one child to be... conscientious or whatever. Didn't want to crowd out the solar system, overtax the support network. You know the lines. So, we only had our little Jadie. But anyhow, we lived our lives as good secular citizens of the FedNet and neither of us really had anything bad to say about Gosnell PTE."

"They work hard for their image," the captain says. "I should say they spend a lot of money to maintain a façade of their image."

"And we bought it," Brigid says. "I mean, you'd hear things—their quiet labs, some ethically questionable behavior here and there which was probably just a misunderstanding or a lone bad doctor, but they did *so much good.*" Brigid clenches a fist. "They said they did so much good. And for those of us not wanting to hear how much evil they commit; it wasn't hard to think they were okay. They did so much good, right?"

"Right."

"Mitchie and I booked a charter ship to take Jadie to Cigam Proxima so she could look at doing her studies there. I couldn't make it—duties. But it would be a fun mom and daughter trip," Brigid says, smiling at the golden cast to the memory as it dawns in his mind.

But a storm cloud rolls over, black and consuming. "Their flight plan had them slingshot-ing around Cigam Prime. Right past Gosnell PTE's most misunderstood quiet lab."

"The Xerxes station."

Brigid nods grimly. "The Xerxes station."

Petty Officer Cavins sucks in some air. "Not the one that— uh, well, my dad. Like I said, my dad worked the controls for a Delta ring back in the day, I mean— it was Gosnell PTE, but... but my dad thought that was heinous. Just heinous. Xerxes station. He never—"

Brigid held up his hand. "Most of the Gosnell PTE's employees openly disagreed with the Xerxes station's decision to 'accidentally' smoke a passenger ship. I would never blame your father for when his company killed my family."

Gosnell Planned Tomorrow Enterprises, a vast company that began its life in biosciences, now had heavy hands in several fields from medical technologies and flesh farms—laboratories that used experimental tissues to grow organs and limbs for various species, to mechanical technologies such as wormhole gates and orbital elevators. They had a growing presence in multimedia productions as well. The calloused rumor was that every decade or so, Gosnell PTE would have to produce a documentary or made-for-TV film to explain a situation in their best interest when they as a company royally screwed up.

Such as when their Xerxes station, a massive facility built into an asteroid that was captured in the orbital gravity of a gas giant, murdered a ship in the weakest claim of self-defense this side of an elementary school playground fight. The Xerxes station conducted morally obscene procedures—pre- and post-birth abortions, living fetal experimentation, elderly euthanasia, et al. on various species. It was highly profitable for the company. It also provided them with a nearly limitless supply of test subjects in the form of embryos.

When all that came to light to the common man, both support and condemnation came down in equal fashion. Mitchie's and Jadie's charter ship just so happened to pass by the Xerxes station during a time when the station had been experiencing heavy protests. Xerxes station later claimed to have been fired upon multiple times, though they could not provide any evidence. They also claimed threats, challenges to their sovereign status and the like.

Mitchie and Jadie's ship was not a luxury transport, but it was considered safe. There was professional security to ensure no traveler-gangs could extort protection money from the passengers. It was deep-cleaned at every port to fight against ship-wide illnesses. It had some nice amenities—things Mitchie and Jadie had never traveled with before. The ship boasted a zero G swimming pool, exterior walks and a library filled with real paper books.

They were not equipped with defensive shields. Offensive weaponry. Soldiers.

So, when the Xerxes station fired two nuclear-tipped missiles at the ship, killing all two hundred and six people on board, Gosnell PTE had to try and explain why. Their explanations turned to excuses which eventually turned to apologies, and they were all the worst kind of flimsy.

Gosnell PTE made a short film about the attack. They left it ambiguous as to whether the protest ship fired on the station. Most viewers got their knowledge of the event from the show, and they shrugged. Went on with life.

"I enjoyed the five thousand credits Gosnell PTE paid me on each of their heads," Brigid says with contempt. "Ten thousand as an apology for killing my Mitchie and Jadie. That's what they're worth to a company that has shelf after shelf, in facility after facility, of flash-frozen infant heads for experimentation."

He gestures. It was another lifetime ago now. "For a company that does so much good, I was starting to see how all they did was evil. FedNet cut me loose on bereavement. Three tours thrown away because Gosnell PTE nuked a ship with my family on it. But, I had an aunt and uncle at the time who were third order Knights 15 13. They've passed now, but when I needed them most, they were there. I found God through their example. My aunt, her name was Brigid, named after Saint Brigid. And even though Saint Brigid is a gal, it seemed right to me.

"So, I gave my ten thousand credits to the Church. Maybe they could wash the blood from it. Use it for some higher purpose. I couldn't. Shortly afterwards I took the vows and donned my monk's cowl. If I can't have my wife and child, a religious life is well with my soul."

Bernhard smiles and elbows Petty Officer Cavins. "But... but all those years later, who was first guy through the airlock when the Knights 15 13 took down Xerxes, though?" He nods to Brigid.

Cavins's eyes light up. "You? Commander? I mean, I know we took down that place—"

Brigid shakes his head. "No. I don't know who went through the airlock first." He lets the burning memory force his bitter smile. "*I* was first in through a hole we plasma-cut into their weapons deck."

"Wow."

"Yeah. And a weapons deck on a medical facility? Armed with nuclear warheads? What does that imply?"

"They're killers," Bonilla says as he leans over on his chair. "You can't expect people who murder babies to not have other things going on, too."

"Things that need nukes?"

Bonilla furrows his brow, purses his lips. "They're killers."

"Agreed."

"But you got your revenge, eh?"

"For us, it wasn't revenge," Brigid says, holding up a hand. "None of us raced through there to murder the staff, make them feel our pain, none of that. We seized the staff. All their patients... the mothers, the children and the elderly, we took them with loving arms. The frozen embryos, we cared for. But, when we were done, we left it empty of everything. All the medical equipment repurposed to crisis pregnancy centers or morally upright labs. We sent stuff to orphanages. Budding monasteries. You name it. Xerxes was hollow. Our bishop came aboard and blessed it. Every space, cleansing it with the love of Jesus Christ. Sprinkling holy water on the walls, leaving thin trails of blessed salt along the doorways. We spent nine days aboard it, praying a novena to the Blessed Virgin, mother of mothers.

"And then we nuked it on our way out."

Everyone on the bridge stays quiet for a moment. Maybe in reverie for the dead, maybe to say a silent prayer in reparations for the vile evil those employees committed without conscience. Then Petty Officer Cavins asks, "What did Gosnell PTE say about it?"

"Who cares?" Brigid says with the righteous indignation of a wronged man.

"Captain?" Lt. Commander Keo says as she leans over a monitor. Younger than Brigid, older than his Knights, Keo has the kind of face that says she knows she's pretty but the kind of hands that have used more mechanic's tools than anything else. "You need to see this."

"Put it on main two," Bernhard says. The ultra high def monitor on the starboard side flicks and a live feed comes in from the top of the ship, exterior. Facing aft. "What in the world?" Bernhard asks.

"That boarding crew, coming down the grappling hooks," Brigid says. "We missed one."

On the monitor a lone Thraw soldier is clutching a tablet device, tapping on it with a secondary hand on the hull of the ship, magboot-ed to the surface.

"What's he doing? Taking notes?"

"We'll find out," Brigid says. "Hopefully he hangs on for a moment more. We'll go snatch him up."

"He should let go. He'd be fine," Bernhard says. "He's got two of his own coming at us. They can intercept him."

"If they won't kill him for failing to stay with us," Lt. Commander Keo says.

"There is that."

"The Thraw are merciless, even to their own. They'd just as soon run him over than pick him up and dust him off," Brigid shrugs and sighs. "We'll go out there and get him. This ship has a brig—" but everyone on the bridge gasps as the Thraw pushes off the hull. He floats out into space, becoming a dot in moments.

"We need to get somebody top side ASAP to make sure he didn't... I dunno... *do* anything," Bernhard says. "Might have been a foot soldier, might have been a sapper or a hacker, whatever."

"Aye, aye, Captain."

"On second thought, send a drone. I don't want to lose anyone while we're running at this speed. Let's get through the wormhole gate and we can have somebody go out there. See to it."

†

The Knights make their way through the showers. A vertical tube with a drain at the bottom and a spout at the top. Two minutes to wet down, then the automation kills the water. Two minutes to soap up, then the automation reactivates the water. Two more minutes to rinse off. Then under the heated pneumatic dryer as it breathes warm air in strong but not stiff currents down on them.

The Knights make their way through medical. Full body scans, a laundry list of all they'd endured since they suited up to descend onto the planet. Hairline fractures, stressed and torn soft tissues. Impact injuries, fluid shock wave injures, radiation or chemical exposures, if any. How long, how intense. Simple bruises and simple aches and pains. Stitches and medical super glue. Tissue fusing and biosupport salves. A few injections and basic nanomeds. No one lost a limb or suffered so greatly they needed emergency intervention. A new organ synthesized and grown on the double, if needed. Even "on the double" means months, but still.

The Knights make their way through the galley. All but Brother Gonzaga take a multivitamin paste and black coffee. Gonzaga never turns down a hot meal, and the ship's cookbot has a liquid egg product and real flour biscuits ready to fire off. They eat in silence, none really that hungry.

"My guts still hurt from the MDE," Gonzaga says, eggs on a biscuit half, ready to be eaten.

"My guts still hurt from being pummeled by cannon fire," Brother Pio says.

"My guts still hurt from being pummeled by one of those Skreeve," Commander Brigid says. "Actually, a couple of them."

"My guts hurt from this nasty paste," Brother Nonnatus says as he slaps the tube down on his tray.

Brother Santa Cruz raises an eyebrow. "Get better guts, then. All of you." They snicker at his comment and lapse back into their silence.

Father Cho finds them, enters the galley with the air of a man who knows how everything will play out not because he is omnipotent but because he is that experienced. Who knows how many times before he has come into a quiet room with hurting people just to make sure they know they are loved? He waits for a moment and then offers his shoulder to the men.

Brigid says, "How about I get Sister Stella Nessa and we can have Mass. How's that for you, Father?"

The crusader-priest smiles gently and nods. "How can I say no to celebrating our Lord?"

So, the Knights have Mass. The source and summit of all faith. Each lights a prayer candle for the soul of Brother Cleopas. Pio lights another candle for the souls of the Thraw lost. For the souls of the Skreeve ruined from the start. He prays to their guardian angels, asks them to be gentle as they guide those souls to their Creator and King. He prays to God for His mercy on them, and on the Knights.

Sister Stella Nessa insists on being on her knees at the communion rail, Rosary weaved through her fingers as she rests her forehead on her hands. Her lips move, graceful, and her near-silent voice goes up to God. The candlelight is like pinholes of light in the weeping wounds through her hands. Adorned with nail-driven love for Jesus.

Brigid kneels beside her, and he tries very hard to hear her praying for the six of them. For her fellow Thraw back on the planet who cared for her, visited her. Provided for her. Those hopefully alive right now, and those she knows are dead in the past few hours.

And then it is time to go on the bridge once again; so he stands and leaves.

The Wormhole Gate

"So, like I was saying, I can tell by the configuration it's a Delta II," Petty Officer Cavins says. His attention going from the ultra high def screen and his monitors and back again. "I'll give you three guesses why these things weren't popular."

Captain Bernhard and Commander Brigid are on the bridge, Bernhard in his captain's chair and Brigid standing nearby. On both the primary monitors is a view of the wormhole gate they're preparing to transit. The gates, functional models of what are commonly known as "Einstein-Rosen bridges," are connecting points throughout the galaxy that allow instantaneous travel from one point to another over vast distances.

They originated as advanced alien technologies, but in time that technology was sold, stolen, reverse engineered, retrofitted, repackaged and put into place by any number of other species. What once was a technology that whoever possessed could dominate entire solar systems with, in time became branded by various corporations or planets and mass-produced. Some gates worked with other brands of gates and were, in a sense, universal. Others were proprietary and transmitted between units of the same registered trademark. Some manufacturers improved on the tech, some failed so spectacularly they, at best, lost entire ships as they transited, never to be heard from again. Transited into a literal void. Others, at worst, malfunctioned and collapsed, causing black hole detonations so cataclysmic entire solar systems were consumed in their blasts.

All wormhole gates require immense power. It was commonplace to put stationary solar collectors in orbit as near to the local sun as could be, which siphoned power and beamed it to the gate itself. It wasn't a constant process—in the beginning it was until the first planet orbited between the collector and the gate; the concentrated solar beam left a considerable wound along its crust—but rather a fantastic discharge that might last dozens of hours. All timed to avoid known interruptions like orbits. There are stories of ships being in the wrong place at the wrong time and getting vaporized by energy blasts, then the gate-owning company hastily covering up the incident.

Now, Brigid stares at two wormhole gates, circles each almost a kilometer in diameter and set so close together they look like an infinity sign. "Is it because they're so close together?"

"Bingo. They're actually *touching*," Cavins says. "There's a whole network of controls and systems right there in the center. Something about only half the energy and materials, some stupid reasoning. Dad said it didn't save them that much and in return, their individual energy fields cause conflict in one another if not carefully monitored, and there was more than one collision as two vessels transited through. Especially if they were going opposite directions or at odd angles to the gate's transit surface."

"That's insane."

"Yeah. I guess Gosnell PTE tried to mitigate it by requiring all vessels, no matter their girth, to center themselves in the ring, they required only one vessel to transit at a time on either side, all kinds of things. In the end, it was easier to spread the rings apart a couple dozen kilometers."

"So, cheap and dangerous. That's why they're still in use in this solar system?"

"Yessir. Arithraw is the only habitable planet in this system, and even then, it's small and mostly low-rent manufacturing, subsistence farming and mud. I don't even think their moons are much more than basic rock compounds. None of it rates much in Gosnell PTE's eyes."

Brigid gives a hollow laugh. "You'd think with how both of them are so into violating God's morality, they'd be chums."

The captain makes a low, gruff sound in his throat. "Maybe they are. Arithraw has plenty of test subjects to supply that vile company."

"That might be something..." Brigid says. He scratches his head and searches through his thoughts. "They're spending an awful lot of resources to reclaim this one nun, even if they think they can peel her head open and extract the identities of the underground church."

The bridge crew stare at him as he works through his thoughts. Finally, Keo says, "Yes, but they think they can wipe out the entire underground church using her, right?"

"I imagine it'd be a domino effect. She's the biggest piece; and from her they can start snatching up everyone. But tyrants like them, why aren't they doing that anyways? What's different here?"

Bonilla shrugs and says, "She's the only one that got off."

The captain and Brigid both look at him. Brigid wags a finger and says, "Now, there's something, all right."

"Yes," the captain says. "No one travels to Arithraw—it's virtually useless as far as the secular universe is concerned. A perfect place for Gosnell PTE to come along and experiment."

"For war," Brigid says. "The galactic culture at large will tolerate their eugenicist lies because they feel good—abortion and euthanasia, mercy killings, the like. Even genetic manipulation and experimentation to better society as a whole."

"But their contributions to making the Skreeve—"

"—their mindless weapons of war," Brigid says. "That's a crime they want to be kept quiet."

"And a crime worth spending these resources on," the captain says.

The bridge is quiet for a moment, and Cavins starts talking as if his side of the conversation never stopped. "Yeah, uh... plus with the Delta II set-up, they usually send an operator on the platform to live for four-month rotations. But if they don't have enough operators, they can extend it up to eight months."

"Jeez."

"It's a one-person job, too. Like going into solitary confinement every time you go to work."

Brigid clears his throat. "You imagine this operator gets a lot of traffic?"

"Why would he? No one comes here but us, apparently. And no one here has the capability to leave."

Brigid snaps his fingers. "That's what it is."

The captain gives him his attention. "What do you mean?"

"The operator. Only we came. We altered our transponder coming in, correct?"

Keo leans back in her chair to address the commander. "Yes, sir. Light freighter hauling base geological components."

"But not our ship profile? Our reactor core signature?"

"No," the captain says.

"The operator must have actually taken the time to examine our ship after we exited the gate. Nothing else to do, right? Realized we were being deceptive."

"Notified the planet's authorities," The captain says.

"That's why they were patrolling like they were. They had already broken the doctor treating her, got whatever beans he spilled. Add in us on our way, and they're rushing around. Ready with the ground assault once we were figured out."

"And the fleet in orbit," Keo says. "They knew."

"Well..." Cavins keeps tapping. Something on his monitor flashes green for a moment and then his entire screen turns over to a different program. "All right. We have clearance to transit out, at least."

"Good," The captain says.

Cavins squints and sits back for a second. Mulling over a thought. Then leans forward again and begins tapping at his keyboard.

"What's on your mind, Cavins?" The captain asks.

Cavins says, "Well, sir, in the transit clearance message, it states we don't even need to slow down."

"Interesting," The captain says, looking to Brigid, who is confused. Captain Bernhard shrugs, says, "They don't normally write that."

"No, sir. Usually, it's a form message. This one checks out, but I don't like that wording. Red flag if you ask me."

Bernhard narrows his eyes. "What's the status on the Thraw ships?"

Keo taps a few buttons on her screen, reads as data comes across. "Nothing has changed as of— oh, wait. They've opened their tubes. Nothing is warming up yet, which is also weird. I would think they'd launch at us before we go in."

"Cavins," Bernhard says. He adjusts in his chair and grimaces like he's tasting something very sour. "Find out where we're scheduled to travel."

"Give me a moment to open a back channel, sir."

Captain Bernhard looks to Lt. Commander Keo, asks, "At this speed, what's our time to transit?"

She glances at one of her monitors. "Four minutes, eighteen seconds, sir."

"You've got three minutes, Cavins."

"Just need a few more... there," Cavins taps a few keys, sees a protocol address as their destination and cross-references it in Gosnell PTE's database. His eyes widen and he snickers out the side of his mouth. "There it is. They've got us transiting right back out the other side, sir. Giving us the U-turn treatment."

The captain laughs. "Right out of our playbook."

"Yes, sir."

Brigid says, "Explains why they've got their tubes open but haven't warmed anything up yet. Give them another minute and they will."

"They'll shoot us in the face and then try and retake the nun," Bernhard says with a grim flatness. "I'm not surprised by the Thraw, but shame on this operator being so easily bought. All right. Cavins, do what you must."

"Yessir."

Lt. Commander Keo leans over. "You think they bribed the controls operator?"

The captain purses his lips and nods. "Oh, I imagine so. Those gigs don't come with a lot of perks, I don't think."

"The operator has to be a Thraw," Brigid says. "Who else would want a gig like this? He'd be loyal to his home."

"Problem." Cavins says. "Just kicked me out while I was changing the transit coordinates. Must be a... a... oh, a rotating encryption? Or I timed out?"

"Hacking doesn't time out. You've been discovered," The captain says. "Get back in there. If you can't do it... Keo—"

"Three minutes, ten seconds."

"—in two minutes flat, tell me. Keo, let's prepare for evasive maneuvering. We'll dip down under the wormhole gate, get behind it and flip about. Sink both those Thraw vessels on our way back while Cavins here gets in and changes our course for good. Got it?"

Keo says, "Captain, they're warming up their tubes now."

"Told you," Brigid says.

"Bonilla, launch a mine at them. Give them something else to think about."

"Yes, sir," Petty Officer Bonilla says. He switches over to the fire controls, sets up the targeting, lines up his shot. "Ready to fire. Permission, sir?"

"Granted."

Bonilla presses a large red button and through his rear-facing camera watches an orb-shaped object leave the stern of the St. Joshua. Proximity sensors all around the mine begin looking for anything within a half klick of it. Once it locates something, it will activate the magnets facing the object and the reaction mass jets opposite it. Chase it. Stick to it. Detonate.

Captain Bernhard looks at Cavins, asks, "Well, we going or are we staying?"

Cavins moves his jaw side to side, says, "I'm trying, captain. Been kicked out two more times. I can get about halfway there and—"

"You've got thirty seconds."

"Aye, sir."

Cavins opens up a notepad on his monitor, hastily types out the entire gate configuration destination sequence. The entire string of letters, numbers and symbols that will send them to Centauri Astoria. Selects it, highlights and copies. Moves back over to the window where he's hacking the gate controls.

"Captain," Bonilla says, "the mine is off. Locked on the first Thraw ship."

"Actually attached?"

"No, sir. Chasing."

"Counter measures?"

"None yet, sir. But they're not literally in a direct line behind us, either. The mine will need to maneuver to get on the correct track line, all that."

Bernhard says. "Cavins? Ten seconds."

Cavins finds the code line in the backdoor program he's got open—for the fifth time in less than five minutes—and clicks. Pastes the entire string in it. Hits accept on the coordinates menu. Turns his head to the captain. "It's in there and accepted, sir. Now, unless—"

"All right. Commit to the gate," Bernhard says. "And pray."

The bridge acknowledges. Brigid looks at Bonilla, asks, "How's that mine?"

He shakes his head. "Still chasing."

"T minus fifty seconds to transit," Cavins says. He looks at his monitor as the location string deletes from the command line, he sees the destination location change again. The screen flicks, and he's out. "Did it again," he says and starts typing furiously.

The captain says, "Fire a disarmed missile towards the gate operator station. Don't hit it but give him something else to worry about. Now."

"Aye, sir." Bonilla launches, punches in the code to deactivate the warhead. Sets the targeting to scoot right under the gate station.

"T minus seven seconds," Cavins says as gets the screen back, swings his cursor over to the code bar and pastes the coordinates. Hits accept and prays the system can change calculations fast enough to make sense of it rather than split the difference and accidentally atomize the ship. He watches the screen acknowledge and he starts to exhale and—

They hit the gate's transit surface.

Expel out the other side. The captain says, "Confirm location," even as they are all scanning their primary monitors looking for Thraw vessels. They see none. Nothing pursuing, no prox mine pursuing that. Blank space.

"We made it," Cavins says, claps his hands once and then begins clicking away at his station. "Confirmed."

"Yeah," Brigid says and points at the right primary monitor. "That gas giant right there is Centauri Michi. Its seventeen moons."

Bernhard smiles and sits back in his chair. Exhales hard and it turns into a relieved laugh. "Yes. And beyond that, Centauri Thomas and its three moons."

"And beyond that, Centauri Astoria," Keo says.

"Home," Petty Officer Johns says with a bright smile. Sitting at his station, engineering reports spooling along his terminal as the ship does its standard post-transit checks. Careening through massive energy fields and traversing thousands of light years in a split second can yield nerve-racking results.

"You're from there?" Keo asks. "I never knew that."

"Born and raised on the east coast. Fishing out my back door. Ore collection to the north."

"Very neat," Keo says. She holds up three fingers, ticks them off as she recounts, "First Centauri Michi, then Centauri Thomas, and beyond that, Centauri Astoria." She looks at the others and smiles. "I've been here once when I was an Ensign. It was a fast trip."

"It's a good solar system," Brigid says. "I went through the Knights OCS pre-classes here. There are two more small planets nearer the sun. One is covered in poisonous, super-heated gases and the other is rocky and just plain super-hot. Centauri Michi has several moons bigger than both of them."

"I say again, very neat."

"Yes, yes. Very neat," the captain says. "Bonilla, that missile missed the gate operator, correct?"

"Yes, sir. Unless the gate operator shifted a hundred meters down in a split second, it missed."

"Good enough." The captain says. "Cavins, did you get just our coordinates in or did you get their U-turn in as well?"

"Got the whole code, sir. They were going too fast to maneuver by the time we jumped. They'd be here with us."

"Fair enough," the captain says. "Set a course for Centauri Astoria. Start checking the ship for damage control."

About the Harlanlocute

The Thraw soldier floats in space, the scar along his jaw deep as a cavern. After letting go of the enemy ship, he remains patient and tries to enjoy the rare moment of weightlessness. He has little else to concentrate on now. Most of his life dedicated to lab research, he has the theoretical knowledge of zero g and all its fruits—no true "up" or "down," the need to exercise if one spends any length of time in it to combat atrophy, all of it.

But his true moment has come and gone now. How strange that his entire purpose of existence culminated in one simple act, and even then, it was rushed. The trial phases are still on-going. But this, as uncontrolled as experiments get. Sloppy at best. He does not do well without control.

He watches as the first ship of his kinsmen charge uselessly beyond him towards the gate. Floating as he is, their ship is little more than a thruster plume as it rockets past him at speeds that would vaporize him if he was struck. Here and gone. Curiously, trailing directly behind it is some small ball-shaped object.

Even at their speeds, they won't reach it in time. If nothing else, these opponents in white metal with their red crosses like brands, these advocates of the *harlanlocute,* they will outrun his kind. Sneaky like the field rodents they called grainers. Hiding under cover of darkness, surprise attacks. Cowardice wrapped in sophisticated armor and weapons.

His mission will be their last hope. And it will work.

The enemy ship transits the gate, and his eyes turn to the other gate. He thinks the plan should be that they exit the one and enter from the other, but it does not appear. His own vessel plows through the gate and immediately exits on the other side. He imagines that if he could slow the visual of it all down enough, he could watch the nose enter the gate and exit the other gate while it's rear is still pushing through the first one.

The enemy ship does not reemerge. But his own does. How they pulled that off he has no idea, but he can venture a guess or two. As it is, as soon as his ship exits back in its ridiculous U-turn, it slows. And by doing that, the chasing sphere catches up. Rams it right up the tailpipe and the vessel explodes.

"Magnetic explosive?" The soldier asks himself, watching the first ship reduce to a cloud of particulates and fading light. And just like that, they have foolishly squandered any advantage they had save one: his experiment. And even that is a far toss from a sure win.

The second ship has already been braking against their forward motion. He can see the plumes of their reverse thrusters approaching. So long as they don't miscalculate, he won't be incinerated in the maneuver. It doesn't matter. His part is finished.

But they home in on his suit's signal. Come alongside, firing a tow line at him as they pass by at rates that would tear him into pieces in an atmosphere but in space simply take him from moving one way to moving another. The tow line clamps magnetically to his suit's anchor point and reels him in.

†

On the bridge, he stands at attention before the ship's captain, a Thraw elder who is missing one primary arm and has milky eyes. His skin is much darker than what it would be if from the region the soldier comes from. Further south, then. Different region. The captain shambles around the bridge, and it is becoming obvious he is in his waning years. Though like most life, Thraw biology displays its age with many traits, the species as a whole key in on how their motor skills reduce. Fine skills go first, gross motor skills go next. From there it's a race to see what organs shut down.

Soon, the captain's uncoordinated motions will be the red flag the National Civilians' Authority Council on Worthiness sees and determines he is unfit for resources anymore.

But for right now, when he speaks, everyone listens. "Success, you say?"

The soldier nods, "Yes, captain."

"Then you have done us honor."

"Thank you, Captain. It was an honor done to me to have been chosen for—"

"Who is the sacrifice?" The captain blurts out as he faces away, hard of hearing or disrespectful. As he does speak a bit of spittle comes with the words.

"The sacrifice?" the soldier asks, confused. "You mean... the volunteer on the—"

"We both know *what* he is. *Who* is he?"

"I did not care to ask his name. In the program he was Subject 02076. He was a former soldier from the high northern regions; one could tell by his excessive shoulder width and pale complexion. Violent criminal of some kind. Disgracefully removed from his service, on death row but given this incredible opportunity. His family was promised the removal of his disgrace upon successful completion—"

"Will he be successful?"

"I don't know. I want to say yes. The experiments are still new. The chemical compounds are still in their trial phases, but as far as I know—"

"So, this is a waste of our time, then?"

"Better to try and fail than to let them see they can walk all over us. As the NCA Emergency Council has already stated, this is about correcting their grave injustice against our proud people. We have been slapped in the face, Captain. We must do whatever we can to cut off their offending hands. We—"

"Look at it," The captain says as he gives the Thraw hand motion which means to be silent. An authoritative move which the soldier respects out of rank only. The captain's gross motor skills have degraded enough to where he can't even keep his saliva inside his mouth anymore. There's nothing left to respect but his rank insignia.

"Look. Look at it. The underground exists though we kill on sight. The underground obviously gets off-world communications to even draw the attention of these... whatevers. These whatevers arrive and even though we were looking for them, they got the *harlanlocute* with no resistance. It wasn't until we—"

"With all due respect, captain, the trap is set," The soldier says.

"Our Skreeve took her back, and even then, it was not enough. How can one soldier—"

"If this works, he will be worth a thousand Skreeve, captain. A thousand."

"And then? Back home? The underground church is emboldened. They don't mind torture, suffering, dying. Their little man on the tree did the same. It is their path to enlightenment."

"We don't mind dying either, and if it is all the same, they will die and be gone and we will live and not be bothered by it anymore. How they value it makes no difference—"

"I don't see—"

"We can control the truths the civilians see. Our Council on Information will see to that as they always do. And when the religious underground starts spreading their claims of the *harlanlocute* escaping with these religious men, we can stomp it down. The mere act—"

"*But will he be successful? Our soldier?*" the captain asks. As if that meaningless philosophical question will change the course of history if only he asks it passionately enough.

The soldier sighs. He wants nothing to do with placating this fool. A stiff drink and maybe a pinch of powdered hallucinations from the shipboard dispensary would relax him. A capitol ship would have one, even if it was on the officers' decks only. His research credentials would get him access. A mild trip where the colors are cool and sweet like spun dune sugars. "Yes. Captain, I understand that in your... more formative years? The beginning of your career, anyways, bioweapons were too cutting edge to be considered functional, but we have made major advancements. Partnering with the company has moved forward our designs by generations over a single decade. Generations, sir."

"The company? That Gobswell logo I keep seeing?"

"Gosnell, sir. Gosnell PTE. Yes, they have—"

"But will it work, I ask you—"

"Yes!" the soldier blurts out. Immediately he regains his composure. Such a sliver of an infraction. One word, as disrespectful as a punch to the face. And with an audience, of all things. Though he is a high-ranking soldier, he is enlisted. His patriarchal caste will never elevate him out of it. Even the lowest member of the bridge crew was an officer. Of purer blood than he.

The way the members of the bridge freeze shows his mistake. "My humblest apologies, Captain. I beg your forgiveness. I... I have dedicated my life to this cause. We are here in some part due to my efforts, and I need them to work to justify my... my everything, I suppose."

The navigator stares at the two Thraw as they interact in their own world, a bubble inside the bridge only those two can inhabit. Waiting for a crease, some indent in the conversation where he can wedge in to say what he needs to say. Finally, as the captain appears to be mulling over his forgiveness or lack thereof, the navigator clears his throat.

"My honorable captain, we have arrived at the gate. Now is the time."

The captain turns, his milky eyes wandering about for a second as if to get his bearings. Focus in on the new change in direction. "The gate's coordinates are programmed correctly?"

"Yes, captain. I have verified it."

"Send it through."

"Yessir."

The navigator runs the program, and on their screen, they watch a small probe travel through the gate. To follow the cowardly soldiers in white armor with red crosses like brands. The *harlanlocute*. A second one follows it but stops short of traversing the gate. It takes up a station-keeping orbit on the Thraw side and waits.

The captain turns his dead eyes towards the soldier and says out one side of his mouth, "This better work. Dismissed."

The soldier leaves, knowing he is not forgiven for one word he used without control. His life hinged on one disgraced and condemned soldier whose name he didn't know, also without his control. An experiment still in the trial phases which he cannot control. Failure will most certainly place him ahead of the captain in line towards a judgement of worthiness from his utilitarian government.

"Maybe *two* stiff drinks, then," he says to himself and wanders the passageways of a ship not his own.

†

The first probe gets on the Centauri Astoria side of the wormhole gate and unfolds its comms reception array, aimed towards Centauri Astoria. Another array unfolds and aims back through the gate. The second probe does the same; aiming one at the other probe and another one at Arithraw.

Communications from one planet to the next.

Part Three:
Atmosphere

Anomaly, Abomination

The drone is a wide, thick ring more like a tire than anything else. It rolls along like a wheel, smoothly cantering down a hill. Its exterior surface where rubber tread would be is a series of slender electromagnets as long as the ring is wide. An array of cameras and sensors in the middle, gyrostabilized inside the turning wheel around it. Scanning, examining, scanning again. Stenciled along a flat section of metal, the insignia HID 0011.

It rolls about the surface of the *St. Joshua* surveying the damage in its assigned sector. By happenstance, the sector where the Thraw soldier had been clinging before. Facing aft on the ship, the drone pauses to take its current information package and upload it to the *St. Joshua*'s automation network. It stays bolt still, a single blinking light as the uplink is established. A second blinking light as the information packet is uploaded. A third light comes on solid, the two blinking go solid as well, and then all three cut out simultaneously.

And it begins rolling again.

It crests a hump in what would be considered the spaceship's roof, then eases down into a declination between two ribs running fore and aft. Its sensor array does a sweep, detects what may be an anomaly under a feature that looks like a cowl stretching across between the two ribs. The wheel makes a wide rounding turn and rolls closer to get a more complete scan. Possible damage to the *St. Joshua*.

While this drone is unaware of whatever the other drones are reporting, part of all their scanning packages is to assess post-combat external damage: scorch marks, impact events, plating or ceramic tiles peeled back, rolled up, blown away. Even foreign objects stabbed into the hull, clamped in place. Mines, explosives.

But this anomaly does not fit those profiles. Foreign, yes. A foreign object is somehow attached to the hull. The first scan does not reveal any chemical reactants, agents, or volatiles. No arming devices. No fuses, no timers. A few mechanical features. Two canisters containing unknown fluids, what little of them are left. Those fluids do not register as known explosive compounds.

Hull Inspection Drone 0011 switches over to a different line of inquiry. Unfolds a different set of scanning array. Its organic sensors, rarely used on a drone that is deployed only on a spaceship. The foreign object attached to the hull is organic.

Under the cowl-feature, a pulsing mass quivers. What used to be another Thraw soldier huddles there. Around it, cannisters of the growth and mutation serums. Tubes tracing through to its veins, injecting. A constant feed. Curled up under the cowl. Out of sight. Hibernating? Pupating?

Transmogrifying, for sure.

What was the disgraced, condemned soldier is unreal now. Its hide translucent; an in-between stage of where it was and where it is going. Not quite a chrysalis, but a good enough descriptor. New musculature roping around underneath it, thickening and swelling well beyond the unaided, normal limit of the species. Its heart pounds inside, the veins snaking off it flexing as they transmit new hot blood. Advanced blood. Thorny spikes growing out from where its bones were once smooth. Armored patches of skin where flexible tissues once were. It is not a Skreeve; Skreeve didn't receive these new drugs. They received their revolting concoctions while still fetal. In an egg. An adult Thraw being gifted with this kind of serum, not even the nun knows about this. This abomination.

The drone rolls up to the thing and aligns its sensor array. Carefully recording everything. A small dish unfolds one section at a time in a clicking circle around a stem, like a metallic flower unfurling each petal. This sensor is extremely sensitive and has the broadest capacity. It will be able to get the best information. A single eye inside the abomination's head blinks and sees this.

The drone is running the requisite battery of protocols for organic scanning and the abomination, huddled up under the cowl, transmogrifying, bursts a limb forth. Strikes the drone with a backhanded swipe. The heavy magnetic wheel of it dents in and half the scanning array shatters into a thousand pieces of useless trash. Rectangle after rectangle of magnet knocked free of the outer wheel, jettisoning into space. The drone detaches from the hull under the sheer ferocity of the strike.

Hull Inspection Drone 0011 casts off into the darkness, soon to become just one more piece of space debris that may get drawn into a planet's gravity well someday. May be struck by a passing object and obliterated. May float aimlessly for a million years, traveling the cosmos.

As it flings one way and the *St. Joshua* the other, it runs one last emergency protocol and a single light on it begins blinking. The Thraw abomination folds itself back up as the overdose of mutagens continues working in its veins. It must finish growing. Because soon enough it must begin killing.

†

Petty Officer Franz from engineering takes the repair patch kit and readies it over the next puncture in the exterior hull.

He has loved walking along the various ships he's served on while they're traveling through space. Contained in his vacuum suit, magboots clinging to the hull, the butterflies in his stomach knowing that magnetic clinging is the only thing keeping him stuck to the ship hurling through the nothingness at thousands of kilometers an hour.

The repair patch kit is a self-pressurizing tube with a pistol grip. On the working end is a circular press that he puts polymer patches onto. Peels off a backing layer with an adhesive strong enough to bond with the exterior hull and resist re-entry. The polymer disc is larger than the puncture in the hull, and he sets it over the wound, pulls the trigger.

The repair kit seals over the damage and that will have to do until they get into dry dock.

He stands and sees a hull inspection drone floating off into space. Obviously damaged, he stares at it for a moment, confused. He can't make out its number; 00-something-something. But they're all 00-something-something. The larger ships have so many they would be in the hundreds, making them 0-something-something-something. The *St. Joshua* isn't that big. Franz watches it disappear like an ember in the wind.

"Johns, come in, Johns."

"Yeah, go ahead."

"You lose a drone out here?"

"I don't know. I'll check, but I'm getting swarmed with info packets here."

"Well, did we go through a micro-shower or something? I haven't noticed anything unusual."

"Were you hit?"

"No, this... I swear I saw a drone all damaged and whatnot just floating off into space."

Silence for a moment, and then Johns says, "Keo says we're going too fast for you to notice anything coming off the hull. We'd leave it behind too fast."

"I know the physics— uh... don't tell her I said that. Just... tell her I understand what she's saying. I'm going to go look. Maybe it ran over something and lost grip."

"You get its hull number?"

"No. It came from forward, somewhere forward of me."

"All right. Give me a minute and I'll send another drone over."

"Copy, out."

Franz walks over and sees a bizarre feature near the primary exhaust vent hood, which is little more than a cowl-shaped feature between two ribs on the ship. "Huh." He goes closer, clicks on his comms as the bizarre thing moves.

†

"I'm getting like, almost twenty-five info packets a minute from the hull drones," Petty Officer Johns says. He clicks through reports on his monitor, eyes only half skimming them. The report packets are gargantuan. 0001-0020 all on the status lines, all transmitting as they gather enough for a complete packet. "And guess what all those packets are telling me? We got shot. A lot."

"All of it line up with data reports from ship's systems?" Lt. Commander Keo asks. As the engineering officer, she sits beside Johns, her engineering enlisted man, and together they assess the incoming flow of information. That flow is a veritable tidal wave. Most of it unnecessary to their task at hand, but there all the same.

On one monitor they have a shipboard diagnostic readout: a bird's eye view of the ship itself with colored lines sectioning out anywhere there's damage. Green is good. Areas colored yellow can wait, orange should be looked at soon and red is immediate. A lot of the *St. Joshua* is red where the Thraw made their final push through the docking bay.

"Johns, am I right?" Keo asks. "They're basically the same info?"

"Yeah. Broadly," Johns says. "For instance—and this is the part I love the most—the computing system that scans all the info, categorizes it and, you know, does this entire job for me, it's dead. Shot up along with this section of waste heat bleed-off, this monitor circuit here, this relay for the—"

"Lucky for us, you know how to do your job. So do it."

"I am. But it's going to take me hours. The system did it in seconds."

"We'll be in Centauri Astoria's outer atmosphere in an—" Keo squints at a nav display nearby, "—an hour, probably less. Then you'll have help. Just keep us flying."

"Yes, ma'am," Johns leans into one display, blinks hard. Licks his thumb and rubs the pad of it along the screen. Clicks onto a line of numbers and scans the read-out. "Oh, Franz was right."

"What is it?"

"It's just... drone 0011 went offline. Transmitted a partial packet... right here... headlined with a distress coding."

"What code?"

"Well, a damage code... it was scanning with— oh, boy," He leans in more, then back out. Types at something.

"Spit it out, sailor."

"Scanning with an organic inquiry array. Found an anomaly on the exterior of frame nineteen—"

"Thraw?"

"—No apparent weapons. There's some kind of non-weaponized chemical apparatus, though, and—"

"And what?"

"Franz..." Johns clicks on his comms. "Franz, Franz buddy. You copy?"

"Captain," Keo says over Johns' head. Concern in her voice. Captain Bernhard looks away from whatever he was saying to Commander Brigid, the urgency from her a magnet. "You need to see this. Both of you," She focuses on Brigid.

She motions to the display as they cross the distance. "A drone just detected an organic anomaly on the skin of the ship. Frame nineteen, center keel."

"Petty Officer Franz was out there, correct?" Bernhard asks.

"Yessir. Patching up the worst of the hull damage."

"Is he nearby?"

Johns says, "... he's not answering, sir, but he said he saw a drone floating off the hull just a moment ago."

"Thraw?" Brigid says at the same time as Bernhard says, "F19 is the primary waste heat vent."

Johns clears his throat. "Well... can it be anything else? Thraw, I mean," He tosses a glance at the captain, trying to answer both officers. Nods. "Yessir. Waste heat vent. Like a... a pronounced hood kind-of thing." Johns is flying through screens of video feeds, fingers clicking on one as the next visual feed comes up, then the next and the next after that. "Its organic scan was incomplete but now the drone is off-line and what else could it be? We already had one Thraw clinging to the hull and now... let me get— for goodness sakes, I can't get a clear view."

"Send another drone over," Bernhard says. "Keep trying to raise Franz."

"Yessir. Already on it," Johns says. His display has the word MANUAL in all red at the bottom corner. His hands deftly press keys as the newest video feed changes angle in a rolling motion.

Brigid turns away from the others and hits his comms. "Gonzaga, Santa Cruz, what's the status on our war-fighting gear?"

Brother Santa Cruz comes back, "Commander, five functional suits of FFA gear that are piecemeal, each with approximately seventy percent ammo load, most with full batteries."

"So be it," Brigid says. Looks at Bernhard. "Five piecemeal full frontal assault kits. It'll have to do."

Brigid clicks his comms, "Knights. Suit up. We've got an exterior walk on the double. Possible combatant on the hull of the ship. Meet in the hatch in five." Acknowledgments overlap and he returns his attention to the displays. Studies the feed Johns is focused on as he controls it.

"Where are you?" The captain asks.

"Coming up on the vent from the portside now, sir."

They watch the display as the drone rounds the last feature in the hull. Space itself is hurtling along past them, the view from the screen sharp and fantastic. The vent hood is aerodynamic by necessity; the *St. Joshua* is atmosphere capable. Many ships in their fleet are built in space for the purpose of only ever being in space. With the vacuum providing no friction, there's no need to design a ship with aerodynamics in mind. Some of the Knights 15 13 vessels look like side-facing tubes, studded with gargantuan boxes and antenna arrays. Things too vast, bulky and awkward to enter an atmosphere of any significance, but extremely effective in space.

The *St. Joshua* is sleek and long, and possesses short, stubby wings, more flap than an actual recognizable wing. The heater vent is forward of them, aft of the nose section.

Father Cho enters the bridge and sees the group. He approaches and the captain steps off to the side. Accepts him with a single hand on his shoulder and speaks quickly, quietly. The priest nods and watches the display.

All gasp.

Petty Officer Franz, magbooted to the hull, is floating limply in space. Some kind of thick chunk of semitransparent, silvery crystal speared in his chest. Frozen rubies trickling out of the wound.

"Franz, buddy... you okay? Franz?" Johns asks, but the tone of his question is answer enough.

"Lord bless and keep him," Father Cho says, makes the sign of the cross over himself.

"Can you pull up his suit?" Bernhard asks. "Get a read on his vitals? Anything medicinal the suit might have administered?"

"No, sir. It's a basic vacuum suit. This was just a patch job..." Keo says, shrugs.

Johns pilots the drone over to Franz and bumps into him. No response. Drives around until they're facing one another. Angles the camera up and it becomes obvious why he doesn't respond.

"All right," Bernhard says with a heavy sigh. "Carry on for now. We'll recover his body when we can. Stay on mission."

The bridge acknowledges and Father Cho recites, "For our brother in Christ Franz, may eternal light shine upon him, dear Lord, and

eternal rest grant unto him and on all the faithfully departed, amen."
The bridge echoes his prayer and that is enough for now.

The drone rolls to the main exhaust and stops several meters away.
Johns adjusts the magnification to turn a blurry and small wad on the
hull into a fleshy, organic sac. A massively muscled arm out hanging out
a tear in it. Its grotesquely abnormal fingers flexing slowly. Like they're
trying themselves out. Or savoring. Something inside the translucent
tissue is moving, stretching. Next to it a few fluid tanks.

"Zoom in on the labels there."

Johns does, sees some familiar placards. The stylized G/PTE in its
universally recognized DNA strand-based logo. The letters are flanked
by blocky gears. Mixing of the organic and the technological. Bernhard
grimaces. "Gosnell PTE. Supplying Arithraw with some kind of
mutagenic compounds."

"Gosnell PTE would be stupid enough to sell to the Thraw, and the
Thraw would be stupid enough to leave all the logos and labels on when
they commit atrocities," Brigid says. The reality of it all is unsurprising
to think about, but very surprising to see it. Brigid rubs his chin. "How
tall is that heater vent?"

"The opening is a bit over two meters, looks like," Bernhard says.

"Two point three," Keo says in an awed whisper.

"That *thing* there is nearly as big as the opening."

Keo sits upright. "It can't really get inside that way, though. It's not
really an open vent. There's layer after layer of honeycomb-style heat
sinks all the way down, and at the base of it is a basically a blower fan.
Even that is connected to a gearbox and motor—"

"Whatever it is, they planted it to continue the fight. A living
boobytrap like a spore on this ship," Bernhard says. "We can't even
catch a break when we leave their solar system."

"It looks too big to be a Skreeve," Brigid says. "Skreeve are bad
enough. But this thing, thank our Lord there's only one."

"Do we know that?" Petty Officer Bonilla chimes in.

Everyone looks around at each other and Bernhard twirls a finger. "Get those HIDs checking, double time."

Father Cho makes a sound in the back of his throat. "I was assigned to Unit #51-Ca when I was fresh out of seminary. We went to a fairly nascent planet in the Quaw solar system. We encountered a predatory beast about that size, maybe a little smaller. Animal, though. Not a corrupted rational soul. Two of our Knights were truly Earth-born, and they took to calling it a gorilla-rhino because of how it looked. I guess that was a close-enough description. I've only ever seen those two animals in pictures. But this... it was terrible. Awe-inspiring and absolutely terrible."

"Yeah?"

"Yes. It got our scent and for whatever reason, it saw us and saw red. It was bloodthirsty. Unquenchable, too. It hounded us for hours—even into the night... and killed three of our brothers. Our weapons were not enough against its hide. Every shot just enraged it more. But the Lord, God of Hosts intervened for us. Little angels in the form of a vast cloud of things like butterflies, glowing in the night air. Bioluminescent. The gorilla-rhino was distracted by them, became preoccupied. I thought it to be so blood simple with its relentless attack on us that it just wanted to kill."

"A raging death machine distracted by pretty little butterflies," Keo says.

"The distraction was all we needed."

Brigid waits for a moment so as not to disrespect the old priest's memory. Then, he clears his throat and says, "We're heading out there. This is some last-ditch effort to get the nun, and I can only imagine it's going to kill her and all of us if it can. There's nothing else that's a possibility at this point. No escape, no back-up. Only murder. Looking at Franz there, this thing can kill, and it hasn't even hatched yet. We'll try and get to it before it fully emerges."

"Wait," Bernhard says. He looks at Keo. "Emergency evac all the heat down to an internal temp of 5 degrees Celsius. Cook that thing. We might get lucky and not have to engage it directly."

"Yessir," Keo says as she begins tapping at her terminal.

Brigid checks the time to see when he needs to step out with his Knights. The captain turns to Keo. She makes eye contact as if that is the cue she needs. Taps a final command button. The ship drastically begins to cool as the sound of the HVAC system growls at the intake ducts.

They all look at Johns's display, see the vent's rim turn red as an entire ship's worth of environmental and waste heat plunge out into space. The abomination quivers violently and boils begin to form on the sac's tissue. Then scorch marks. Whatever is inside squirms as if in panic. It presses its elbows out through the tissue of the sac, heaving and stretching. The one arm that was protruding begins clawing at it from the outside. Anything to escape the heat.

But before much else happens, the exhaust shuts off in one final click. Blown out. Even the super-hot red lining the vent begins to die down, cooling off in the frigid expanse of space.

"That's it?" Bernhard asks.

Keo leans back, speaks, and as she does her breath is a cold cloud before her. "Yessir. The emergency evac protocol is just that: an emergency. It's designed to dump everything in a big hurry in case of reactor overload, all that. I know we wanted more, but from an engineering perspective, that was a fantastic procedure. Very *very* efficient."

"It's still alive. Look."

On the screen the abomination slaps a hand against the inside of the sac, presses out. One claw pierces the tissue. A burnt-brown fluid leaks out, freezing to little icy gobs, trailing off into their engine plume.

"My turn, then," Brigid says. He clicks his comms channel, says, "Knights, form up. I'm on my way. Briefing will be in transit."

Bernhard watches as the crusader gets to the bridge hatch, asks, "I can look at the report, but who are our patron saints for this op?"

Brigid turns his head over his shoulder and says, "Saint Michael. Saint Martin De Tours. Saint Xohig SomphambiXo."

"Yes, yes. All fantastic warrior-saints. We'll pray. See what else we can do from down here."

"Thank you, Captain," and Brigid walks out, the hatch sealing behind him.

Petty Officer Bonilla rubs his hands together, looking at the HVAC register nearest him to see if it's putting out heat yet. Petty Officer Cavins leans back in his chair and digs around in his back pocket. Withdraws a watch cap and puts it on.

"Let us place this in the hands of our Lord," Father Cho says, his silvery cloud of breath like incense around him. He makes the sign of the cross over himself and the bridge crew does the same. "Most Sacred Heart of Jesus," he says.

"Have mercy on us," they follow.

"Most Sacred Heart of Jesus,"

"Have mercy on us."

"Most Sacred Heart of Jesus..."

Controlling the Fight

Commander Brigid gets to the rallying point outside the exterior hatch. Brother Santa Cruz waits there with a portable rack, hanging upon it the commander's armor. Brigid dons it, and as he does a moment passes between him and the other Knights when not so long ago they were at the same lock waiting to go outside with Brother Cleopas beside them.

Finally, he nods. Clears is throat with a cough. Checks his helmet's comms and uses eye flickers to interface with his Visuals. Scrolls through radio channels, asks, "Johns, you on this one?"

"Yes, Commander."

"Status on that thing?"

"Actively squirming, sir. My money is on it trying to hatch."

"Okay. We're en route outside."

"Copy, sir."

Brigid switches back over and asks, "Everybody got the briefing?"

"New Thraw super-mutant getting ready to hatch outside on the hull and it's already killed somebody?" Brother Gonzaga says.

"Torching it with a super-heated dump of the entire ship's HVAC didn't kill it?" Brother Nonnatus adds.

"We've got about twenty minutes to get rid of it before we enter the planet's atmosphere?" Santa Cruz asks.

"God is the perfect embodiment of pure love?" Brother Pio says.

"Yup," Brigid says and turns to the airlock. Cycles it open. They step inside. "Where's the nun? Still in medbay?"

"No. She's in the chapel with Father Cho," Santa Cruz says.

"Father Cho was on the bridge."

"Well, he must have left her in the chapel. They *were* together there. To my knowledge, the sister is still there. Deep in prayer."

Brigid raises an eyebrow. "She's always deep in prayer," He says, "Okay, then. Blessed be the most Sacred Heart of Jesus,"

"Amen."

"Blessed be the Immaculate Heart of Mary,"

"Amen."

"Patron saints of the mission, please intercede for our victory. Saint Michael,"

"Pray for us."

"Saint Martin De Tours,"

"Pray for us."

"Saint Xohig SomphambiXo,"

"Pray for us."

The atmosphere drops to nothing inside the lock and the strobe lights flash, prepping them for the outer hatch to cycle open. Brigid says, "Captain Bernhard says he'll do us a favor and stay out of the Centauri Astoria's atmosphere for longer than the estimated twenty minutes. Not sure how long—the ship is pretty damaged. We've been decelerating for quite a while now. He's ramped up the decel to buy us some time, but if he goes too long or too hard on that we'll need to re-accelerate to get back to the approach vectors, blah blah. If it takes us that long to blast this thing off the hull, we're in trouble."

"Is it still in the egg sac-thing?" Santa Cruz asks.

Brigid shrugs. "Still hatching. Let's go interrupt it," The airlock cycles open and Brigid exits, gun first.

"Roger—" Gonzaga begins. Johns's voice comes across the comms, screeching with a burst of static as he talks over Gonzaga. "—advised, the thing— hatched. Took off. I'm looking—"

Nonnatus is second out the lock, and sees Brigid sweep and clear, turn left. Nonnatus begins to follow, covering their right and Brigid is struck so hard from out of nowhere his gun shatters. The pieces fling off into the void. The commander falls over, wildly sliding down the length of the ship. Flailing to catch himself before he's left behind in space or incinerated in their thrust plume.

"Contact!" Nonnatus shouts as he rushes forward, creating a gap between him and the abomination. His voice over the radio speakers becomes distorted because of his volume. "Contact aft! Commander down!" He opens fire at the thing rushing towards him.

†

Whatever that was, Commander Brigid lost his breath with it. He tumbles, rolling wildly. The blackness of space, ever-expanding, tumbling in his vision. Distant stars just a scattering of pinpricks spinning about with it. The hull rotates into view, and he has enough sense to reach for it. The click of his mag-gloves latching down onto it like a welcome prayer. His body slaps down on the hull and bounces off the other way. Equal and opposite reaction. He sees his feet pointing up away from the hull. To the stars. They should be on the *St. Joshua.*

Head rattling. Shouts and heavy breathing in his helmet speakers. The tether his rifle was attached to floating free now, a bit of broken metal still lashed to the end of it. He flexes, twists. He looks down at his chest, sees a fine dust of something he must have just picked up sprayed along him. Some twinkling crystals, too.

He turns to where he was looking near the vent and there it is, massive as a boulder, arms extended. So ugly. It was larger than two meters tall upright, with a shoulder width of at least one and a half meters. Must have formerly been Thraw, but so mutated now. Still with the bipedal stance, primary arms like tree trunks and so long they're almost another pair of legs. Its secondary arms bizarre—especially the left one, a blackened claw-thing for its hand, and bundled close to the body.

Its face grotesquely misshapen, an upside triangle. Its hide now a ghostly translucent, and with its distorted skeleton underneath, there are bony spikes growing off it and puncturing out through the skin. Weird shapes inside its organs, and they twinkle like lights as well. Brigid thinks he's seeing stars through its body. In its previous life as a Thraw, it must have been tattooed. Remnants of ink lines still draw shapes on its new skin, but even they are hideous.

There are sacs on its primary forearms, and they are undulating like toothless mouths chewing. They have thick orifices on the ends. Organic barrels. One of the arms squeezes and a crystalline spike emerges from it. Ready to fire.

"What did they do to you, poor soul?" He asks, and as he speaks he sees a little bit of blood spit up onto the inside of his visor, smearing the information along his Visuals.

†

Brothers Gonzaga and Santa Cruz spill out the airlock, barrels raised and blindly firing where Brother Nonnatus is aimed. The abomination is a tremendous blur as it dodges, scrambling in a terrific rush for its size. Commander Brigid's observation from when they met the priest comes to their minds, reads *take note how fast this species moves. Now imagine the combat.* Brother Pio rushes out last, going opposite of the others, trying to get behind it.

Nonnatus rushes for Brigid, whose one hand is holding him to the hull. Gonzaga and Santa Cruz fire. The rounds strike the abomination and barely penetrate before it stops them cold. The flesh ripples and disperses the impact, its whole body gelatinous to the point of nullifying the transferred energy of being shot.

"What is this thing?" Gonzaga shouts.

"Just the next obstacle," Santa Cruz says. His gun sending vibration chattering up his suit in the deaf expanse of space.

A crackle of static in their ears, "Wh— they do to y— poor sou—" in the commander's airy voice.

"How is it clinging to the hull?" Nonnatus asks, clomps against his magboots to get to the commander. Every step they must disconnect, sense contact and reactivate. Unimaginably slow in the adrenaline rush of life or death. He looks once towards the abomination, a heaving bulge of bone-white mutation, and turns away.

"Couldn't tell you," Gonzaga says, clomping his own way off to the side. Looking at its bare feet with long, slender toe-like protrusions that make its footprint almost a half meter in diameter. "Suction cups? Feet covered in goo?"

"You gotta keep that thing from getting me until I right the commander!"

"Working on it," Santa Cruz says. More shots, more of its skin jiggling like slapped blubber, more of it not being affected by gunshots.

"That thing started off as a Thraw?" Gonzaga asks as he moves to triangulate on it with Santa Cruz's position. He sees Pio emerging behind it, angles to him as well.

"I guess," Santa Cruz says the same time Pio says, "Our blessed Lord, I hope not."

"What happened to it?" Gonzaga asks. He spends a three-round burst nearer its head as opposed to center mass. Watches its eyes react with a flicker. Thick plates fling across them like eyelids turned ninety degrees. A single round sparks off one and ricochets into the hull, ricochets again into space.

"They mutate their eggs. They mutated this too. I guess."

"I'll ask God when I die," Gonzaga says. "Whatever it is, let's pray they don't do this again." He sees the abomination roll an eye towards him, lift an appendage. An arm, or what used to be one. A pillar of muscle with an unnerving throbbing going on in ropy tubes under the skin. Its forearm is grotesquely larger than its upper arm. Looks like a cross between an ovipositor and a seashell. It aims it at Gonzaga, and a pore at the end of it quivers so rapidly it looks like a blur. Spasms once. Like a gun firing.

Gonzaga kicks back, both his magboots locked down on the hull. He falls backward as far as he can, his gun floating by its tether next to him. His voice over the intercom suddenly coughs hard enough to sound like a wretch, his breathing instantly heavy and shallow.

"Gonzaga!" Santa Cruz shouts. But his brother Knight remains still, a silvery crystalline spike sticking out of him like a spear. His suit vacates a burst of internal atmosphere, followed by frozen blood droplets.

†

Hull Inspection Drone 0017 rolls up higher on the curvature of the *St. Joshua*'s bulk and its camera array zooms in tighter.

Petty Officer Johns still in his chair, his display still showing MANUAL in the bottom left as he pilots the device. Captain Bernhard has thrown the display feed up on one of the primary monitors. The entire bridge crew watches. The Knights' radio chatter is on but low, filling the bridge with an ever-present murmur of battle communications and labored, tense breathing.

Father Cho rubs his chin, snarls. "Today's version of my old gorilla-rhino, but this one courtesy of Gosnell PTE."

"How many of your old unit survived that thing, Father?"

"Four. Four Knights out of seven, if memory serves."

"We're only starting here with five," Bernhard says. "We've got to shift those odds. Petty Officer Bonilla."

"Yes, skipper?"

"Where does it need to be to fall into the scope of a defense cannon?"

"Ten meters out from the keel. That's all," Bonilla absently points to his display. One of his monitors is split-screened between six different cannons' cameras. Waiting for that thing to enter a safe-firing field.

"Not there yet?"

Bonilla has his hand on his terminal's controls, scrolling. "They're about seven meters out from the keel, give or take, but they keep moving around. That thing has been in my sights twice now, but a

Knight has been downrange both times. I need it to— there. See it? They just did it a third time. Everybody is in the firing line. It's about five meters now, sir. Going the wrong way."

Bernhard presses the comms button. "Knights, we need that thing further out from the keel. Ten meters at least. Ship's defenses can kick in if it's there and you're out of the way."

"Roger," one of them responds. On screen, they watch one Knight grab at their commander, struck and upside down almost off the skin of the ship. He rights Brigid and they watch the abomination scramble.

"Captain," Lt. Commander Keo says.

"Go ahead."

"Initial scans show that thing was most likely an adult Thraw before its mutation. Bipedal, four arms. Two primary, two secondary. The growths on its primary forearms are different. The—"

"Bioweapons?" The captain asks.

"Seems to be. Those bulges on its forearms are glands. Secreting a resin it hardens into projectiles. Just shot something into—" she squints at the monitor, "—Brother Gonzaga, sir."

"Vitals?"

"What you'd expect for someone who was just lightly impaled, I think."

"*Lightly* impaled?"

Keo sheepishly nods her head. "My words. His CeramaTex took a pretty good bit of the impact. His flesh has been punctured but appears to be very shallow. Started to vent to space before his suit reacted. Contained about sixty percent of his internal atmosphere. Fairly shallow wound. His suit's medical kit is responding."

The captain watches the other Knights engage in a firefight. A trio of heavily armed warrior-monks forming a loose, flowing triangle around a grisly enemy. Buying time. Wasting ammo. Watches the abomination's bizarrely gel-like white flesh take the rounds, jiggling like a hand slapping hefty fat. But nothing penetrates too deeply. "Why are they not getting closer to the guns?"

"Sir, they're trying," Bonilla says. "That thing is controlling the fight."

Bernhard breathes heavily. Father Cho pats him on the back. "I remember these times, friend. With my gorilla-rhino and the butterflies that distracted it. Be a little butterfly, eh?"

The father's quiet nudge rocks Bernhard back on his heels just a tad as if the ship maneuvered under him. He breaks a smile and raises an eyebrow. "Johns?"

"Yessir?"

"Ram your drone into the thing."

"Aye, aye."

"Try and lead it into the guns."

"Will do."

"And be ready with another one if we need it."

"Yes, Captain. Right away."

"The rest of you, keep praying."

The bridge acknowledges. Father Cho catches the captain's eye. "I'll go back the chapel. With my sister in Christ."

"Father, that thing is here for her."

"I know."

"We need to get her—"

"I will watch out," Father Cho says. "She's with Jesus. Let us pray and then we will hide."

"Father. This isn't going well." He points to the monitor.

"But," the priest says, "It's not going well, *outside.*"

"For now," Bernhard says, and the priest leaves the bridge. He nods, turns to the primary screen. Watches the drone zooming towards the danger.

†

"Five on one—" Brother Pio says as the abomination aims its left arm at him. The resin sac bulges, pulses, the pore at the end blooms open. Quivers. Pio's Visuals draws a track line from it outwards. Sees where it's going to shoot. Right into his chest. His suit calculates reaction time and the abomination fires.

Pio's suit jerks, canting off to the side and the bizarre crystalline projectile flings off into space. "Close!"

Commander Brigid is back on his feet. Draws his sidearm, yanks the ruined tether from his suit and flings it up over his head. He and Brother Nonnatus bring their fire to bear onto the thing.

Brother Santa Cruz grabs Brother Gonzaga and tilts him back up. Gonzaga groans and looks down, sees the bizarre resin-like crystal protruding from his suit. How his suit's emergency rupture system sealed the wound with foam. His Visuals unspools a list of reports and damages. Medical feedback. How much atmosphere he lost. He slaps at the resin spike sticking out of him. It shatters and leaves a puff of dust like what's all over the commander.

"I'm going to avoid that next time," Gonzaga says.

"Can you get back in the fight?"

Gonzaga adjusts himself in the suit and sprays a burst of fire at the abomination as it gallops a loping arc, trying to reposition itself behind them. "I got a bit more firepower in me."

"Good."

The commander clears his throat, says, "Pio, you, Gonzaga and Santa Cruz line up, backs to the keel. Lay into it. Nonnatus, go there—" he throws a position dot to Nonnatus's Visuals, placing him opposite Brigid seven meters, "—the three of you push it outwards, Nonnatus and I will keep it in your line of fire. Get it to the ship's defense systems."

The three rush together and begin to unload. Nonnatus falls into position and off-angle from Brigid to keep him out of direct lines of fire. The abomination steps this way and that, head on a swivel as the

Knights coordinate. Their fire prods at it. Its forearm sacs undulate as they form new projectiles.

Each Knights' Visuals put tracking lines on the organic muzzles of the thing's arm weapons. So, as it raises one to fire, they can dodge. And they push.

Captain Bernhard comes over the comms. "Almost, Knights. Brigid and Nonnatus need to stop moving alongside it or you'll be in the line of fire. Two more meters."

And as if it could hear their comms, the abomination plants its feet and swipes at the nearest Knights. Arms raised, aiming. It fires one high and watches Gonzaga dodge it. Tilts it head like a dog trying to understand its master, then snaps off another projectile at Nonnatus's feet. It takes the Knight by surprise. His magboots are sluggish to click off and on, and the crystal spike hits his left foot.

"Got hit!" Nonnatus says as he does what he can to dance out of the way. His boot flashes a yellow warning on his Visuals. "Loss of power at thirty percent." He fires a volley at the thing's face, trying to double his efforts to push it back.

"It's figuring out a better strategy," Brigid says, aiming for its face too. "Lay on the headshots." They turn their fire to blinding it. The plates that snap closed over its eyes jitter and twitch, open and close. It shoots its projectiles a bit faster. Wild shots near their feet.

"It's forming those spike-things quicker now," Nonnatus says.

"We caught it right out of the egg sac or whatever," Santa Cruz says, taking a hit across his ankle. "I imagine whatever its natural defenses are, they're turning on, smoothing out."

"Working faster. More efficient."

"More the reason to stop it here," Gonzaga says. "I should have brought some high-yield explosives."

Brigid barks, "Get it to the cannons. Those things will make short work of this."

"Yeah, but it's not budging," Pio says. "Last stand right here."

"Keep pushing!"

"Our rounds aren't enough."

Over the horizon of the ship, something else comes zooming towards them. The Knights all look at once; their suits pulling up another contact and waiting to assign it friend or foe status.

Drone 0017 buzzes along its wheel-shaped axis and unfolds two small nozzles, aims them behind itself and down. Builds up speed and puffs a quick airburst through the nozzles as it cuts its magnetic hold. Sixty pounds of metal fling up from the hull and hit the abomination in its chin. Its head snaps back as the drone reflects off, hits the hull with a clank of its magnets turning back on.

Santa Cruz fires at the exposed neck, three rounds hitting dead-on.

The drone backs up, rolls across the thing's toes and it swipes so hard at it, its claws shoot sparks off the hull.

"Dig in! Final push!" Brigid commands. He and Nonnatus plant their feet and work their sides. The other three lay on the last of their ammo stores and the thing takes one more step, both arms getting ready to shoot again. The drone rolls wide and over the lip, out of sight under the *St. Joshua*.

On the edge of the ship, the abomination's flat nose suddenly flares alive and active. Something, somehow, unbelievably caught a scent. Whatever atoms it's detecting in the void of space distract it for just a moment.

The ship's terminal point autocannon ques up with a whir. Half a second. A pill-shaped protrusion on the hull, it rotates, its double-barreled turret adjusts its horizontal position down a click and barks to life. An unzipping sound reverberates through the hull as 20mm rounds of armor-piercing projectiles machine gun forth. Hit the beast. The abomination reacts as if it had been set on fire. The unbroken line of fire punches through the monster in a lightning-fast barrage.

The Knights watch as it dances in reaction. Stung by a hundred white hot bees in a split second. Holes everywhere on it. It collapses to the hull's surface as the cannon cuts out, both barrels rimmed in the same super-hot red that the vent was.

Santa Cruz looks at the abomination and narrows his eyes to slits. His Visuals busy scanning whatever is going on with it. "You guys see this?"

"I see it bleeding pretty bad," Gonzaga says.

"Is that blood? Looks like a... a gel? More resin?"

Brigid's eyes widen as the abomination pushes back to its feet. "It's filling in the bullet holes..." They all raise their weapons again, open fire. "Give a second burst from—!"

And the abomination swings down over the lip of the *St. Joshua*, out of sight. Almost immediately, alarms from the ship spool up on their Visuals.

BREACH BREACH BREACH BREACH BREACH—

The New Gorilla-Rhino

The chapel on the *St. Joshua* is a holy and restful place, a place where Father Cho and Sister Stella Nessa can be on their knees before the Blessed Sacrament displayed on the altar, even if the disconcerting unzipping sound of the terminal point autocannon prominently bleeds through to them.

The right bulkhead of the chapel is a port side exterior wall of the *St. Joshua*, after all. And running around beyond it, the four-armed cosmic horror the Thraw left for them.

The chapel is a rectangle. The only door to it is at the rear on the short side, the altar and tabernacle opposite. The long sides are filled with pews. The right bulkhead to space itself, the left one to the passageway running down the interior of the ship.

At the forefront of the chapel is a wooden crucifix—Christ in His full suffering on the cross. It reigns over everything inside. Underneath it a Tabernacle, a gilded and ornate box blessed and designed to hold the Eucharist. Next to it, mounted into the bulkhead and off to the side, a lit red candle, a signifier that the God of the Universe is present in the form of bread and wine inside the Tabernacle. The miracle of transubstantiation flying through space in a solar system far from where Christ appeared on Earth.

Closer to Father Cho and the nun is the altar, a wooden table with a slab of polished marble along the top. The front of the altar is a two-meter long, hand-carved depiction of the Last Supper. Resting on the surface of it is a monstrance, a blessed and decorated container that is designed to hold a the Eucharist so it may be adored by the faithful. Their God on display, even more fully than venerating a crucifix or picture of Christ because He is the transubstantiated substance of the Blessed Sacrament.

Then the altar rail. Along it, the two devout seeking quiet communion with their Lord. And, because of the nature of the fallen universe, the sounds of gunfire outside the chapel. A burst and then it quits. But even in the burst it must have fired hundreds of rounds.

The compartment behind the bulkhead where the crucifix sits is a machine room that houses the TPA that just ceased firing. The compartment is two meters wide and three tall, filled with power cabinets, bearings, gearing and the motors to move the cannon. All in a neat stack up to the overhead. And from there, the exterior seals and the pill-shaped servo motor-assisted swiveling cannon. A track up one side for the belt-fed ammunition to climb to the gun. A container on the other side to collect the empty casings as they're expended. While there are twelve total TPAs on the ship—six each top and bottom—this one, chewing through the abomination outside, is the only one intruding on their silence.

It goes quiet, and Father Cho looks up. "First, the Knights firing, then the defense gun. Now... now we wait for the all-clear."

Sister Stella Nessa, on her ancient knees, forearms, and wounded hands on the rail, Cleopas's Rosary intertwined between her fingers. Her forehead resting on those hands, eyes closed. She looks up, serene. She takes a deep inhale, shakes her head.

"No, he is still with us." Her voice in Father Cho's universal translator says, "I have been praying for the Arithraw who turned himself into... that. What a wounded soul. Jesus loves him."

Father Cho smiles. A pocket moment of bliss. "What a hard saying, when Christ asked our ancestors to pray for our enemies. I've had my struggles with it."

"Then you have not been wronged enough," the sister says. "I do not wish for enemies, but it is nice having those who need my prayers. I am still useful that way."

The port side bulkhead smashes inward toward them. The deafening sound of it shocks them both. Three powerful beatings like a bell ringing and then the unmistakable *pop!* of atmosphere forcefully bleeding out.

"He is still with us, indeed." She says.

Father Cho grabs the nun and lifts her, fighting the drag of vacuum as it sucks the words from his mouth. "We've got to get—"

And the room opens up to the void of space.

†

BREACH BREACH BREACH BREACH BREACH—

The Knights rush as fast as their magboots will allow to the edge of the *St. Joshua*'s wing. Brother Santa Cruz gets there first, his gun leading the way. Without hesitation he kicks one leg over the lip onto the underside, straddling both top and belly of the ship for just a moment before he swings upside down. Keeps going.

Brother Pio next, then Commander Brigid. Brothers Gonzaga and Nonnatus get to the lip and hear Santa Cruz say, "Inside! Get back inside the ship! It's torn a hole inside!"

Gonzaga down on his knees, gripping the edge. Leans over upside down. The Knights tromping back up to him, he sees behind them a mangled wound in the hull. Emergency sealant foam bubbling out of it, hardening in seconds and keeping the ship's atmosphere contained.

"Commander," Captain Bernhard comes across the comms.

"Go," Brigid says as he races back to the airlock. He sees the stars shift almost imperceptibly. Looks at Nonnatus beside him, mouths *course change?* Nonnatus shrugs.

Bernhard says, "In about four minutes we'll be within range of Centauri Astoria's planetary defenses."

"We getting a live escort?"

"I didn't request one since we left the Thraw on the other side of the gate," Bernhard says. "Even if they launch now, we'll be inside the atmosphere long before they reach us."

"Okay."

"My point is, even though the planetary defense stations are automated, we can get them to aim at the abomination."

"That means firing anti-aircraft munitions at the ship. *Our* ship," Brigid says, breathing heavy. They reach the airlock and activate the cycle. "This thing is big, but you're talking about shaving a gnat off an elephant hide with those guns."

"Oh, I'm well-aware. I've got my nav tech charting a course to make a close pass. Like I said, just keep it— did it damage the hull?" A clip of an alarm klaxon is going off on the bridge. Brigid can hear it as the captain keys up.

"We're going in go fetch it now. If we can get it back outside in time to let the planetary defense shoot at it, we will."

"*Outside*? Why is it not outside? Where is it?"

†

The abomination shoves through the bulkhead and into the chapel. The holes in its mutilated body now filled with the crystalized resin it produces. Through its quasi-translucent skin, its black organs have shifted out of place with the resin filling, pushing them. A strange rectangular box-shaped organ inside as well, with what might be veins or cables coming off it and snaking elsewhere. Haphazardly stuck to it are smears of the emergency sealant foam. Must have been working through the outer and inner hulls as the agent released.

The thing's nostrils shudder, breathes deep. Tours its head along the chapel for just a moment before its eyes settle on the nun. Father Cho carrying her to the rear exit, eyes on it. The thing lets out a gravelly wheeze, joyous even in its bizarre tone.

It steps forward, the sacs on its primary forearms pulsing as they secrete more resin to form into spikes. Its fists, almost as large as Father Cho's head, clench and release, clench and release. Fingers ugly and bony, swollen at the knuckles. Claws like stalactites. Its secondary arms folded into its chest. Its left secondary hand an odd multi-segmented claw rather than the same fingers of the other three. It licks its misshapen mouth. Steps forward, wearing the bony protrusions from its skeleton like nightmarish armor.

It inhales deeply, snorts loud enough to startle the priest. Inhales deeply, exhales forcefully. Following a wafting line of scent in the air to them. It fires a resin spike and it strikes the exit violently. The priest stops, turns.

"Here for her, my poor friend?" Father Cho says, setting Sister Stella Nessa behind him. "Smell her out, did you? Even in the vacuum of space? I am impressed. But not afraid."

He looks at the abomination as it slides forward into the walkway between the rows of pews. This thing used to be like her. He can see the species resemblance but can also see how it has grossly changed.

The abomination growls and opens its arms wide, lowers itself at the torso. A bull getting ready to charge. All its pointed features seem to flex make itself look larger, huge.

"Intimidation by size? A bird spreading its feathers to appear dominant amongst rivals. But you look so in pain, my poor friend. Tortured."

Sister Stella Nessa lays a gentle hand on the priest. "See, upon his neck, that symbol?"

Father Cho nods. The nun says, "It was a mark back home. A breed of soldier proven through combat trials. The fiercest, the most difficult to kill."

Father Cho smiles. "I see. You think you are difficult to fight, difficult to kill?" The abomination roars and steps forward. Strikes its claws against one another and sparks come off them.

"To quote Saint Maximillian Kolbe, who is worlds greater than I could ever be, *I see Mary everywhere. I see difficulties nowhere.*"

Father Cho edges back, driving the nun towards the exit. He reaches the last pews as the thing takes a giant leap towards them. Father Cho withdraws his TechHaft, ignites it. A spiked ball on a chain blaze forth, and Father Cho swings it over his head. Spins it once in a great rotation.

Father Cho whirls the energy weapon at the abomination. The ball slams upside its head even as it tries to block it, grab it. It topples and Father Cho shoves back, putting the nun through the exit and into the passageway. "Run, sister," He says solemnly and shuts the hatch on her.

He turns and the thing is on its feet, rushes forward, swinging its arm trying to take his head clean off. The priest ducks and rolls outward, swinging at its leg as he moves. Its claws rake along the hatch where the nun had gotten out, wrenching together metal from the frame with metal from the hatch plates. Twisting. Father Cho takes one look at the two metals worked together and knows that hatch isn't going to open very easily now.

The swipe to its leg opens the skin. Resin oozes out in a thick rush. The priest scrambles as the thing turns to him. Father Cho stands and backs up, eyes flicking from the hatch to the abomination's eyes. *Where is it looking?*

"My poor friend, I have been in worse positions," he says. Listening for the thunder of magboots to come. "I am ready to die, at peace with my Lord. It will be a good death."

He begins to whirl the weapon over his head again. A circle of light over him like a weaponized halo. The thing raises an arm, and the tip of a spike slides out from the fleshy muzzle of its launcher. Father Cho smiles and inhales deeply. The thing roars and fires. Father Cho swings. A cloud of shards and dust plumes around him.

The abomination grabs a pew, bolted to the deck. It heaves and the wood of it snaps, a great whipping crack and the wood breaks free. The thing throws it. Father Cho leaps back, hitting the left bulkhead. The pew sails through the chapel and hits the altar. A chunk of it breaks off, sails over the top of it and strikes the stand holding the Tabernacle. It rocks violently.

The priest shoves off the bulkhead, barreling towards God in the Eucharist. He dives and the Tabernacle tips precipitously. Another wooden crack, another impact as a second pew cleaves the communion rail into pieces. Father Cho lands under the Tabernacle as it falls on him. He slams his hand along the seam of the double door that opens to the inside. To the Hosts. He hugs the gilded box, feeling one edge of its golden ornamentation run like a knife down his forehead. Blood fills his eye. But the box does not spill its glorious contents. He sets it off to the side, rolls as another pew strikes like a javelin at his feet.

He stands, TechHaft in hand. As the abomination grabs another pew, Father Cho ignites it, spins it and hurls the whole thing. It helicopters through the air, strikes hard just below the abomination's neck. Wraps once around its body and it roars again. The energy chain sizzles along its flesh. The thing grabs the TechHaft and squeezes, shattering it. The energy cuts off in an instant, leaving a charred mark in its shape.

The abomination rushes at Father Cho and he ducks behind the altar. Hears it inhaling hard, following the scent of his blood. He moves around the altar and the thing commits to rushing at him from one side. As it does, he leaps to the other, bounds down the single step and through the busted communion rail.

He is struck hard on his left shoulder by something hard and angular. As he collapses, he sees the splintered pieces of the crucifix scattering. The fully intact wooden Jesus tumbles with him and he takes it up. He stands, his back to the bulkhead. He turns to the abomination and bares his teeth in defiance. The thing already has its arm raised, and it chuffs and fires.

Father Cho is hit by a resin spike low and under his heart, scraping his ribcage as it punches him against the bulkhead. Knocks the wind out. Pierces his back on its way out. He sluffs down but is held aloft against the bulkhead. Nailed to it. He can barely cling to the crucifix.

The abomination rushes forward, howling.

†

The Knights stampede to the exterior hatch of the chapel. There, Sister Stella Nessa holds herself upright against the far bulkhead. She sees them and delights. Her smile, an awkward thing for human eyes, is beautiful.

Her voice across their universal translators says, "Inside. The priest and the poor soul." Spoken unremarkably as if they asked her what was in her purse.

Commander Brigid hits the open button and nothing happens. He hits it a second time. Brother Gonzaga begins to pound on the hatch as the commander tries a third time. "Back up."

The Knights do. Brigid ignites his TechHaft. A blazing Merovingian axe comes to life. He tilts it over his shoulder. Aided by the strength-enhancing properties of his suit, he swings and the laser weapon chops into and drags a clean line through the metal of it.

"Gonzaga, get her to the bridge." He chops a second time, crisscrossing his first strike. It makes a triangle of dangling metal from the top of the door down. Brother Pio punches it and it wrenches loose. They see the mangled chapel inside. They see the priest, commotion. Hear roaring.

†

Father Cho watches the abomination close the gap between them. Hatred in its eyes. Pain too, but also seething hatred. It regards him for a moment, then the wooden statue of a ruined man in his hand. It bends its mouth in what must pass for its smile. Holds its arms out to its sides. Lolls its head off to one side.

"Mock if you must, my poor friend," Father Cho says. "He is your FSather too, and He loves you."

It drops the pose and leans in. Saliva making a trail out of one corner of its mouth. Eyes huge and empty, each showing the priest's full reflection in it. The bony plates on the sides of its head, ready to jerk over its eyes, quiver by the ligaments that pull them either way. Excitement. It licks its mouth again. Its nostrils flair. Turns its head, ready to follow her scent. Get this over with.

The door is banging from the outside. Red molten lines carve into it, their impacts booming inside the chapel.

"But, as I have said," Father Cho coughs out around blood, "I have been in worse positions."

The thing smiles and clicks its teeth and Father Cho swings the wooden statue up by its feet and drives it into one of the monster's eyes. The bony plates surge forward, too late. Cocks the statue off to the side in its eye socket as it fumbles back, screeching. It swipes at the statue, and it falls. The thing covers its face and yowls, screeches.

Father Cho grabs both his fists into a ball and slams it down onto the spike. It shatters and he pushes himself off the bulkhead. Collapses on the deck and crawls with everything he has between two pews. Under him and with him always, the marred wooden statue of Christ. He grabs at it, hugs it close as he does what he can to tuck under the pew.

"My Lord, my God. How I have loved You," He rubs the crucifix along his shirt to clean off the filth from the abomination's eye. "Please forgive me for using Your image to stab this poor creature. I love You."

The abomination begins pounding into the ends of the nearest pews. Raging. Tears one out from the deck, then another. As it beats on the one Father Cho has hidden under, a new sound fills the chapel.

The door bursts inward and gunfire rattles the sanctuary. The abomination leaps from where it is beside the priest. Father Cho lays along the cool deck, the shattered wood remnants of a pew over his head. Nestled. He feels nestled, even though he is covered in blood and wood fragments. Dying. But his Savior is in his arms, and he is loved. Cranes his neck to see down the length of the chapel. The shattered Communion rail like kindling snapped and tossed off to the side. Stabs of it remaining in place here and there. The altar abused but intact. The Tabernacle still where he left it along the back bulkhead. Its most precious cargo inside.

By its legs and feet only, Father Cho watches the shock-dance of the abomination being shot. It must be getting flooded with small arms fire. It races back to the port side bulkhead. Father Cho sees chunks of emergency sealant foam fall like dirty clumps of snow. The unmistakable click-chatter of the Knights in full vacuum armor shuffling through the chapel to coordinate fire. It goes silent, and his ears fill the quiet with their ringing.

Suddenly the wild droning sound of the vacuum of space fills the room and Father Cho can feel himself losing air and being drug along the deck to where the abomination was. It must have pierced through, going back out into space. And then it stops, as abruptly as it started.

Father Cho pulls himself along the pew, hand over hand until he emerges in the aisle between the two rows. Sees the Knights cluster around the bulkhead. Even then the ragged metal flowered out from where the abomination came in, the sealant foam to preserve the atmosphere. And in the center a patch of new foam. The thing must have gone back out onto the exterior.

Santa Cruz says, "I'm so tired of that foam."

Father Cho hears Brigid shout, "Keep that drone on it, I don't want to lose sight of it." Then, to his men, "Back outside! They're lining up the planetary defense systems to take a shot at this thing! Thirty seconds."

"That'll get us too," he can hear Brother Pio say.

"I'm sure they'll try really hard to not blow us out of the sky."

Father Cho looks up through darkening eyes and sees another Knight come pushing through the mangled door. Looks to his brothers, then looks down to him. Startles. Rushes up to him. Brother Gonzaga's eyes look down and his whole body grabs the old priest. "Hang on, Father. Medbay is around the corner."

"No rush," the priest says as he settles comfortably into the all-consuming burn of his injures. So hot, it's almost numb now. His wet and deeply red hands come up around the Knight as he gets lifted off the deck. The chapel passes around him as they rush into the passageway. Too quietly for Gonzaga to hear, Father Cho smiles and says, "I keep telling everybody, I have been in worse positions."

†

Petty Officer Johns sits at his terminal, the camera view of Hull Inspection Drone 0017 filling his screen. The bridge has it up on one of the main monitors as well. Sister Stella Nessa waits inside, lost in prayer as she perpetually is.

The bridge crew watch the wounded side of the ship, sealant foam bubbling forth and stiffened. Their eyes drift from it; the action went into the chapel where there are no cameras.

But suddenly the foam bursts outward in chunks and the abomination slaps its two primary arms out onto the hull. Heaves and drags itself out.

Captain Bernhard taps the comms connection, "Knights, the thing is exiting back out onto the ship through the same hole it went inside."

As acknowledgements start flooding in, the captain turns to Johns, "Keep that drone on it, I don't want to lose sight of—"

As if in reaction, the abomination sees the drone. Johns backs it up. Even so, it swings hard, its lanky but giant hand fills the screen. The camera feed jostles violently and then spirals frantically. Views of the stars replaced with a sweep of the *St. Joshua* replaced with the stars and the *St. Joshua* again, over and over.

Johns huffs and scrolls through command prompts for HID 0017. Takes it off-line. "It served us well," he says as he queues up another drone.

"Gets eyes on that thing. We can't afford to lose it," The captain says.

They switch through stationary camera feeds on the ship's hull. One gets a glimpse of the abomination shuffling past, then nothing.

"Lost contact, sir. I'm trying—" Johns flips through the feeds, trying to recapture a visual on the beast.

The captain swallows fury. "Get it back."

All of Them Willing to Lay Down Their Lives

Brother Gonzaga hefts Father Cho's body into one of the surgery pods in the medbay. Slams his open palm down onto the emergency eval and interdiction button. The pod fires to life and a scanner array begins running up and down the priest. A pressure cuff takes his bicep and gently inflates. A surgical mask folds down over his face, floods with oxygen. Needles on slender articulated arms find his veins.

"The works, Father," Gonzaga says as he tries to playfully point at the priest. "Just for you." The Knight feels fake and deflated. He drops his hand and steps back.

The priest's eyes flutter and he smiles. Tries to speak but cannot. His lips part enough to soundlessly mouth *thank you* and Gonzaga waves a hand to brush it off.

"Her," Father Cho finally wheezes. Points past the Knight with a finger that has a clip-on blood-oxygen monitor. "Her."

"Yes, Father. Her. Of course," Gonzaga stares at his priest for another moment. The blood, the grisly chest wound. All his various injuries up and down his arms, his face. Gonzaga hadn't seen the fight, but he'd seen the aftermath. The chapel he knew an hour ago was ruined. And here is the father. An old priest. Standing up against what Gonzaga had only fought in full armor with automatic weapons. He'd gotten the better of it while he was grievously wounded. What a hero. What a guardian angel.

"Her. Yup," Gonzaga drops his smile, pats the pod over the old warrior and leaves him.

In the passageway, he takes a single bounding step to the right where the other Knights are. Commander Brigid comes over the comms. "Gonzaga, status?"

"Father Cho is in a surgical pod; I'm heading to your location."

"Negative. Get to the bridge. Guard her."

Gonzaga looks down the passageway to the starboard side cargo bay. "Yes, sir."

"Let me know when you're in position."

"Roger," Gonzaga runs to the bay, an idea forming.

†

"Have you ever seen the rails they fire out of the Planetary Defense Platforms?" Brother Santa Cruz asks. "I mean, like, *really* ever stood next to one of those things?"

The airlock finally cycles open to the passageway and the Knights rush in, hit the button to cycle outside.

"I've seen rail gun projectiles everywhere," Brother Pio says. "Aren't they usually just depleted uranium or tungsten slugs or whatever? Little metal pills, just about?"

"Mostly for the small arms stuff, yeah." Santa Cruz says. "The ones in my rifle are pretty small. Don't need to be huge, but these defense platform things... they're anti-aircraft munitions. They're like ten meters long each."

"Should make short work of our boy, then," Brother Nonnatus says. His eyes are fixed on the status dial of the airlock. The strobes flash. A few more seconds and they're back out on the hull.

Santa Cruz keeps going, says, "They're designed to create a fluid shock wave through a ship that will tow metric tons of debris in its wake, right out the exit wound. It'd be like hitting a man dead center with a hydraulic ram at... I don't know. A million kilos per square inch. What comes out the exit wound—"

"Why do you do math?" Pio asks. "You're terrible at math."

"It's not literal. The point is—" the airlock cycles open and Commander Brigid rushes out. Nonnatus too. Pio and Santa Cruz shut up. Game time. Guns up, they rush onto the hull.

"Fan out," Brigid says, sweeping the upper hull of the *St. Joshua*. "The latest report is, it slapped another hull drone right off the ship and into outer space. Then they lost visual of it. It could be anywhere. Clear this and when we're all in position, we'll move as a team to the underside."

The Knights all roger up and spread out. Mingled amongst them are more Hull Inspection Drones. More eyes. Santa Cruz watches one of them wheel itself to the edge of the ship and flip over, disappearing under the angle of the starboard side.

The Knights work their way aft. At their backs, the front of the ship and the colossal spectacle of the planet consumes their portion of space. It takes up most of their field of vision, the majestic swirling whites of clouds. The deep blues of Centauri's three oceans. The vast patterns of greens and oranges that make up much of the planet's forests. The richly detailed browns of the mountainous region they're descending to, where their commandry is. Rocky and steep with sheer cliffs leading down into blackened and abysmal crags, but in other areas draftsman-flat shelves of carved rock hundreds of meters long. Santa Cruz can almost hear the chopping buzz of the helicopters the permanent host of Knights use to travel the mountains.

"Commander," Captain Bernhard says over the comms. Santa Cruz finishes his sweep and sends a message through the Visuals he's in position to go upside down. Pio and Nonnatus do the same.

"Go," Brigid says.

"We're still within range of the nearest Planetary Defense Platform. Between our little maneuver and our brothers down on the surface logging into the platform and adjusting its orbital compensators, we've bought ourselves two whole minutes. A gift from God on scales like this."

"Roger. We're moving to the belly. It's got to be there."

"I've got Petty Officer Johns and Lt. Commander Keo piloting drones. They're all out there on automatic except for those two. We're looking along the belly now."

"Check the nooks and crannies. Father Cho got it good one time. I imagine it'll be nursing its wound."

"Will do."

"Knights," Brigid says as he sends the message to prepare to go over the side. "If it wasn't up top, it's down below. Make this the last effort. Stop it before it finishes its suicide mission."

"Are we sure its mission is to kill her before it gets killed?" Nonnatus asks as the four Knights step over the edge. He flips and spends a half second fighting the change in their perception of technically being upside down. In the nothingness of space, there is no true up, no true down. Just orientation. Their guts adjust as they move.

"No one followed us through the gate. It's got nowhere to go if it were to snatch her up again."

"I think we've already covered this, but best guess," Santa Cruz says. He takes a position by the bridge and starts sweeping. "I can see the logical chain here. The planet's government wants the religion stomped out. They hear from a torture subject that there's a stigmatic nun who's become a touchstone to her religion. A pilgrimage site. One after another of the faithful goes there. Sees her. Prays with her. They, no doubt, have been in contact with other members of the underground. Their brains together form a world-spanning web of every member of the hatred religion."

"And her brain is the central node," Pio says.

Santa Cruz gives a harsh laugh. "Why do you do English? You're terrible at English."

"Am not. I'm better at English than you are at math."

"*Node* violates the simile of a *web*, but I'll allow it."

"Lock on, people. More searching, less banter," Brigid says.

"Yessir," Santa Cruz says.

From somewhere distant, Gonzaga's voice clicks into their comms. "So, not to completely disobey the commander, but they do the brain-thing to her and unbury the underground. One final genocide and they're free of Christ."

"Never free," Nonnatus says. "Our Lord, our God is everywhere in all things. But the church on Arithraw might be pruned into a dead branch, yes."

"Yes, yes. You know what I mean."

Pio says, "But we got her out of there. We got her off their planet, and then off their ship."

"And so they booby trapped ours with this monster since their guns and missiles didn't work," Santa Cruz says.

Brigid clears his throat the way his Knights know he does when he's been ruminating on something. "That still doesn't answer how it would get her back to them. How would they do the brain harvest to her?"

"Contact!" Nonnatus shouts for the second time as he rounds a feature for the landing gear. Opens fire. The other Knights spin and can only take a step before they see Nonnatus's head snap back with a spike jutting out of his helmet.

†

"Engage! Engage!" Commander Brigid commands as they form a semi-circle around the creature. At the same time the abomination rushes quick as a spider barreling towards something caught in its web. It charges across the underside of the *St. Joshua* forward towards the bow. It shoots another spike, aimed at Brother Pio, but again his suit draws the track line and helps him dodge.

"To the bridge!" Brother Santa Cruz shouts.

Captain Bernhard gets on the comms and says, "Herd that thing outward so the planetary defense systems get a clear shot."

Brigid is grabbing at Brother Nonnatus checking his suit for air leaks and says, "Man down, I repeat. Man down. We need a drone or something that can get him—"

The chatter of gunfire through their suits adds to the confusion. The gleaming jewel of Centauri Astoria growing by magnitudes in front of them. The angle of the ship as it gets in position to have a gnat skinned off its elephant hide.

Santa Cruz moves and fires, his small arms rifle doing nothing to the thing. Brother Pio is the same, both letting small bursts fly to keep it distracted and trying to prod it outwards. Santa Cruz snarls. He swings his gun down on its tether, the built-in magnet on its forepiece snapping it to his armor. Out of the way. Draws his rail gun and aims for its head.

He fires once and hits a bony plate. A shard of it snaps off, flings into space. The impact violently knocks its head off to the side, but it's not enough. The abomination reacts in utter rage, neutered silent in the vacuum. Spins to Santa Cruz. Pio maneuvers, getting a better angle. Santa Cruz fires again and the thing twists hard at its hips. Bringing up its arm, fires a resin spike at Santa Cruz. He dodges and the thing races upward, clambering over the port lip. He fires one more round as the thing clears the lip, hitting it in its foot hard enough to kick its whole leg up and out of sight.

"Keep it topside!" Captain Bernhard says. "It's our best chance. We're only seconds from re-entry and we've—"

Another blaring alert pops up as Brigid drags Nonnatus's limp body off from where he was magboot-ed down. He looks down the ship, his Visuals unspooling a mechanical print of the *St. Joshua*. Not too far away is a service hatch leading into the forward armory. If he can just get there... "Pio! Gonzaga! Santa Cruz! Where are—"

BREACH BREACH BREACH BREACH BREACH—

†

Inside the bridge a deafening *pop!* cuts through the entire space as the overhead punches downward. Three claws deform the metal and shove through, curl up and rend back a streak of the hull . The rush of the atmosphere getting sucked out turns into visible air currents as the freeze of space solidifies water molecules in the air.

The captain starts to shout but his voice is drowned out in the roar of the vacuum. Everyone on the bridge scrambles for emergency oxygen masks. Petty Officer Johns dives over to Sister Stella Nessa, strapped down in a flight chair, and roughly strings one over her face.

"Don't worry, sister. This is just— one second..." He adjusts it to work with her alien features, then goes to undo her clasps so he can get her off the bridge before the abomination climbs inside. He looks her in the eyes and smiles, then jerks violently and stops moving. His own oxygen mask begins to slowly fill with red and he falls over, a spike driven into his back.

There, the abomination hangs upside down in the damage it dug through the hull into the bridge. It heaves itself out of the jagged metal mess and the ever-growing scab of sealant foam. Drops to the deck. Captain Bernhard leans up with a gun in his hand. Opens fire. The abomination spins and grabs him by the throat, slaps the gun out of his hand and hurls him across his bridge, flinging him back-first into the primary monitor mounted on the other side of the room. He crashes down in a cascade of sparks.

Petty Officer Bonilla gets across the bridge, firing from a handgun. He moves in a semicircle, weapon trained on the enemy. Sights steady on the thing, popping off rounds. Buying time. The abomination raises an arm and fires a resin spike. Bonilla ducks and weaves. The spike hits behind him, shattering a console. A second spike comes on its heels, and Bonilla takes it hard in his upper chest, near his right shoulder. He coughs and falls backwards.

The others dive to the deck, scramble. Petty Officer Cavins maneuvers in a squatting position around a series of desks. Grabs a rifle from a compartment in the decking. Stands up to shoot and sees the great thing next to the nun. From where he is, there's no good shot.

Lt. Commander Keo rushes over and the thing whirls to meet her. She has an emergency flare in her hand and shoots it at its face. The brilliant starburst of red alights along it while it roars, swinging. At the same time Cavins comes about with his rifle. Shooting, watching its ghostly flesh jiggle and disperse the shockwave of the rounds.

Keo grabs Johns, looks to Cavins, "Can you get the captain? Bonilla?"

Cavins looks behind him, "I'll try."

But the abomination swings on Keo and clips her. She tumbles away towards the hatch, Johns' corpse rolling with her. The thing swings around and grabs a monitor screen off the nearest station, throws it at Cavins. Strikes him on the head and he crumples as the monitor shatters around him.

Turning back, the abomination sees the nun and smiles gleefully, like a demon having lured a soul to damnation. It grabs her. It reaches out with its left secondary hand with the odd multi-segmented claw. Snatches the nun by the head with it, its fingers draping down her face like moss over water. It becomes apparent the fingers aren't really fingers. They're black shiny metal, like insect carapaces. Designed for something else besides the articulated movements of appendages.

Rows of tiny lights along the hand light up. An electric whirling sound fills the room. The boxy organ inside its chest hums to life and flashes a sequence on it. Cables like veins that run off it shimmer with the effort as it leaves the box, travel down its secondary arm and into the carapace fist.

The door to the bridge opens and Brother Gonzaga stomps inside. Outfitted in a safety orange mech loader from the starboard side bay, he can look at the abomination at eye level. The suit is a metal frame, riveted along the joints, striped with reflective lines. A battery pack on the back, flood lights up front. Hydraulics and servo-assisted gears on the joints. Forks on the arms to lift pallets.

The abomination spins around, cruel smirk on its face. Gonzaga looks down to the nun and sees her head under the thing's probing technological hand. X-ray-like flashes of her skull appear and disappear tens of times a second inside the carapace fist. Scanning.

Harvesting.

"Get away from her, you—" and the thing fires a spike at Gonzaga. It hits a cross member built into the suit and he's peppered with shards. Gonzaga shoves forward, clamping a pallet fork onto its primary right arm. He thrusts his other pallet fork towards its face, and they struggle over the nun.

Gonzaga can hear the hiss of hydraulics flexing his loader suit, see a fitting feeding a cylinder start to bubble oil out under the strain. He struggles against it still, trying to think of a way to keep moving the loader's arms while grabbing for his weapon.

Keo appears from around the corner dragging the unconscious captain towards the exit. She is bleeding from the forehead and limps as she moves, but her eyes have a determined set to them. Fierce. Cavins comes with her, his hand pressing the back of his bleeding head. He's got one hand on Bonilla, who has gone white with blood loss. Cavins lunges near enough where the Knight is struggling against the abomination and grabs Johns by the ankle. Reaches for the nun and he gets hit a second time by a backhand. He pinwheels into the others, and the whole mass of the bridge crew tumbles into the passageway. The hatch shuts fast enough to where Keo has to yank her foot out from getting closed on.

Suddenly a laser-bright cone shoves down through the hardened sealant foam. It sizzles like frying fat and peels back, blackened by the heat. Brother Santa Cruz drops inside. He and his TechHaft drop to the deck. He moves up, the gigantic drill bit on the end of his shaft still spinning. Overhead, new sealant foam begins to gurgle out to fill the hole.

He jabs at the abomination with the Techhaft in one hand, pulling his rail gun off from around his back. He swings the long barrel up, aiming for its mouth and pulls the trigger just as another spike hits him in his hand supporting the gun. The shot goes wildly up, punching through the overhead and creating a worse wound in it.

The atmosphere *pops!* again. The wide wound spills out into space whatever the life support system managed to pump back into the bridge. Gravity weakens as the Delta V dampener system begins to fail in the maelstrom. Sealant foam tries to repair that, but the tear is too wide. Spatters of foam collect at the edges, unable to close the gap.

Santa Cruz falls back into the free-floating bits of his demolished rail gun. His right hand destroyed by the spike. He kicks off the deck, thrusting with his TechHaft again. "Pio, where are you?"

Pio says over the comms, "Sealant covered the hole you made. Then you shot through the roof?"

"Didn't mean to."

"Coming down."

"Hurry!"

The abomination drops the nun as the black box in its chest flashes a rhythmic sequence of lights that reminds Gonzaga of a finishing flurry. She floats off the surface of the deck in the weakening gravity, still exhaling little plumes of condensate on the inside of her mask. Her hands bearing the Wounds of Christ still glistening with blood. A single drop of it detaches from her hand and becomes a tiny globe ascending through the bridge.

Gonzaga stabs a glance at the whole thing—her, the embedded tech in the beast, the assault he'd just witnessed—says, "Brain harvest," and they clash again.

†

Commander Brigid drags Brother Nonnatus through the access hatch into the armory and the system automatically cycles it shut behind him. He gets him on the other side of the manual air lock, and it becomes quickly evident the armory is not designed for two men in full battle armor. Crammed in, Brigid monitors the fight on his Visuals through the other Knights' cameras. Each display only a little bigger than his thumbnail.

His atmosphere read-out is good, and he gently pulls off Nonnatus's helmet. The crumbling remains of the spike fall away. Nonnatus's entire mouth is in ruins, but his throat and head appear fine.

"C'mon, brother," Brigid says as he stands and looks for an emergency first aid kit. One is on the far bulkhead, past a rack of the solid red telson rockets for the dropship. Brigid huffs a tired laugh and moves around them, gets the kit, sees the set of manual control buttons on the side of the rockets. "That is weird they put those controls on the outside."

He rushes over to Nonnatus. Brigid checks Nonnatus's suit medical systems and sees what all it's done since he was shot. He draws out a dose of some wake-up cocktail, administers it. Nonnatus's eyes flutter open and he mewls, rolls off to the side.

"You've got to get up, brother. We're down, hard. I need to know you're okay to—"

Nonnatus waves him away, appearing as if he's fighting off nausea. He makes choked moaning sounds and turns back to the commander. Tries to nod. His eyes begin to glaze over with the new dose of painkillers coming in. Brigid must force himself not to wince and turn away at the damage to his Knight's face. He pats Nonnatus's shoulder lovingly, a wave of pity rushing in. "You've done good, brother."

Nonnatus uses a hand signal to blow off the compliment. Fumbles around and finds his helmet. Electronically pushes the controls for his

Visuals to a small interface that is attached to a flap on his armor. Sends Brigid a text message. *I've done good at being the canary in a coal mine.*

Brigid laughs. "I know you're not okay. Not okay enough to get back in the fight. But are you okay enough to get yourself to the medbay? Can you walk yourself to it?"

Nonnatus gives a hand signal. *Maybe.* Stands slowly. It's a struggle. Brigid can hear someone in the passageway. He jumps up, opens the hatch. Sees Lt. Commander Keo, Petty Officer Cavins. Sees them dragging the others.

Brigid steps out, asks, "Survivors?" as he motions to the limp captain and crew.

"Mostly," Cavins says. He peels his hand off the back of his head, sees the slick blood all over his hand and forearm, groans. He looks to Petty Officer Johns, shakes his head.

"So be it. I've got to add to your burden, though," Brigid points to Nonnatus.

Keo shrugs and wipes sweat off her brow, leaving a smear of blood instead. "Of course."

"And I'm going to need somebody on the sticks to this plane. Can you remote pilot it from somewhere?"

Cavins nods. "Yeah. Engine room."

Brigid takes him by shoulder, nods to his bloody mess. "Are you in the shape for that?"

"Maybe. You'll know I'm not if we crash."

Brigid nods, looks back into the armory. Down at his magboots. "Good enough. We're in pretty deep. Those of you who can, pray, and do it fast."

†

The rail gun wound is wide enough that sealant foam can't bridge the gap. Brother Pio jumps down through the tear and lands on the abomination. He pulls out his TechHaft and ignites it. A short, thick sword appears in the laser-brilliance, and he begins to chop at the monster.

"Took me a minute—" he starts as the abomination swings him wildly, fighting against all three. "—sorry... the foam— couldn't get through..."

The thing swings again and Pio flies off into the bridge. Hits hard across the captain's chair and flings off into a console. He stands up and runs at the dogpile. Leaps again. Gets back on it and stabs.

An alarm sounds in the bridge. The last functioning monitor turns red, alerting them that they passed the window for the planetary defense systems to help.

"Not too bummed about that, actually," Brother Santa Cruz says as he attacks the thing as best he can with his TechHaft.

Pio swings his sword one more time and severs its right secondary arm. The left one, still with its black metal claw for a hand, snaps out at him. Gouges his armor.

Brother Gonzaga re-clamps both his loader grips around the abomination's body. It's fighting to get free, and absolute dread fills Gonzaga's guts. "That hand... the box blinking inside it... brain harvest— hard drive. Must have all her— all the pilgrims' faces there... I think if it gets back outside the hull—"

"Somehow they'll collect it." Pio says, fighting. He looks down between his legs, sees through the translucent skin of the beast and sees what a must be a comms transmitter/receiver just below the flesh. Close enough to erupt out of it and send the data.

"Not a *total* suicide mission, then," Santa Crus says.

Gonzaga swings one loader claw up and grabs the abomination by the head from underneath its jaw. It roars and jerks. Pio shifts forward a good deal, nearly falls over its shoulder. It drops a hammer blow, strikes Pio hard along the back. Takes him and throws him into a console next to it. Pio grunts over their shared comms and falls limp. Santa Cruz reaches down for him, but it kicks Pio away. Pio flies across the bridge again, hits the same chair. Wraps around it and slumps.

Light spills out over and through the rail gun blast in the overhead. Flames spring up all along the jagged edges of the metal. Santa Cruz looks up, swallows hard. "Re-entry."

"Get it to the flames," Gonzaga says as he shoves up on the thing. Santa Cruz rams his TechHaft into the abomination's armpit and activates the drill. It gouges into its flesh. He wedges himself between the abomination and the console, uses his entire body to shove up, driving it deeper.

Gonzaga rams both his loader clamps around the thing's body, locks them in place. The hydraulic fittings leak; globules of black shiny oil peppering out under pressure from the lines. They float through the air, intermingling with the dots of blood from the nun.

Gore spills out from the drill hole and the abomination snaps the carapace-fist from its secondary arm onto Santa Crus's face shield. The helmet crushes inward near his eye. It fires a spike at the same damaged area and then hits him hard enough that the combination of the threefold attack knocks him back. He collapses. The TechHaft falls.

Gonzaga looks up, sees the re-entry flames burn white hot and hits the loader's emergency release button. All the straps holding him in pop loose into a rat's nest of tangles.

He struggles to get free of the mess of straps, he shouts, "Santa Cruz! Pio! One of you gotta get the nun and get away from us! Hurry!"

Pio floats motionless, still unconscious from the force of the strike against him. Santa Cruz groans. The sound is weak; from a million miles away. Gonzaga can see crimson droplets forcefully spraying out of the gouge in his helmet. Santa Cruz stirs, his ruined hand curled up protectively against his chest.

"Hurry, brother... we're out of re-entry... but not too far out for..."

Santa Cruz rolls as if he doesn't do it right this second, he'll never move again, and grabs the nun by her ankles. He rolls away, towing her with him.

Gonzaga heaves one more time and the abomination's carapace-fist shoves through the loader's roll cage. Snaps open and closed at his face. He jerks his head side to side, but the arm keeps trying. The very tips of the fingers find his neck and clamps down. Weak for a hand that just crushed Santa Cruz's helmet, strong enough even with only the fingertips on his flesh.

Gonzaga struggles. Can't talk. Can't breathe. The abomination's primary arms grab his arms. It bends them and he can feel muscles burn sharply, joints stress too far. One of his eyes rolls far enough to see that Santa Cruz drug the nun halfway across the bridge before collapsing. He's twitching hard like he's having a seizure.

The abomination leans in, licking its mouth. Its ruined eye from the crucifix a gaping wound, a deflated hole. No resin filling for that. It sneers, speaks in a voice that sounds like it's burbling up from hell and his universal translator makes it crystal clear, "I have won."

Gonzaga prays for help. His guardian angel. The abomination's guardian angel. His confirmation saint. His name saint. The patron saints of the Order. The patron saints of the mission. Jesus Christ, Lord and Savior. God the Father. The Holy Spirit, paraclete.

Gonzaga's vision goes black around the edges. His throat burns and he can feel the starving tingle in his fingertips. He gurgles once and finds himself immersed in the sandy yellows and oranges of the noon day sky of his colonial settlement in the Verities System.

Death has come yet again. And it's not so uncomfortable, either.

But a single dot in the bridge floats through his vision, light shimmering across it as it comes nearer. A lone droplet of the blood from the Wounds of Christ lazily travels upwards, floating free in the bridge amongst the rest of the fluid droplets.

It comes to them, face to face, and Gonzaga sees the droplet, aimlessly floating along with a million other globs of blood and hydraulic fluid and sweat and whatever else. He sees it, so minuscule and pathetic next to this Goliath of a beast, killing him even now. Killing everyone.

But that holy droplet. Untouched by the violence. None of the things of this world. Taking its time as it goes where God directs it, floating on the bridge. Exuding love. A small red ball. Pure.

Gonzaga prays, "Lord Jesus Christ— king of endless glory... I offer myself— to You as a— a living sacrifice for my brothers. For— For her. . . For her people. Use me— for... Your victory."

The droplet turns sharply and floats into the abomination's ruined eye socket. In an instant the thing seizes and screams in agony. Gonzaga reflexively heaves in a breath, free of its grip. And as the abomination writhes trying to scrape out the droplet of holy blood, Gonzaga is immersed in gratitude to God.

"For Christ!" Gonzaga shouts and he slams a fist down on the loader's emergency thruster's button. The thrusters, designed to give a quick burst of course correction in case the loader was ever to fall out of the open dock into space, blasts and lifts off. The deck beneath them is slagged by the intense flames, the rest of the bridge fills with roiling black smoke and heat.

The abomination is pincered by the loader. They all rocket up and out through the massive tear from the rail gun damage. The abomination hits its shoulder on the side of the hole but the force of the rockets drive them up. Out. The hull falls away under them, propelled into the sky.

Gonzaga struggles inside the roll cage to escape. The upper atmosphere of Centauri Astoria unfolds around them. Behind them as they climb, the trail of rocket smoke belching out of the bridge as the *St. Joshua* darts away. The thing looks at Gonzaga as the Knight smiles, finally freeing himself completely of the straps.

"I'm not going make it, big guy, but I'm too keen on letting you kill me either. I'll pray for both of us. God bless you."

Gonzaga flings himself out of the roll cage. He freefalls down towards the surface, praying for the soul of the monster they've been fighting. Praying for himself, asking Saint Joseph for the grace of a good death as he reaches terminal velocity. Praying for his brothers' health and lives after their silent get-in-and-get-out mission became a rolling gun battle across two solar systems. Praying for the dear Sister Stella Nessa and her wonderful graces. Praying to Brother Cleopas to intercede with the Father on his behalf.

"I'll see you soon, brother. I love you all." He shouts joyously in freefall.

†

The abomination rockets up into the reaches of the atmosphere, and its roars thin out in the lack of air. The sunlight is unimpeded, and it glistens in the golden rays. It reaches high enough and the thrusters begin to burn out. The abomination writhes in the pincer grip, leans forward, rounding its back. The transmitter/receiver exits its body, begins to unfurl a communications dish it will aim back towards the wormhole gate. Towards the satellite patiently waiting for the brain harvest results. The abomination tries to laugh. Tries to bask in the success of its mission. Its entire body buzzing with pain, either from its wounds or the terrible way it was mutated.

But its work is done, and all to destroy the useless church of the fake god on its home world.

The thrusters give out and it is too high for gravity to have much effect. High enough for the planetary defense platform to begin tracking the object. Not far now. Not at all.

The abomination tears at the loader's hydraulics, pulls itself free from a gripper. The transmitter/receiver array verifies its connection with the satellite, begins to maneuver so it can line-of-sight project the brain harvest information.

From hundreds of kilometers away, the defense platform fires a tungsten javelin along a magnetized rail at nearly the speed of sound.

The black box inside the abomination performs one last check of its information. Formatting the neural impulses examined and copied from the nun's brain. Prepares the connection sequence with the satellite, sending a test blip to make sure they're speaking the same language.

A flash of silver through the sun's rays overhead. So quick it's here and gone in the blink of an eye. The loader and the demonic mutant vanish in a cloud of destruction. The thirty-meter-long javelin hitting them might as well be an asteroid against a fly. Laid to rest, and with it the black box and all its information about Thraw who dared to think their God is not only real but loves them.

Its plume of obliteration shimmers in the sun, glimmering like a comet of jewels as it cascades along the skyline. Free of its pain and rendered beautiful.

†

Commander Brigid exits the airlock hatch, climbs onto the surface of *St. Joshua*. He pulls out two items with him, clicks on his comms. "Cavins, you read me?"

"Yes, Commander?" Petty Officer Cavins says.

"Will we be able to land?"

"Yessir. I think so, anyway."

"Good. I'll try to be in touch, Brigid out."

He looks down at the surface of the planet, still so many kilometers away. Prays, "Saint Michael, I don't even know what intercession to request..." He jumps off the hull of the ship, slides one of the two red telson rockets between his legs.

Activates the manual control and locks his magboots and one glove to it in the most awkward pose he's ever been in. Tucks the other rocket under his arm as the booster kicks in, shooting him off at a speed he instantly regrets.

"Do it for Brother Gonzaga, do it for Gonzaga, do it for Gonzaga..." he mutters to himself. Chants over and over. His suit gives a warning for his bursting heart rate, the adrenaline dump he just got.

In his Visuals, he's got a lock on Gonzaga's suit. In freefall, several klicks away. The rocket closes the gap in moments, however, and for the first time Brigid wonders if the rocket carries a warhead that arms after a certain distance or simply needs impact to trigger. Better not find out the hard way.

He leans this way and tilts that way, correcting for the dumb-fire rocket. Its propulsion system wasn't built to carry hundreds of pounds in extra payload, and as he nears Gonzaga the thing begins to falter, losing thrust. He gets to where he guesses he can make it and jumps off before he thinks too hard, still above Gonzaga and wildly careening towards him.

"Hey! Gonzaga!" he shouts over the comms. "Above you!"

†

Brother Gonzaga rolls in his plummet, sees his commander in freefall above him, arms wrapped around something as the dying flame plume of a rocket fades behind him. The dying flame corkscrews a half kilometer above, then explodes.

"Grab me!" Commander Brigid shouts as they come within several meters of one another. Gonzaga isn't wearing his full-frontal assault kit like Brigid is—wouldn't fit inside the loader mech—but he has a stripped-down version of it, including breathable air canisters. He yanks one off his suit and wrenches the head off it, using the compressed burst of air to aim himself at Brigid.

They reach out and grab hands. Clasp and pull in. Gonzaga lets go of the cannister and the two Knights grab in a hug.

"Our Lady of Mercy! Commander, is that a rocket? I thought Santa Cruz was teasing about you—"

"I guess not," Brigid smiles. He looks down and sees a patch of mountain rising to meet them quickly. "If we pull this off, we can top anybody else's brag for a lifetime to come."

"Pull off what? What if we don't pull it off?"

"It'll be a good death."

Gonzaga puts it together and shrugs.

The mountain coming towards them and the Knights aim the rocket's thruster at the ground. Wrap themselves around it and magnetize their boots and hands to it and one another. Brigid poises his finger over the manual engage button, waits until he can see the floes of dirt and pebble on the very hard surface below. Hits the button.

The thruster bursts forth in fire and smoke, slagging the earth underneath them. Kills their freefall velocity and starts to rock side to side as it exerts towards the ground.

"Jump!" Brigid shouts and Gonzaga does. He falls a few meters and off to the side, avoiding the plume. Brigid kicks the rocket off away from them and falls. Lands on scorching hot earth. He scrambles out of it and collapses next to Gonzaga. The rocket flies up into the air and spins wildly. The thruster puffs out a belch of black smoke and cuts off. Falls down the mountainside. They're on a cliff face, and the rocket falls below it, out of sight.

Gonzaga whoops and says, "That wasn't so bad—" and the rocket strikes something with its explosive, blows up. A volley of shattered rock and fire spit up over the side, pepper them with the outskirts of its debris.

Brigid waits, holds up a finger to Gonzaga. As everything dies down, he nods. Lowers his finger. "*Now*, that wasn't so bad."

"We got a beacon for them to find us?" Gonzaga asks, groaning and yawning all at once. He stretches out slowly, his aches and pains causing him to shout a few times. Lays down on his back, stretches out again. Groans.

"Yeah," Brigid says and lays down on his back as well. "Plus, they'll know where to pick us up from that explosion, I think." Brigid says. "I've got my broadband homing beacon on. Just a matter of time. You want to turn yours on? Do you even have one right now?"

Nothing.

"Gonzaga, brother, you want to turn your broadband—"

He looks over at Gonzaga, and the man has fallen asleep. Brigid lets a small laugh out and he reaches over to the controls interface on Gonzaga's armor, finds he does have a beacon. Brigid activates it. Then lets out a long, relaxing breath. Eases his head onto a patch of soft dirt amongst the hardscrabble and watches the clouds pass overhead.

He smiles as two Saint Christopher-class multi-rescue ships roar across the sky from behind the mountain. In a tight formation, the ships maneuver with such impressive synchronicity that Brigid thinks they both might be auto controlled by one pilot or AI.

"Lord, guide them," he says as the ships begin their work.

The jumbo ships swoop in to intercept the *St. Joshua*, which by now is wobbling in flight and leaving behind a smoking trail. The multi-rescue ships position themselves over the *St. Joshua* and extend rigging to attach to it. In a moment the battered ship is secured and the multi-rescue ships ease it down off to the horizon where a landing pad and overhaul base are.

A glimmer of sunlight falls on Commander Brigid and he is moved to thanksgiving. He gets up. Kneels and prays, "May God bless the work of our hands. Thank you for everything, especially Brother Cleopas and Sister Stella Nessa. Thank you for their witness today, and may it serve as a reminder to the Thraw that You are good and they need Your love."

He remains on his knees for some time, Gonzaga peacefully snoring behind him. The edge of the plateau they crash-landed on, and the view from it is awe-inspiring as it gives way to the vast of creation beyond. And even as a rescue helicopter rises up and homes in on his beacon, he stays on his knees. Hands clasped, weeping for his fallen and giving thanks to the loving God for giving Brother Cleopas and all of them the opportunity to die for something great, and holy.

All Our People Are Here

Centauri Astoria is a small but lush world. The blues of its three oceans are more baby blue and translucent than many other worlds, and along the surface there is a harmless bacterium that shimmers like flecks of gold in the sunlight. The green of the forests is darker than one expects before seeing it for the first time. Deeply green, so much so it looks black at some angles. There are orange trees mixed in, and they add spice and warmth to the earthen color palette.

The grain of the wood of the most populous tree in the nearest forest looks like sandstone. A light blonde in color, it is so dense it requires a special blade to cut. Its leaves are wide and thin enough to flutter in a breeze, and they hang low. Brigid has always loved walking underneath the trees for that very reason. It is like being petted by silk.

His shoes off in the mossy grass, he strolls slowly along the grounds of the Basilica not only to enjoy the texture but to carefully navigate the small, rounded stones that populate the topsoil like chocolates in cookies.

Along the planet, which is one of three major epicenters for the Knights 15 13 that directly report to the grand home planet, there are numerous industries that third-order Knights 15 13 live their lives to support.

All the usual industries for any self-sustaining world: the sprawling farms, efficient factories, schools. Centauri Astoria also has the second largest aeronautical installation of the Knights. The *St. Joshua* is being repaired and overhauled by some of the finest and most experienced airline mechanics in the Order.

Their northeastern ore mining and refineries contribute structural materials throughout the Order and their oceans contain unique nutrients that they synthesize into medications.

But the Basilica at the center of the major town, the tallest building of it, is a jewel. A tribute to God, reaching high to the heavens and

225

226 CARL MICHAEL CURTIS

showing the greatest achievement of the universe is to strive to its Creator.

The stained-glass stories high, sunlight passing through and illuminating like rubies, emeralds, topazes, diamonds and a thousand more. The rose window is a glorious tribute telling its holy message in picture to anyone with eyes to see. Its choir tells its holy message to anyone with ears to hear. Its incense telling its holy message to anyone with a nose to smell. Its stone, metal, ceramic and glass walls, different slabs here and features there, telling its holy message to anyone with touch to feel.

But today, its symphony of church bells ring fifteen times and pause for a breathless moment. Then ring thirteen more times. Everyone gathers there to pay honor and give thanks to God and celebrate the lives of their own.

†

Petty Officer Heratio Franz is laid to rest at the Basilica, with the local Bishop himself presiding over the funeral Mass. Franz receives full honors as a secondary member of the Knights of Those Washed in the Water and Blood from His Side, Aeronautical division, and even though his body was incinerated upon re-entry on the *St. Joshua*, his belongings were sent to his home planet of Cigam Proxima where his family interred his Rosary and collection of prayer cards with a stuffed animal his youngest child donated.

It is beautiful, celebrating Franz's life and his act of rushing into the Thraw and Skreeve invasion, fighting for the nun. They listed his numerous other commendations, and his service to God and the Order remained untainted to the end.

†

Petty Officer Joseph Johns is laid to rest at the Basilica, with the local Bishop himself presiding over the funeral Mass. Johns receives full honors as a secondary member of the Knights of Those Washed in the Water and Blood from His Side, Aeronautical division, and since Centauri Astoria is his home world, his parents and siblings can bring his body back east to their family's ancestral plot.

It is beautiful, celebrating Johns' life and his last act of heroism, situating an oxygen mask on Sister Stella Nessa's face so that she may live, when he could have stood from his workstation and retreated from the damaged bridge. His was the closest seat to the door, and his were the best chances of survival. Greater love hath no man than this, that a man lay down his life for his friends.

†

Brother Ezra Josemaria Cleopas is laid to rest at the Basilica, with the local Bishop himself presiding over the funeral Mass. Cleopas receives full honors as a member of Knights of Those Washed in the Water and Blood from His Side, special operations division. A marker with his name and details on it is christened on their wall of honor in lieu of a burial.

It is beautiful, celebrating Cleopas' life and his last act of heroism, taking sufficient damage through his full-frontal assault armor to endanger his own life while selflessly participating in the rescue of Sister Stella Nessa, and then making the ultimate sacrifice to save his brothers and sisters from a full-scale invasion of the *St. Joshua* and to terminate the threat of the Thraw mothership. Greater love hath no man than this, that a man lay down his life for his friends.

†

In the Commandry's medical wing, Captain Bernhard, Father Cho, Brothers Nonnatus, Santa Cruz and Pio all recover from their wounds while remaining in medically induced comas. They are all housed in the same stasis dorm, however, and their visitors can come and go, seeing the entire group lined side-by-side along a wall.

Sister Stella Nessa, herself in bandages and rolling with her an IV stand and monitor, prays with Brother Cleopas's Rosary at the foot of their beds. She suffers from migraines after the brain harvest, and her vision has dramatically reduced. Even in the medical ward, pilgrims come to her and ask to pray with her, holding her Christ-wounded hands gently. Just to be close to a living miracle.

Commander Brigid visits every day, and for hours. He and Brother Gonzaga take rotating shifts being at the nun's side. Though any force of evil would be not only suicidal but incomprehensibly delusional to attack Centauri Astoria or any Knights 15 13 stronghold, the Knights themselves do not doubt the depths of stupidity that evil will plumb.

Brigid walks into the medical bay where his friends and allies are all bedded down in medpods. There is the slight form of the Arithraw nun, curled up on herself as she quietly ticks away at the slag-metal beads in her hand. She prays so deeply that she is in a fugue-like state, a resplendent trance. Beside her, the wall of a man named Brother Gonzaga. He sits silent as a shadow, calm as a pond under heavy clouds. An arm around the nun, engulfing her. A settled avalanche of his love and protection. His eyes closed, head tilted back not in sleepiness, but contentment.

Brigid approaches, eating hand to mouth from a small, crinkled paper sack. He tosses a small kernel of food at Gonzaga. It hits the man, and his eyes flutter open. Watches the kernel tumble down his chest. Settle in his lap. He stares at it, stares at his commander. Takes the kernel and eats it.

"Too sweet."

Brigid smiles. "It's Saint Honoratus of Amiens feast day. Local calendar."

"Sure. It can be that."

"Patron saint of bakers and pastry chefs?"

"Sure," Gonzaga says, smirking. "He can be that."

Brigid snorts. Shakes the bag and rattles the sweetened kernels inside. "You ever had these?"

"Just did. Too sweet."

"One of my favorite reasons to come to Centauri Astoria, these things."

"That, and you said something about walking under those trees, correct?"

Brigid sits down beside Gonzaga and exhales long and slow. "Yes. I love the embrace of those leaves as they just kind of... swipe along me. Their texture is really comforting."

"This right here—" Gonzaga wags his eyebrows and points his chin at the nun, "—the best comfort you could ever ask for, short of being in our Lord's arms."

Brigid nods. "I'm jealous."

"I love hearing her tiny voice. Without my translator, I hear her words in her native tongue. Before, I thought it was harsh, you know? Ugly. Maybe the Lord has been working in my heart through her. I'm sure that's what it is. Hearing her now is just... It's like, uh... I don't know. Sweetened kernels and weirdo trees. Beautiful. My favorite." He winks.

Brigid laughs. "Not better than that?"

Gonzaga laughs now. "Probably. But, if I'm being honest, Commander, you *really* look like you enjoy those two things."

They sit in silence for a moment, and the quiet huffs and clicks of the medpods gently working to deliver their friends from their injuries; it all drones comfortably along. The sweet odor of her wounds competes with the astringent of the environment.

"Checked on Nonnatus lately?" Gonzaga finally asks. The nun continues to pray as if the warrior-monks were not speaking next to her.

"Last report I saw was looking good."

Gonzaga nods. "Yeah. His face was destroyed. I'm glad they can rebuild it for him."

"We'll have to tease him about actually being handsome now." Brigid smiles and cracks a kernel between his teeth. "I saw Pio's bones are well on their way. That's good."

Gonzaga nods. "Yeah. I saw him get pummeled. He took it like a champ. All those compound fractures."

"Pio is tough. And his patron saint, Padre Pio, that guy is constantly working miracles for him. Constantly."

"Got to love him."

"Our Pio is what they call a *spiritual child* of Padre Pio, and I don't blame him. It's a whole thing. A whole devotion. What about Santa Cruz?"

"Lost his right eye among the facial bones damage. Plus, his hand. It was gone too."

Brigid raises his eyebrows. "His sharpshooter eye?"

"Yeah. That monster-thing grabbed his helmet and squeezed. They installed a morally acceptable replacement in there yesterday. Cybernetic. He might not need a scope after this."

"It's so funny you have to put the qualifier *morally acceptable* on there," Brigid says. "That's all we have on this planet."

"I know. As opposed to morally unacceptable, which we've had plenty of lately." Gonzaga looks off at some distant point on the wall or even beyond it to the other side of the universe. "So, Gosnell PTE is in the business of mutating Thraw now, eh?"

"To be fair, they're in the business of mutating everything. But yes, I guess so. They have a million tentacles out there and I'm sure we Knights and everyone else have seen only a handful."

"What's the plan, then?"

"The Master Knight is communicating with the others. We'll know soon enough," He points to their team, shrugs. "Us? Got to get back up to speed. Get healthy. It'll be a little bit for us yet."

"We got a new guy coming?" Gonzaga asks, his face carefully stoic. Replacing Brother Cleopas will only ever happen by way of filling his office, not the man himself.

Brigid nods, eats a kernel. "Yes. Yes, we do. Brother Becket, from Spec Ops Unit #3-3a."

"#3-3a, they took a rough hit, didn't they? Just a few weeks ago?" Brigid shuffles a few kernels in the palm of his hand, blinks a few times. "Yeah. Seven went in on a mission, Becket and one other guy made it out. They were both hurt pretty badly, and from the report I read Becket had to carry out the other survivor. Under fire. The other Knight is being removed from combat status permanently."

Gonzaga adjusts where he is sitting a little bit and looks over at the nun. Leans in and kisses her head as he thinks about this Brother Becket. "Sounds like a fighter. I like that. Glad to hear we're getting such a man, then."

Brigid chews a kernel. "We did well, getting that fella."

"Good," Gonzaga looks around. Sees Santa Cruz, Pio and Nonnatus one after the other. Sister Stella Nessa with Cleopas's Rosary in her hand. "I'm going to stay for a while with you. All our people are right here."

Brigid looks down to the crucifix on Cleopas's Rosary, even now in the wounded hands of the woman who loves Jesus so much He has united her to His suffering. She eases up and looks heavenward in ecstasy, the supernatural joy across her face something magical for their souls. "Beautiful," he says.

The risen Christ, this religious sister, his warrior-monks, all in their mixture of disrepair and healing. No doubt Cleopas is at the feet of God, praying for them and their souls, their missions. Gonzaga waits for his reply. Brigid touches his double pendant around his neck. Memories of his wife and daughter. He settles in and his shoulder leans on the huge man beside him. Relaxes.

"Yes, brother. All our people are right here."

A note from
behind the scenes

Early readers are hard to find. You write a book and then ask somebody to interrupt their busy life and scour a Word document. On top of that, you want feedback. Constructive criticism. Keep a watchful eye while they're (hopefully) enjoying the book. How's the pacing? Notice anything that's inconsistent? Did you like their cool space gadgets? And, most importantly, *did we get the faith correct*? Turns out there were a lot of details that needed tweaking. A few that required a full-on overhaul. Maybe one or two that demanded highlighting and unceremoniously deleting.

These early readers were invaluable in their help in shaping this novel: Matt James, Luke Knott, Doug Fitzpatrick, Eric McCormack and the lovely Donna Sayles. Great insight and suggestions from all. Mr. CMC is indebted to the lot of you.

Amos King is a great friend for numerous reasons. Among other things, he provided answers about space and physics to the silly questions we had. If we got them correct, it was due to Amos. If we did not, the blame rests on our shoulders.

Catherine Lueckenotte withdrew her red-hot editor's pen from its sheath and performed surgery on this book. From the obvious (*"Are you missing an entire word here?"*) to the secluded (*"Your readers won't notice this, but still…"*) Catherine took the lump of a novel we gave her and whittled the best thing she could out of it. She did not, however, proofread this postscript, so if it's grammatical garbage, that's on us.

Patrick Sayles came up with the space-art for the cover. We don't know how. We understand words, not images. One day he just shared a photo folder with us and started uploading stuff. "Pick one," Patrick said. We did. It's on the front of your book now.

Chuck Regan is a guy Ryan knows from way back. Chuck is an artist by trade. A real, bona fide artist. He does lots of things, from designing advertising campaigns to professionally massaging people's feet, but he's an artist at heart. He did the lettering, spine and back cover. Again, we don't know how. We understand words, not images. One day he just emailed a file to us and said, "Use this." We did. It's wrapped around your book now.

God bless you all. Don't die between now and the next book. There's more work ahead.

Carl Michael Curtis, January 2024

Carl Michael Curtis is the pen name of Catholic authors Joe Ralston and Ryan Sayles. *Stigmata Invicta* is their first work together, and the beginning of the *Knights 15 13* series.

Joe Ralston has spent his life collecting memories, stories, and experiences. From his days as a ranch cowboy, riding bulls, working as a bouncer, soldier, police officer, doing executive protection, and as a construction scuba diver to being an adventurer and explorer, he has dedicated himself to the pursuit of adventuring.

Ryan Sayles married his high school sweetheart. Through his wife's selfless generosity, his quiver has been filled with seven arrows. He drove boats for the military and policed in bad neighborhoods. Now he is a tradesman. He's published several secular novels in the crime genre.

Milton Keynes UK
Ingram Content Group UK Ltd.
UKHW010733220224
438165UK00001B/27